The History of Light Book 5:

THE BOOK OF TOUGH

KEVIN HINCKER

THE HISTORY OF LIGHT
VOLUMES 1 THROUGH 5

THE CURSE AT THE END OF THE WORLD

THE BOOK OF TOUCH

THE HISTORY OF LIGHT BOOK 5

KEVIN HINCKER

A WORD ABOUT THE CITY

Skysill Beach Master Plan

Skysill Beach is an art colony on the Southern California coast. It is stylish and quaint, wholly dedicated to taking money from tourists, and hosts a multitude of art galleries that *compel* shoppers to buy, using special ultraviolet paint. This is a town where ghosts and psychics and magic *light* are the pressing mysteries. Ringed by high coastal hills, resting in a bowl tilted toward the Pacific, it feels at once wild—filled with parks, pressed against the sea, separate from the outside world—and oppressively controlled. An unseen power oversees the painters of Skysill, who have lived for generations, trapped without knowing it, in a city they can never leave.

THE FIVE FAMILIES

1. **ASPECTU** *sight* [*The PAINTER*] *
2. **AUDITUS** *sound* [*The MUSICIAN*]
3. **SAPOR** *scent* [*The HUNTER*]
4. **NIDOR** *taste* [*The ALCHEMIST*]
5. **TACTUS** *touch* [*The DANCER*] *

* Prime

THE THREE PSYCHIC PATHS

1. The offspring of either Prime and AUDITUS - <u>The Path Before</u>
2. The offspring of either Prime and NIDOR - <u>The Path Beneath</u>
3. The offspring of either Prime and SAPOR - <u>The Path Behind</u>

THE HIGHER COLORS

CHAPTER

ONE

Caroline and I hung in a sunset sky of cherry bowl *light.* The moment felt endless. Ghost eyes like ours can stare straight down the sun's red core, where the drama is, so that's what we watched. A dark stripe of pelicans passed between us and the horizon. Far below, waves crashed.

Caroline and I were finally touching. We hung, and we hung, and her ghost palm lay on my ghost arm, and you might think a moment like that, stretching out, with the girl you've been trying for so long to reach, would be sufficient unto itself. Or whatever that saying is. But I'm a person with attention management issues, as everyone knows, and I'm also less interested in a view than a lot of people, so as the sunset went on and on and on I found myself growing bored. This sun hardly seemed to be moving.

Does it seem like it's taking <u>forever</u>? I asked her. Partly I asked it just to see her ghost lips move when she talked. A fully mobile ghost like her was a revelation. She really existed. Unbelievable and flexible. She was like Bigfoot, but smaller and prettier.

It does seem like an extra long sunset, she agreed.

Are you bored at all?

It's so beautiful, she breathed. *Like time's slowing down, just for us.*

So a little bored is what you're saying?

Her ghost hair whirled, tips trailing *light,* and her head turned to watch me. I pivoted my whole ghost body to face her. I wasn't at all flexible, of course. Even before this strange, multi-body person that I'd become, I was never very flexible. And as a ghost it's worse. I have the one arm stuck stiff. I can't nod or sigh. I can't walk. But those were all things Caroline could do. So maybe there was hope. Could that be right?

I still had flesh me dangling from my waist, staring at Caroline. He really liked to look at her. He's very easy to forget about when he's not talking. Because of all that, I accidentally bumped his head on Caroline's knee as I reoriented to her. The sky is a smaller place than you'd think.

His dark flesh hair was stirring fetchingly in the ocean breeze, but other than that he looked like shit. Covered in snot and tears, his eyes unnaturally wide and pretty bloodshot, his mouth held open. It was how we looked when we were overwhelmed. Like someone had given him a word problem we'd never be able to solve. Below him, a thousand feet down, Skysill Beach spread among dusk-dream sand shadows.

She came right up to me and ran her ghost fingers up my frozen ghost arm and I felt it. It was a faraway sensation, but it was the first sensation my ghost had ever felt in all the time I'd had him. And then Caroline was an inch from my chest. Looking up at my ghost face, fingers tracing my neck. She pressed herself against me. The setting sun lit her ghost lashes.

We no longer had telepathy. We sent no bio-magnetic pulses into each other and flashed no *light* messages. There was none of the polarized undertow madness which had marked our relationship to this point. We were just normal—the two most normal ghosts on the whole continent, at least that I knew of. So it was probably just outlandish coincidence when both of us ghosted the same words at the same moment.

I want to kiss you again, she and I said.

Her lips came up to me, open. Her eyes gathered *light.* We were going to do it. It was finally going to happen. She looked as eager as I felt, though my own ghost expression never changes, which probably conveys an impression of confident self-control—though I dislike misleading people that way.

Caroline, however, knows all the self-control I have or do not. She's been in my brain.

Our ghost lips met. And like the very first time, on her beachy sidewalk, holding each other, blissing out in front of her psychic shop—the kiss where our polarity flared to life, the kiss that more or less doomed us—this kiss was astonishing.

But only because of all the things it was missing.

It went on a long time, I'll give it that. I was like the sunset. But I barely felt anything. Just a distant impression, her lips a million miles distant. Like a kiss in a bottle. Like getting *xoxo* in a text. Just an idea.

She floated back off my mouth, head tilted to the side.

Well, that was not what I expected, she said.

Maybe we need to warm up.

I spent a lot of time thinking about that kiss. I'm pretty warm.

Let's try again, I said, because I'm an optimist, and my best problem-solving strategy is to keep trying the same things over and over expecting different results.

I could tell she was dubious, but she floated back up. She already saw the way it was going to be. We both saw it. But at a sight like that, the sight of all my dreams going up in *light* smoke, my first impulse is, I assume it's not real. Some people say that's my first impulse for everything.

We gave it another go but had no better luck, and then there was no denying it. We had a distinct lack of connection. A lack of closeness. I knew I wanted to have those things. Closeness. Connection. It was just ... hard to picture. Like we might be missing a gland.

I was afraid this was going to happen, she said.

Let's try again, I said, pursuing my strategy. She shook her head.

No Ash, she told me. *It won't change.*

We spent hours in a car kissing just a month ago—or just four months ago, depending on how you're counting. It was insane. Remember? Kissing's our thing. We just need practice.

No. This isn't a thing that practice changes. It won't change until ...

Until what?

The sunset still bathed us. It was the longest sunset I'd personally ever experienced. The *light* from it fell on her, painting her unhappy. I disliked this *light.* She sighed.

I guess it's time we talked about the elephant in the room, she said.

That's a challenging proposition for a person like me, who doesn't pay very close attention to the room. Whole circuses go by where I'm preoccupied with my issues and fail to notice even a single elephant. But I know better than to show that side of myself when there are people I'm trying to impress, on the rare occasions when that happens. She wanted to talk about the elephant. What elephant, I wondered? Then I had an idea I didn't like. It was my only idea, however.

Do you mean ... our thing? I asked finally. *How I sort of ... realized I'm in love with you? Should I not have said that?*

She smiled and shook her head, and I thought she looked sad, and I was definitely not used to that. Ghosts with expressions. I wanted her to try out some different expression.

No Ash, she said, *that was perfect. It was the best thing anyone's said since I got to Skysill. A little delayed on your part but who cares. Plus I'm in love with you, too, so it's real convenient.*

Yes. Convenience. It's really the overlooked romantic ideal, isn't it? So then ... you're saying it's some other elephant?

She just watched. I didn't think she was going to say it, whatever it was. I started to wonder if this was a test. I hoped not. Historically, those have all been too hard for me or I forget what day they're on. What elephants had there been?

Oh—the end of time? I asked.

She shook her head. *The end of time's an elephant, that's true. But it's not keeping us apart.*

Is it Aeternus? I was just guessing now. She could tell. I knew I'd never get it this way, but I couldn't stop. *Or ... are you only supposed to date other psychics? Are there unwritten rules? I hate those, they're as bad as the other kind.*

You really don't know.

She waited for me to deny it, but she was resigning herself to having a boyfriend who could no longer read her mind. I hated abandoning her to a confession like ... whatever this was going to be. Because isn't that the highest good we can do for the people close to us? Know enough to say the things they can't bring themselves to say on their own?

Okay, I actually don't know, I finally admitted. *What're you talking about?*

I'm talking about being a murderer, Ash! That's what's standing in our way.

You're ... It took me a minute to remember. I had flesh me nod—since I couldn't—to show her how fast I'll catch on when people point out the obvious. *Sure, that's right, the TV repair guy. The animal killer. My god. That?*

I managed it. Locked it away all those years. But now everything's unlocked inside.

But that wasn't murder.

You may need a refresher on the word.

Yes, I do admit that happens to me with "words," but not this time. That was not murder. That was justice!

Oh Ash. Justice for who?

For ... Justice wasn't my area of expertise or a concept I'm comfortable or acquainted with, though I know it has problems with blindness and seeing, much as I do. The only thing I know about justice is, it's a thing with an unreliable payoff. You might seek it, but seeking is almost always more satisfying than finding. Still, in this case, I felt the case was open and shut. Like the cops always say. Only this time, it was true.

What you did was absolutely justice, I began insisting, with really no idea what I was talking about but pretty sure I was right, the charming way I am. *It was justice for those thousands of innocent animals that shit bag killed. Just to feel them die. Just to feel the power. The worst kind of addict. Addicted to abuse. That wasn't murder. He deserved to die.*

I know I should try not to make sweeping pronouncements like that, though I'm drawn to them. I think I pronounce them all wrong since I seldom get the effect I'm after. Caroline, for instance, couldn't even look at me now. Instead she was seeing the shit bag I'd pronounced with such certainty.

He had two kids, she told me, her face a ghost mask. *I saw them. In the vision. He had a little girl and a little boy. And I murdered their father. Like Aeternus did yours. I can't hide what I am from myself. Not anymore. I'm no better than Aeternus.*

This was not the time to get into my complicated ideas about murder, I knew. People died in various ways, and yes, murder was one of them, and it was sometimes sad, or uncomfortable or boring, and then after people were murdered or whatever else, they didn't go away. So what was the big deal? Death wasn't the end. For me personally, death was very inconvenient, because of the ghosts building up in my kitchen in front of my refrigerator so it's hard to get my marmalade. But that was me.

In my frustration, I fell back on complaining.

But didn't I hear your ... I heard your story, I complained. *I did the thing, I released you. Isn't that supposed to ... free your spirit? I guess that's what I thought. All the other ghosts looked relieved. You asked me to forgive you, remember? I totally did!*

Halfway through my complaint, she'd started nodding. Not like she agreed with me, but like something was becoming clear to her. I like to think the complaints had somehow helped since they were all I had to offer.

I know, she said, *but I guess it turns out you forgiving me wasn't the solution to all my problems. Imagine that. And I don't mean that the snarky way it sounds. Just—what's keeping the two of us apart now is <u>me</u>. Those two kids had lives they had to live after I took their father.*

An asshole who mind controlled, and tortured, animals. Just to be clear.

She did a slow turn in the air. I did it too, to see what she did. We peered west along the horizon, to the Skysill shoreline curving down from the north, then east toward our citrus-sunset inland hills. Looking for something and not finding it. In my case because I didn't know what it was.

Caroline paused when her survey brought the wreck of Three Paths into view. It'd been leveled by me accidentally, over the course of several of my battles. It must have surprised her to see it like this since at the time she'd been kidnapped, and then killed by a shard of stone, her house had been perfectly fine. Though, hadn't she seen it subsequently, as a ghost? Or had that been ... the timeline honestly wasn't crystal clear. Timelines had stopped working the way they used to.

When did that happen? she asked, at her ruins.

You don't remember anything from when you were frozen?

She'd been floating and mute since the quorum battle. I wondered how far back I needed to go to explain why her house was just a pile of rocks and why it hadn't been as much my fault as it might appear.

Being dead was a blur, she told me. *I only remember bits and pieces.*

When you say being dead, you mean what exactly? You're dead now. Right?

I mean when I was frozen. On the <u>outside</u>, I was frozen. But inside ... I'd get little blips of what was happening out there. Like somebody dropped a photograph into my cave. But I was not the only person there. I wasn't really in control. There were others. Like, past lives? A long chain of them. We were ... something vast. She turned to me. *I was me, and I was multitudes.*

Because I leave my brain to pretty much do what it wants, I suddenly had an image of Samantha, and found myself wondering what it was like inside her? Was she multitudes? If so, I hoped she liked those other people—because Samantha was never going to be what Caroline was, a moving-around ghost. She was stuck in there forever.

Did you talk to any other ghosts around here? Can any of them talk? I asked. A long shot. Maybe she'd chatted with Samantha. She shook her head.

I was barely connected to this world. I doubt any of them talk. Plus a lot of my time in there ... I was screaming. I felt all the things I did while I was alive, and it was bad. While all the other ones behind me ... they were talking about getting to the water. A sea. A great ocean.

She stopped, remembering.

Ash. That's what I need. I need that great sea. It's for ghosts. To wash us clean.

It didn't sound great to me. In my circles what she was proposing we called the *geographic fix*. The geographic fix is, if you can only go somewhere new, some magically perfect place, you can start over and all your issues will be fixed.

My problem was, I actually did know of a sea, which might or might not be her fantasy clean-me-off sea. I saw it every time I sent a ghost on vacation. I just couldn't remember seeing any of them come back.

So ... where is this sea? I asked, offhanded like I can be. *This so-called sea. And when I say so-called I'm not suggesting it doesn't exist. That's just my spirit of pioneer skepticism.*

It does exist. I feel it.

So, could that sea be in ... the Undying Land? I hated bringing it up like this, but I wanted to know what we were up against. Not that that's ever helped me any.

The Undying Land is ... I think yes, maybe ... Ash have you seen it?

I mean, yes there's <u>an</u> ocean in there, or something. That's pretty *attractive to ghosts. After I release them, that's where they all fly off to. It might be a coincidence.*

For the first time since she'd suddenly reappeared in the sky talking and flying around, Caroline looked, momentarily, like she had no idea what was going on. She was facing west, looking at the blue Pacific but seeing different water. I had no idea how she'd come as far as she had, kidnapped by Aeternus, mind controlled, stabbed dead, entrusting deep murder secrets to someone like me for god's sake, then getting reborn and only *now* she had no idea what's going on? It was mesmerizing. She had reserves I found hard to understand.

Whether her murder-guilt was appropriate or not, she felt it was keeping us apart. Now it was pointing her to an ocean I had real questions about. But why should we complicate things with an ocean, when I had an alternate theory? A more real-world theory of what was keeping us apart, and what to do about it. These theories rise up to me, from time to time, from the deep well of bad ideas I've nurtured over the years.

Okay, listen, I said, *here's why we can't get together, or whatever our problem is, I mean I don't think we have a problem, we don't have to kiss —one thing I know is this: you're a fully moving-around ghost who touches things and feels, while I'm a ghost hooked to a flesh body. There should be different names for those kinds of ghosts. Our problem is, I'm just very numb. I barely feel anything. It's not you, it's me. And the good news is, I have an idea how to solve that problem. It's pretty easy.*

She only had to think for a second, then she'd decided what she disliked about my idea.

Nothing's ever easy, she said. *Plus that's a bad idea.*

No, it makes perfect sense, I'll just die. And presto! We're the same, so we can touch.

She looked at me like I wasn't thinking it through. I get that a lot. It used to frustrate me.

For one thing the problem's <u>me</u>, she insisted. *It's what I did. It left me*

... missing something. Plus your dying plan wouldn't work, I'm sorry to tell you. I know you worked on it a while.

I was nodding inside my mind, where no one could see, because of course my plan was broken. She's at least as good at plans as I am. I may have the quantity, but she's got the quality.

If you die you'll be floating around with your arm out .... she said.

... and then who'll send me to Ghost Disneyland? Right. I get it.

Ghost Disneyland?

I don't know what it's called. The next train station. Where the ghosts get off.

That's poetic. That's nice, Ash. Now think about this, you poor thing, I hate adding stress but if you die it won't be just <u>you</u> stuck with your arm out. Every ghost in the world is stuck at that point. You're the only one sending ghosts to Disneyland. They need you. We all need you.

"My arms are getting *really tired*," flesh me said softly. He made it clear he was complaining, but without sounding bitter or resentful, a skill I'd never mastered. I'd forgotten him again.

Caroline turned from the ocean and looked at my knees, surprised—she'd forgotten him too. He's like furniture. And looking over his shoulder she noticed the wreck of Three Paths once more. Her breath caught.

Ash, I know what to do, she said, speeding off through the air. *I know how to find it!*

I was of very mixed minds as I followed. On the one hand, I felt like we'd all gone a long time without anyone *knowing what to do,* so this was a welcome change. On the other hand, this sea was a dangerous question mark. Why were these ghosts drawn there? I went sliding sideways through the air, dragging flesh me along, and caught her only because she stopped to stare above the ridge-top mansion, now a wreck of shattered stonework.

The fires were all out by this time. The devastation was comprehensive. I saw tender little trails where feet, probably psychic feet, had gone back and forth, excavating, dragging items from the carcass of their home. Mostly items to bring to the

Bradley Building. Here and there a broken gargoyle glared up at me.

My god, she whispered, surveying. *What happened here?*

It's complicated, I admitted. *But different people were trying to kill me and your castle fell over. Don't worry, no one was inside. No one you'd miss.*

You did this?

Accidentally. Technically the Gray did it. And Amelia.

I was happy to see she wasn't upset about her house. I found myself wanting, ever more powerfully, to hold her. I did think we were missing something, despite all my assurances to the contrary, which everyone knows shouldn't be taken at face value. I wanted to hold her because of how she glowed. The grace of her, floating. Because of her cowboy shoes and the soft planes of her neck—all of that would've taken my breath away if ghosts had breaths. And I felt, surely, *surely* there was some small adjustment we could make to find a way to be normal. Normal felt so close. Closer than ever. Close enough to touch.

I'm just glad none of it fell on you, she said, *I never liked this place that much. Now come on. We're going up to the Closure House.*

She shot her ghost over castle wreckage toward the far side of the compound where a ravine held the side of the mountain open. Like someone had pulled out a slice of pie. A path went toward the opening over greensward.

Before I could follow, flesh me groaned.

"Please can I go down?" he begged. "Down?" He pointed. The ruins were only twenty feet below us. "My arms are *so tired*. I'm thirsty. Let me down."

He sure looked like he could use a rest. I peered for a likely landing spot. I saw the tree where I'd put him earlier when the Aeternus Dancers had ambushed us, and that reminded me of Aeternus himself. Still unaccounted for—though I'd watched him die, I hadn't seen his ghost anywhere.

The tree made me nervous. Everything here was making me

nervous, suddenly. There's always supposed to be a ghost. Plus the last time Aeternus got flesh me alone, he'd tried to end the world with him. I wondered, should I be taking that kind of risk with the world again?

"Down, down, I promise I won't go anywhere," he begged

I have the world to think about. You know how you are.

His nod was a sad acknowledgment of all his tendencies. Caroline had paused, and now floated, curious to watch me talking to myself this way.

Aw, she said in a nurturing tone. She had great sympathy for flesh me. *Nobody comes up here. He'll be okay a few minutes on his own.*

If you'd ever seen him make toast you wouldn't say that.

But he was trembling. He was probably going to fall if I didn't sit him someplace. So I chose a clearing free of sharp objects and sinkholes and poison and dropped him off, instructing him *stay*. He nodded, very solemn. I promised I'd find him water, speaking loud enough for Caroline to appreciate how nurturing I could also be, then flew after her, leaving him on a gargoyle.

CHAPTER

TWO

*Y*ou're real sweet to him, she approved as she took me into her ravine.

I know, I agreed. *He's a lot of responsibility but I think he reminds me of myself a little. I just hope he makes better choices than I did, that's my only concern.*

This way, Caroline said, dropping the subject of me talking about myself as she shot up the shadowed, zig-zagging cleft. Three Paths and flesh me fell behind as I flew around the first slanting canyon wall.

Below me wove a copse of coastal oak with groupings of eucalyptus, a well-tended rivulet of woods. A trio of white gravel paths ran twining through the trees, crisscrossing, circling back, and starting again in little eddies and glades. After a few canyon twists the trees fell behind. The ravine continued, tighter and deeper, and the three trails ran on, through deepening popsicle-orange sunset light. The shadows grew on the canyon floor.

The air began to press, increasingly thick, like nothing I'd felt as a ghost because usually ghosts feel nothing. This wasn't a welcome change. It felt oppressive but seemed imaginary, like other things in

13

my life, and I'd have put it down to nerves but ghosts lack those too. It was something portentous. A volcano feeling, moments from eruption—though in reality I doubt you can feel that, or how do you explain Pompeii?

Then, faintly, the drums began. Thick, deep, slow, somehow distant but also coming from everywhere all at once. A timpani behind the sky.

Caroline, I ghost hurried to catch up, *hey, do you feel this? Do you hear ...*

She was slowing. I caught her as she stopped. Below us, a basalt courtyard, hewn into the floor of the ravine, stretched between sheer canyon walls. The three trails we'd been following merged there, into one, a channel chiseled in the stone. The channel led to an opening in a three-sided stone tower. No door, just an arched hole.

Behind the tower, the ravine ended.

Caroline put her hand out to stop me floating forward, which I had definitely not been about to do. Towers make me nervous.

Something's not right, she said.

It's pretty creepy, I agreed. *Is this your Closure thing?* I like starting with simple questions that have obvious answers. I think people appreciate it. Plus they're usually my only questions.

It is, she nodded, staring. *Closure House, but where's ...*

She took a slow turn, scanning the high walls, looking back the way we'd come toward Three Paths hidden far below. I copied her. Not a bird called. Nor a cicada sounded. All you heard were those drums—which had begun to beat louder. The whole sky was a drum. Very unsettling and doomy and super weird.

What are those? Drums? I asked. Simple. Obvious. But she ignored me.

This is all wrong. Where's the Path?

Maybe tell me what's going on, I said. *So I know how disturbed to pretend not to be.*

She got a faraway look in her ghost eyes. I'm not sure how much farther you can be than a separate dimension from your boyfriend but she looked super cute doing it. Then she spoke and it had a pledge of allegiance quality, so I knew it was a poem, and I hoped it wasn't one of those riddle poems that put me to sleep.

The Paths of time wind 'round the world,
twining high in starlit air.
And where they land, a Closure makes
a door for walkers, brave and fair.

I nodded.

That's so awesome, I told her. *Can you say it a normal way?*

The Paths of time circle the Earth without touching it, except in a few places called Closures. Psychics can sense the Closures. We're drawn to them. In those places, Monarchs, or walkers strong enough, can literally step onto the Path.

By having a vision.

No, by literally walking. That's how I came looking for you, remember? It's two different things. Having a vision's like looking at the Path through a window. To actually walk the Path, you need a door. Monarchs walk the Path to protect our people, so everyone can do their job without being eaten. You know the shapeshifters.

We've met. So the Path touches in Skysill. And this tower's the door. Am I right?

She nodded, happy I was making myself sound smart, though that trick has a short shelf life and almost instantly she'd returned, warily, to scan the steep ravine.

It was partly the drums. They were filling that canyon with increasingly surreal echoes and a sense of dread. Which, usually a sense of dread sends me straight to the bar, unless I'm already at the bar in which case I stay there. But I had a job to do here, I saw. A job talking Caroline out of something.

Okay, I ghosted, very casual like I sometimes think I can be, *so I guess why you're here is to walk the Path. To go into the Undying Land, like when you rescued me. You're thinking the Path can get you to your ocean.*

Don't worry, Ash, I wasn't leaving today. I know I need to go, but ...

I'm not ready. I'm not ready to say ... . Anyway it doesn't matter—the Path should be right there but it's gone. It's not touching the world. I don't feel it.

Her worry mounted, her eyes narrowing at the tower—an expression that looks fantastic on seemingly everyone but me. She made the tower seem incredibly fascinating so I looked too. It was wedged like a shim into the point where the canyon walls came together. I estimated it at three stories with absolutely no confidence because my track record estimating things is mixed at best. There were no windows, and just the one door hole. I was confident estimating the door hole. Near the top of the tower, an enormous clock face had been carved with Roman numerals but no hands to point the time.

We should be feeling it, Caroline said. *We should almost see the Path here, like a shiver in the air. But nothing's here. Like a door's closed. Like the Path's sealed away.*

Ohhh ... I remembered out loud so both of us could hear it, for efficiency, *that's right, Phyllis and Jorge said no psychics can get on the Path. No psychics can have any visions. I think it's making them stir-crazy. I mean, they were obviously already crazy, but—*

When did that happen? she interrupted as, in the background, the drumming grew.

After you died, I told her, thinking back. But that's not the direction I'm best at, and it's where I tend to lose focus, so I went cautiously.

Let's see ... it was after Nolear Fa died and the curse got half lifted— and we figured out Aeternus was Nolear Fa, by the way—my god there's so much, yeah, Aeternus, Nolear Fa—thankfully Samantha blew him up, I mean I guess I'm thankful but black shit up my lungs wasn't great, better than being dead I assume, but who knows? Anyway, Phyllis and Jorge and me and Amelia ...

I drifted to silence under her speculative ghost gaze. Her careful listening was disorienting. Around us the orange stone cliffs bounced light from a sun that, honestly, was like, *never going to set.*

She was struggling to make sense of something I'd said. Then her face cleared.

Oh, she nodded. *I see. You're not doing it on purpose, okay but Ash, we're in a hurry now. And your style of letting facts out slow as pond water's going to be a little impractical, though it's charming. Can you go faster?*

How fast?

Just focus and say it, clear as you can, without making a novel. What do you mean the curse is … half lifted?

Her organized Monarch instructions were so attractive to be around. They reminded me of the rooms and hallways in her brain house. As I started talking I could almost see her filing things into her drawers and cupboards. Almost. But not quite.

I covered all the things that hadn't happened to her because she'd been dead, that had happened to the rest of us, starting with the half-lifted curse. It seemed to be half lifted because the terms of fully lifting it were that the Inmortalis Nolear Fa and the ghost warrior Ti'eirl both needed to be dead, and those terms had been half met. Nolear Fa died when Samantha blew him up while he was sucking the Asher Gale juice out of Asher Gale—but now Ti'eirl was apparently still alive somewhere, so the curse was half lifted, and our world left as a shadow realm of death, somewhere far, far up shit creek.

I paused to make sure my speed was right and she was following me, which she was, which didn't surprise me but did surprise me because I have a hard time following myself a lot of times. She spun her finger in the air though, like, get on with the story Asher, these drums and this pressure are driving me insane, so I jumped back in.

We'd be looking to Veronica for explanations to a lot of this, I told her, but Veronica, though currently not dead, was in suspended animation with Amelia obsessing over her, which if you knew my sister's relationship history you totally could have predicted since they always leave her one way or another, though Caroline was less interested in Amelia's relationship history. So I shifted to an account of Samantha—waiting for the moment Aeternus was most vulnerable to kill him—who was the one ghost I'd never be able to send on vacation because Amelia had *wandered* her goblet into a never-never void.

It was all entertaining to Caroline—because she likes me, not because I'm good at explaining things—until at last I got to what Phyllis told me about the psychic's inability to get on the Paths, or to have visions. They all lived at the Bradley now. They'd already been crazy, a lot of them, and now they were bored too, though Phil and Dale were keeping them distracted with presentations on Tahitian cruises and tax-advantaged bonds. Caroline was uninterested in anything to do with Phil and Dale. I skipped the rest of that part.

I did mention human births had stopped and people were getting really old, really suddenly and then dying—how could that not be important?—and I sort of complained how the ghosts were in the way all the time everywhere.

All of which naturally segued into my theory that the moment the throne atop Mount Obitus sank into our world under my palms, our world became a land of death. The whole Earth. I admitted this to be a little more conjectural than some of my theories, since I hadn't checked any other parts of the world, because in a lot of ways I didn't care enough, and instead I'd been mooning around the penthouse watching her for the last few weeks, but one way or another, I told her, it was clear the world was fucked.

Then I took a deep breath, in my mind at least, and then I felt like I should stop. Sometimes I don't know when to stop but in this case I'm pretty sure I nailed it. I waited for whatever questions she had, since you'd think there'd be questions. But she just watched me.

It's amazing watching your brain work, she marveled. *It's like a tornado hit a hospital.*

Because of the bodies.

There's bodies just ... everywhere.

Is it too much?

No, I like it. It's what makes you different from other boys.

Normal boys, you're saying.

Exactly. Now you stay here. I need to test something.

She turned back to the triangle tower, newly armed with my theories. I wondered if any of that would help. She drifted forward, slow, above the carved-out path in the courtyard, toward the tower door, holding her palms up and out like a person walking in a dark room hoping her face doesn't hit a wall.

I heard a smudge of sound, a voice, a whisper lost under the drumming … calling my name? Something that was, at least in part, only in my mind. Something familiar.

Caroline pressed toward the tower and as she got closer found it harder to walk, or float, or whatever. All the while the drumming rose and fell, but increasingly rose. It was beginning to sound like a mob pounding on a door. An impatient mob.

Caroline had angled forward, gathering herself to shove, when the air itself began rippling. With every drum beat a mirage wave expanded everywhere, like each beat was a rock, and the whole world was a pond. The ravine walls distorted, the sky went sideways.

And then, from far away, beyond or within the open tower, came piercing shrieks.

Caroline spun.

Run, she said, *figura!*

Run is a funny thing for one ghost to say to another but I got the idea. She blew past me calling my name and I followed, sluicing back down canyon the way we'd come. I could have blinked but I didn't know if Caroline knew about blinking, since she was new to ghost life, or if she did know, whether the two of us could blink to the same place—blinking was a mystery.

The pounding faded as we flashed along. The world stopped rippling. By the time we'd issued from the mouth of the chasm to ghost out above the Three Paths ridge, where the sun had still not set, the drums far up the ravine were just a suggestion in the air.

Flesh me stood by his rock, right where he'd promised to stay, jumping up and down and waving. When he saw Caroline he smiled and looked relieved.

We reached him and slowed and I spun to with my questions.

What was all that? I complained politely. *It sounds like figura … like a horde of monsters trying to get in. Is that possible?*

I have to find Phyllis and Jorge, she said, *they'll know what's going on.*

The psychics are all at the Bradley, I told her. *Fastest way to get there is blink. Do you know how? Disappear one place, appear somewhere else?*

She got a faraway look, started nodding, recalling a memory.

I see, she asked. *Does that really work?*

Sure. See that gargoyle? Imagine you're floating beside it.

A moment passed. Her expression didn't change. I had no idea if she was imagining anything but then suddenly she vanished and appeared beside the gargoyle. Despite our numerous, overwhelming, possibly insoluble problems, an amazed giggle escaped her. She blinked back and forth several times and ended up beside me. She reached to touch my arm.

A million miles away I felt it. A shadow of all the things I wanted. A promise.

We'll get this figured out, she said. She seemed more hopeful than any part of our situation could really warrant. Usually, I'm the one filled with unwarranted optimism, though some of that's booze. This sober hopefulness of hers was refreshing.

I'll fly flesh me down after you leave, I told her. *He can't blink.*

She nodded. I saw, very clearly, that she wanted to kiss me again, but when she resisted that impulse I was glad. A person can only take so much disappointment. Her hand on my arm was bad enough.

See you soon, she said. Then she looked up the coast toward the Bradley, imagining it. A moment went by. Nothing happened. After another moment she closed her eyes for clearer visualization of the Bradley, but she didn't vanish like she was supposed to.

What—? she started to wonder. She lifted her hand as if to point up the coast—and the moment she was no longer touching me she blinked away. A second later she blinked back.

Update, she said. *You can't blink if you're touching another ghost. Bye honey. It was real nice being brought back to life by you.*

And she vanished.

And then it was just flesh me and the ruins we'd made and the sunset. I actually wondered if there was some problem with the sun. I asked flesh me to sigh, for both of us, just to vicariously get my weariness into the world. Then I had him climb back to his post, clinging around my neck with one arm while standing on my toes, and up we rose. I headed us out over the city, going toward the beach.

So I was facing the sun, which was just touching the horizon, when it went out.

CHAPTER

THREE

eep black midnight consumed us in the span of a second —violent, instantaneous darkness. I've seen a lot of things in my life. Very unusual things. I'd started thinking of myself as, *just about impossible to surprise.* But the sun going out was very surprising.

It died without a sound, without fade or flare. It wasn't an astronomical event, like titanic forces clashing in the sky. The light just *stopped*—the sun was on fire one second and then there was a round, black disc in the sky in its place, and darkness deeper than grave shadow everywhere I looked.

The Higher borealis was gone. The lights of Skysill were gone. The black coin hung before an arm of the Milky Way, which was the only way I saw it—silhouetted before star shimmer like a hole in the heavens. The light from those stars hit the ocean and spread the only murmur of illumination.

"What's happening?" flesh me wondered. "Look at me."

I didn't look. The ghost body I wore, that I'd grown so accustomed to—upright, pivoting and flying under my control—was listing sideways. Like gravity had gone off. For one second I assumed flesh me had done something. Was he overbalancing us? And then … where *was* he—I tried but could not shift my ghost to look. I no longer had power to move me. I could only float, a leaf on a black pond, stirred by any ripple that hit me.

A moment later my twirl brought flesh me drifting into view. He was untethered and floating in the air beside me, like an astronaut on a spacewalk, staring everywhere wide-eyed. He waved his arms like he wanted to tread water—though we'd never learned to tread water—or rather we had but only in the existential sense—and I wondered, what was he doing? Your first move, when the sun goes out, is let go of your ghost and float off in the air? He's a fucking mystery.

"Look at me," he complained. "What's going on with me—"

Be quiet let me think! I shouted—knowing of course how unlikely that was to help. It was simply what I'd been reduced to. *The sun went out?* I thought. *WHAT THE FUCK … THE HELL … IS THIS?* Because I lack practice keeping my thoughts to myself I thought this out loud and flesh me heard and went arm churning faster, really freaking out. He did not like me asking what the fuck. He counts on me having all our fucks in order. It's actually a lot of responsibility.

At precisely that moment both of us realized he was sinking. Ghost me randomly drifted but flesh me went slipping slowly down out of the air. When he realized it he grabbed for my chest, but fists aren't the tool for grabbing and he spun himself in outer-space circles, dropping past my ghost knees, but just as he was out of range he reached above his head with both fists and clamped a ghost foot.

Then down we both dropped, through darkness like interstellar space, heading for the starlit ground, flesh me a diving weight dragging me to the bottom of the sea. Or maybe there wasn't a bottom. I could take nothing for granted now. You take the sun for granted, but once that's off the table everything else goes with it.

Below I thought I saw the Pacific Coast Highway, and slowly made out blacktop running along a bluff. On the inland side a neighborhood of shadowy residences and storefronts rose, not far from the psychic district. Off the ocean side was a sandy cliff and a strip of state beach. The water wasn't stirring at all. Dark, motionless car shapes dotted the road. *Nothing* moved.

Nothing but my bodies dropping from the sky.

When flesh me hit the pavement his legs folded. He went to one knee, head bowed, fist knuckling the road like a preacher blessing a coastal highway, maybe someplace Jesus had driven. Because he'd unclamped my ghost foot I was left floating three yards above him. Still at a loss for *what the fuck?*

At which point Samantha bloomed in above the dark coastal asphalt.

She floated in right below ghost me near my kneeling flesh. She wasn't accompanied by her usual Higher pyrotechnics. Only a weak *dominion* cloud surrounded her. The *light* making up her ghost kept flickering in and out, fading then refilling what appeared to be a Samantha-shaped shell. I do not know much about ghosts, but that didn't look good.

Beside flesh me kneeling on the road she flickered in, spent a second there like a string of dying Christmas lights, then blinked up beside me in the air. Then down and back up, then again, and again, fading while the dead dark missing sun grew harder to see.

Ohhhh, I thought, out loud again, as it dawned on me, *charades*.

I figured it out pretty quick. I know it frustrates people. It probably frustrates ghosts. How it sometimes takes me a moment to catch up. But honestly how many unprecedented, completely novel circumstances am I expected to process *at one time*? Processing things isn't even one of my strengths. It's too much. I have my various bodies, my girlfriend I can't kiss, the end of time, a realm of death, the list goes on and now the sun goes out? I mean *please*—as I sometimes argue to myself as the bar closes—what do people *want* from me? All I ask is walk a mile in my ghost shoes and see how easy this shit is.

Samantha wanted us merged. That's what she was flickering. *Get in one body,* she was saying, which was super clear as soon as I stopped talking to myself about what everyone expected of me. Samantha was expending the last of whatever ghost energy remained to her on this motionless, sunless, fade-away highway, begging me to merge. Or maybe *begging* is the wrong word? I'm not a word person. All I know is you don't have to ask me twice. Not once I realize you're actually talking to me. Which I admit can take a while.

What are you waiting for? Cross them! I shouted at flesh me a little unfairly. I think he'd been waiting for me. By now he and I are like a wrestling tag team, a coordinated dance of fantastical lunacy. He crossed his eyes without even thinking—that's the way he does everything, so not a big deal—and sucked ghost me toward him.

Dominion bloomed up as we two Ashers superimposed. The hot *dominion* accumulated in a ball and shot down my arm toward the fork flesh me still—thank god—held from lunch. And then some funny things happened. And by funny I mean horrible.

One thing was sudden terrible-agony, a stage of merging bodies I thought we'd evolved beyond, although terrible-agony comes up so often in so many different circumstances these days it should never be a surprise. I felt *dominion* pile driving through me like boiling fiberglass, igniting every nerve.

Then another funny thing that happened was, after the *dominion* current slammed the fork it kept going. It did not stop in the fork, did not glow the fork, or duplicate the fork or any of the ordinary fork things, but surged out where my flesh hand knuckled the ground and made a river into the earth. *Dominion* came from somewhere and went somewhere, and I was the wire it traveled.

Like the very worst old days, I couldn't move, kneeling, two bodies superimposed with *dominion* spasming me. Once again I'd become an open circuit, the same thing Samantha did to me making me kill Julian. And the pain ... what I'd called *terrible-agony* in the past had been nothing. Just training agony. This was the real deal. *Dominion* ramped up, blasting out my hand into the ground, growing from garden hose to firehose to torrential river-flood, then scaling beyond description. It was unspeakable pain. And practically nothing's unspeakable for me.

The only way to handle a thing like that is disassociate. Escape somewhere in your mind, where nothing is real. Fortunately, that's a solution I'm practiced at, and so I just let go. I left me. I went with the flow.

I was carried down the river of *light* and out, as I had been at Damely's, as I had when I straightened the Bradley with *dominion*. But this time when I came out I wasn't filling a metal pole, or filling a building. I was filling ... the world. I left all my old things—bodies, illusions, good plans, bad judgment—and traded them for nothing but a sense of direction: into. *Dominion* took me down through the veins of the world into *everything*.

I sensed myself fill what could only be called the Earth, though usually I'm shy about that kind of language since I've got preexisting manic grandiose tendencies which there's no sense encouraging. But I felt it. I poured in, and expanded, my mind inside the *light,* spreading through the planet. Filling the world with ghost energy.

And along with these feelings came *visions*. Not pretty ones.

I saw the Earth devastated. Everything shattered. A dark disk in the sky. Cities leaning, empty, oceans dried, mountains thrown over. In this world, people still somehow lived, but they weren't going to last. Because monsters stalked them. Figura.

The intensity of *light* hit a critical level and then I saw ghosts. The world covered in ghosts. Frozen ghosts, one arm out. Lost. The bleakest thing I'd ever seen, or had a vision of, or whatever was going on. This was the dark at the end of the world.

Far off, then, I heard the voice again. The one I'd heard behind the drums at the Closure. Saying my name? Calling me. And among the ghosts, a figure appeared, distant but ... someone I knew. I knew the voice. I recognized the figure. Didn't I? Who was she ... *who was calling my name?*

Far behind, like a tick on an elephant, flesh me clung to the world and burned, brighter-hotter, faster-wilder, harder than any sun and screaming, channeling *light* through the planet's mantle with no way to stop. Melting. Failing now. Not slowly.

The sun flashed then, stuttered like a car engine catching. Why it's always a car with me I do not know, they are my albatrosses. But it flashed and I couldn't help a mental image—my best kind—of me behind a wheel turning a key, the sun a galactic motor ... turning ... catching. *Fire.*

The engine roared to life. Light exploded.

My bodies snapped together as the essence of the entire world— again, not language I'm comfortable using—shuddered and stared back up. Filled with nuclear flame, the sun seemed suddenly to blur in reverse, rising out of sunset, rising to late afternoon, then noon, backward until it stopped, beaming down late morning dapple, as if nothing in any way out of the ordinary had just happened. Normal, late morning dapple. A few high clouds.

I felt exhausted, but retreating to a healthy dissociative state had been the right move. My mind, such as it was, had come through unbroken. And here it was late morning again. Of what day, I wondered? I supposed that technically it might be the same day, since the sun had never fully set, but those thorny questions I like to leave for historians and meteorologists.

My body lay curled on its side in a crater. How I came to be in a crater was not clear. It was a smallish crater, relative to some I'd seen, but it was deep and blasted in the middle of the Pacific Coast Highway, an inconvenient place for a crater of any size. The sky was a circle above me. I heard tires skidding—when the sun came back on, the traffic did too—at breakneck speed, as they say. There came screeching, and the sound of one car hitting another car, and then the undercarriage of a sedan spun into view above me and stopped, hanging sideways, one wheel spinning in space. More impacts from cars further back up the chain all dominoed up to the vehicle above me, pushing it further over the top of my hole.

I knew that escaping the crater was the prudent thing but I was *exhausted*. There's only so much dodging around a person can do before it's too much dodging around. If I was slated to die when a car fell on me in a hole then that's just what was going to happen. I'd been utterly drained by the thing I'd done to the sun. Whatever that'd been. My mind shied from it.

But a distant corner of that mind, my mind, was asking—*hold on ... did I just restart the sun?*—which is dangerously similar to thoughts assorted counselors and court-appointed representatives have warned me about—all my life they've warned I should ground my thinking on a smaller scale—like no, I have no influence over celestial bodies. I'm just normal. But then something like this happens, and it's clear I was right all along.

On the highway above, a siren beeped. Just once. Wearily, I thought. Then silent red and blue reflections began. I heard a car door open, and the vehicle looming above me rocked as someone large climbed out. I heard boots. And foreshortened above me I saw my favorite peacekeeper glaring down in his peacekeeping uniform.

"Hen," I called, without moving. My energy was returning, little by little, but I decided I'd play semi-dead for a minute and collect a little information. What I'd do with a little information was anyone's guess. Something dangerous, probably.

"You," Hennessy told me. His voice was breathy and weak. He had gauze and tape bandaging his throat. I remembered the last time I'd seen him, I'd been *Gray* and he'd had a dog eating him.

He looked over his shoulder at the highway behind him and saw things he did not like, then peered back at me with a similar expression. "What is it you are doing in this pit?"

"Just resting," I guessed. "Hey, did the sun go out just now?"

"Get up," he wheezed, ignoring my questions. He wasn't buying my helplessness—cops preternaturally sense real helplessness. It draws them like virgins draw Huns. He knew I was no virgin. It was one of his enduring disappointments. "Out. Out of the hole. Now."

"I might be injured."

"Are you injured, Gale?"

"Emotionally and psychically yes I am."

"Get out or I will send dogs to pull you out."

It seemed to me a pretty healthy sign that he could talk so nonchalantly about dogs after what'd happened to his throat. I guess for cops being eaten is just the price you pay for the privilege of safeguarding the public with guns.

I stood, and it was not easy. And I tried to climb up. I really did. But it was no good. How'd I even get into that hole? I had no idea. It hadn't been here when flesh me landed. The walls were sandy, and I was weak. Hennessy finally had to throw a cop rope to me, from the kit peace officers are issued so they can pull people out of a hole, I guess. He had me tie one end around my waist and then dragged me up. I hardly had to work at all.

When my head popped over the edge Hennessy reached under my arms and heaved. I came out like a champagne cork and he dropped me on my knees and stood panting and untying rope. I glanced at the late morning sun, shining cheerfully or whatever, then back at the mass car accident behind Hen's car, then over at the beach where there were some seagulls. When Hennessy got his breath back he looked where he'd dropped me.

"Put your hands behind your back," he announced, taking out his handcuffs.

I accidentally shook my head, which is something they hate, and asked, "No. What?"

"*Now*," he said.

"But Hen, I didn't—"

"*Do not call me Hen,*" he shout-wheezed, phlegmy and horrible. "Do not do a single thing but put your hands. Behind your back. *Now.*"

"You're arresting me?"

Was he blaming me for the hole? Were holes illegal? These questions dragged an entirely new train of questions into view, which is the problem with being at all curious about anything. Once the questions start, they never fucking end. And I wanted to know about the sun. Had Hennessy seen whatever had happened? Had everything gone dark for him?

But all my questions died on the vine of my brain when a sudden chorus of honking turned Hennessy away from me, back toward the traffic jam, and for just a moment I got a really good look at him from behind.

He had a ghost coming out of his back.

It wasn't a complete ghost, or it hadn't fully emerged. The face of a ghost head was buried in the back of his flesh skull. A ghost neck, torso, ass—all the way down the ghost legs to the ghost feet, embedded, moving with him. A monkey on his back. A huge, Hennessy-shaped monkey of *light*. Was this Hen's very own ghost me—a ghost Hen—emerging? Was it because of the thing with the sun?

I considered what tack I should take bringing it up.

"Hen," I started, but flinched when he snarled, "No, I mean sorry, *officer* Hen—how do you ... feel? How's your head feel? Does anything feel different at all?"

"How do I *feel?*" he asked. He pointed to his throat. "Imagine how I feel. And this, of course, is not the worst part. Do you know what the worst part is?"

"Something with your 401k?"

"The worst part is when I emerge from a hospital and resume my duties, I discover, among many other things, my service revolver missing. The department is investigating. An investigation is very bad. But here you are. The person last known to be in possession of said revolver. I have men searching all your places. It is one more detail I must worry about."

"I didn't take your gun," I told him, which was either technically not true, or technically true, but in either case failed to satisfy him.

"For various reasons, I cannot afford an investigation," he told me. "So. You, emerging here, in your way, from this hole, you I am arresting. We will go to the station, find a private room, and craft your official statement. Which will not involve me. Or it will be the last confession you ever sign."

"It doesn't matter, you can't read my signature anyway," I told him, "and look, we have *way* bigger problems right now."

At which point he drew out his gun and pointed it at me. A different gun obviously. He pointed it at my chest. He looked very willing to do whatever it was that came next. He didn't care. Just another dead painter. That's the way it is in Skysill Beach. It's a very dangerous place to be a painter.

"Hands," he said.

And then almost without noticing it had happened, I popped a ghost. What now, I wondered? A new ghost somewhere—Samantha? Someone dying in the pileup?—I spun my ghost body but saw no dead bodies and no new apparitions. No Samantha.

But what I *did* notice was flesh me. Who wasn't flesh me. He was the *Gray*.

So *this* is the new thing that happens, I complained to myself? It was obvious to me what was going on, because I'm best at the wild conclusions that aren't obvious to other people: when there's a ghost, I'm going to pop out and leave flesh me behind, and when there's danger I'm going to pop out and leave the *Gray*. I'm a fucking jack-in-the-box. Or a whack-a-mole.

Hennessy, with instincts honed by years of cop action, tightened his grip on his gun and eyed the *Gray*. He had no idea what'd just changed but he knew something had. He'd never seen anything like it but he'd seen enough to know he had a problem.

The *Gray*, his own instincts honed by years of who fucking knew what, lay on his side and smiled up. Magnetic and glorious. Like a magic, smiling, brutal, prince of violence. And as he did it, he took a deep breath. His smile grew when he saw Hennessy's gun.

"Gale, this is your only warn—"

Which is as far as Hennessy got. From the ground, the *Gray* sprang, a blur of action. Hennessy had no chance. Hen's gun went off —of *course* he'd been willing to shoot me—but the *Gray* was somewhere else. The *Gray* reached the gun and grabbed the barrel. Hennessy pulled but went nowhere. Like he was having a tug-of-war with a backhoe. I doubted this had ever happened to Hen. He owned all the higher-weight classes.

But no one's in the *Gray's* class. He was bio-magnetized to the ground.

The gun was torn from Hen's hand with at least one finger broken, you knew it had to be broken, but Hen, a pro, went for his baton. The *Gray* got it first. He waved it in Hen's face for one second. Then he took Hen by the bulletproof vest.

With one hand he lifted Hen, the uniformed acres of him, held him up there where his arms and legs waved, then slammed him down on his back. Then, still smiling, he snatched Hennessy's wrist and bent it backward. It looked excruciating. He put his knee on Hen's throat, fast and efficient, some kind of Judo, which I guess you automatically learn if you're a sociopath killing machine.

The *Gray* bent to Hennessy's face and whispered, "You should have left my friends alone."

Hey, I ghosted, and the *Gray* looked up at me. *Thanks, great. That's great for now.*

"Not great it's *awesome*. He's about to scream super loud and die hahaha!"

Yeah, okay, but let's not kill him.

"He was going to kill you."

We don't know that.

"Yes we do," he snorted.

Hennessy's wrist looked like it was about to break, but he focused on the *Gray*. Hen had cop pain tolerance—or else, like those dinosaurs, it took extra time for nerve impulses to get to his brain. I know I'd have been screaming, but that's actually my first impulse for everything. Hen was trying to figure out who the *Gray* was talking to in the air.

"Gale," he wheezed, checking the emptiness of ghost me, "what is this? What—"

"Shut up!" the *Gray* sallied, happy as shit to twist a little harder, and that broke Hen's wrist. We heard it. Hennessy heard it. He screamed then.

Stop! I ghost yelled. *I'm in enough trouble! There's a hundred witnesses. I can't go around maiming police—let him go!*

"Haha—who cares about *witnesses*? He was going to shoot you. Oh. Did you want to get shot? Ohhh ... is that what we should try next?"

No but thank you for asking. Here's what I do want to do next. Listen, okay? He shrugged, but stopped killing people for a moment.

First I want you to let go of Hennessy. Then, if you don't mind, I want you to take our body to the Bradley Building. Can you run it back there? And don't kill anyone on the way? Just go back, as fast as possible, no battles, and when you get there, let flesh me out so he can sleep. He's been up since several sunsets ago, doing shit to the sun and he's worn out. And look at Hen. He's not hurting us now.

Hennessy had passed out. The *Gray* scrutinized the cars, the houses around us, doing professional threat assessment like a presidential security detail, only crazy. He came to the same conclusion I'd come to. There was nothing here to kill a ghost me. He dropped Hennessy's limp arm.

"Later I want to go cliff diving," he told me.

Let's see what happens. I'll meet you at the Bradley. I need to check out these half-ghosts.

"Why?" he scoffed. He had no respect for ghosts. Other than me. I hoped.

Because no one else is going to, I said, wishing I could sigh. Hennessy stirred and raised his broken wrist with his broken finger to his bandaged throat where the *Gray* had him pinned.

Go before he wakes up. And don't kill anyone! Got it?

He shrugged. Then he was gone so fast that none of the witnesses saw where he went. He left me hanging above the hole Hennessy thought was mine watching a crowd gather to take pictures of Hennessy on the road. Every single one of those people came with a ghost growing out the back of their body.

Ever since the very first ghost I'd seen—Samantha—my sensitivity to ghost theories had grown. Now I felt myself haunted by ghost theories everywhere I turned. Everything I saw was tied to one ghost or another. I had a theory about these half-ghosts but I was struggling with it. It was a pretty extravagant theory.

Everything had been normal—as far as ghosts went anyway, and taking into account that nothing that ever happened in my life was normal—and then there was the thing with the sun. Before the thing with the sun people hadn't had ghosts coming out of them.

The theory had two versions: one, the thing with the sun had created these ghosts, or two, they'd been hidden inside people all along and I'd squeezed them out by pumping so much *dominion* into the world. Like soft cheese through a grater was the image that came to me, because I'm so visual.

Number two was the more gruesome and it felt right. I'd squeezed them out of hiding. Which, did that mean ghosts had been inside us all along, ever since the curse that created this world, eons ago? But if *that* was true, what'd been happening to the ghosts of people who died before I came and started releasing ghosts? Or whatever I do?

All I knew for sure was I wished they'd go back where they'd been because this was a sight I'd have a hard time getting used to. Half-visible human forms emerging through the backs of people disturbed me like those frogs with two heads. I hoped it was just a local phenomenon, something that affected people near the *dominion* circuit that I'd momentarily established with the planet. Because what if the whole town was like this? Or the world? It would be super distracting and horrible.

I floated through the traffic jam crowd. Hennessy's cop lights still flicked red and blue over the scene. I found that even the people in the last cars, who'd remained in their seats, were ghosting half twins. Like when I'm seeing double for the various reasons that occasionally happens.

After Caroline died I'd spent a week or two alone shut up in the

Bradley Building, and it felt like time to get out again. To see the sights. I hovered up, over the sidewalk, looking for people. Everywhere I saw them, they were growing a ghost. These growths didn't seem to be harming anyone. No one seemed to notice or mind. It was just strangely disturbing. I rose higher to get a better view and be less disturbed.

Skysill as a whole had been reduced, I began to think. By something other than earthquake damage. Everything felt somehow smaller, and thin. People, plants, buildings. Birds and waves and clouds, they all seemed somehow less significant. But as I continued upcoast toward downtown the town re-solidified and appeared more real. Even the sunlight fell thicker. One thing did not change, though: there were fewer cars.

It was the tourists: there weren't any. I swept through downtown into the gallery district and found every store empty. And yes, you could blame the road closures, the sidewalks all yellow taped, the earthquaked roofs—but because the power of *compulsion* called them, there should still have been a crowd at every counter. We *always* have buyers. When tropical storms level sixty miles an hour onshore winds, and rain drops visibility to zero and there's flooding, people still come. *Compelled.* But not now.

The only people I saw were locals. All of them sprouting ghost twins.

I passed the Bradley and continued north. And as downtown fell behind, the world began to thin again. The waves lay back flatter and the breeze weakened. I stopped when I got to the Charles. Point Marshal, just across the highway, seemed to be some kind of boundary. Beyond that point, the light stopped appearing at all substantial. Like we had a sphere of influence around the city, the psychic district at one end, the Charles at the other.

I was already there so I ghosted into the bar. I was overjoyed to see some of my most familiar drunks in there. It wasn't crowded but it was functioning. And there was Selena, regarding the drunks with disdain. Whatever else might change, a drunk always needs his bartender's disdain. Sometimes that's the only thing that seems real to him. I allowed myself to be reassured, even though these drunks and a bartender all had ghosts on their backs. You can't have everything. I can't, at least.

There my superficial tour of the town concluded. I'd come to no decisions about what was happening with ghosts in Skysill, whether I'd caused it by restarting the sun, or if any of it should concern me at all. I'd seen nothing to stop me going for my body, bringing him to The Charles and getting him drunk. And though I wasn't sure if that was the best idea, in situations like this I always err on the side of getting drunk being a good idea.

So to the Bradley I ghosted. Sunlight grew more substantial the closer to downtown I came—when you knew what to look for, it was pretty obvious. As I floated up outside the Bradley Building the world seemed basically normal, with all my usual caveats. The only thing missing were visitors. In many ways this was the Skysill I'd always craved. A quiet, seaside art colony no one ever visited or lived in other than me.

The Bradley lobby was crowded with psychics when I ghosted in the front doors. Phil or Dale or someone had found dozens of cots and arranged them around the walls. There were kid psychics and old people psychics and all the other kinds. They all had ghost doubles. I saw Ambrosia waiting by the elevator in her medical scrubs with a second Higher Ambrosia of *dominion* wedged into her from behind. I kept wondering how these ghosts could breathe, though I knew ghosts don't. Who knows why I wonder the shit I do?

When the elevator came, Ambrosia stepped in and I ghosted after her and we rode up in the kind of companionable silence where one person doesn't know the other person is in the elevator with them. Ambrosia got out on 3 and I followed, again just out of habit. More cots lined the hallway walls, and psychics were everywhere. This was Asher Gale's office floor, where Phil had put the Monarchs in his office, which had made him feel pretty important. He refused to put any psychics into the Penthouse. He'd reserved that for me. He was like my Lord Chamberlain. He was having the time of his life.

Thinking of the Monarchs made me think of Caroline. I'd known her for many months, depending on how you counted, but Caroline never came to visit the Charles with me. To really know me you needed to see me there, since that's the bar I grew up in. So I thought, though the experience would be less intoxicating now that she was a ghost, I'd ask her to come get a drink with me. She could watch flesh me swallow and we could banter.

The last time I'd seen her, she was headed here to confer with Jorge and Phyllis—though now that I thought about it, what could she have accomplished, since those two wouldn't even know she was there? She'd probably been wracking her amazing brain to figure out a way to signal them, though I happen to know you can't do anything to signal anyone. Being a ghost is like living behind a one-way mirror.

I blinked up to the Penthouse. I was going to grab my body, swing down to Phil's office to pick up Caroline and we'd make a day of it. I blinked into the bedroom, where I hoped the *Gray* had managed to put flesh me to sleep, and there I found flesh me, stretched atop the sheets, drooling like a baby. And, floating beside him, gazing down with an expression rapt and hungry, was a ghost.

It was the ghost of Aeternus.

FOUR

*W*hat, I asked myself in confusion, *is going on here, now, again?*

And I floated in one place for a longish second or two. History has shown that ghost me is not an action hero. Ghost me is slow in an emergency. Flesh me is pretty fast, and of course, the *Gray* is in another speed class entirely, plus he himself is often responsible for whatever emergency needs to be addressed and has prior warning. But ghost me? I process crisis information slowly, and I think it's fair to say reluctantly. Ghost me prefers denial.

Get ... away! I ghosted after far too long, slowed by questions like, *where did Aeternus come from?* And, *what is Aeternus doing here I thought he was dead?* And *well he is dead so I wasn't wrong about that at least.*

Aeternus noticed the ghost yelling and turned his head my direction and my brain slowed again to realize more questions, like *wait—Aeternus turned his head?* And—*wait Aeternus isn't frozen and he's now reaching for flesh me?*

I flung my ghost straight at Aeternus's chest. Was it great strategy, I do not know, but your options as a ghost are slim and none. Crashing into other ghosts is your power—that and snarky observations, and those get me nowhere—plus garden variety denial, which is honestly the most useful in almost every case.

Just as I crashed into him, he blinked elsewhere. My momentum —or whatever I had—carried me toward the closet. Behind me Aeternus blinked back in. When I turned he was smiling.

Hello Asher, he ghosted.

His lips moved. All his Bollywood good looks moved. He wore his loincloth like a three-piece suit and though the umbra eye was missing from his chest he looked in all other ways exactly as I'd seen him last, kissing me to death in his underground torture theatre. His leading man curls shifted as he watched me.

Someone had touched his object. He'd been sent to the ghost beyond, and like Caroline, had come out here. Who did it to him?

I was filled with a panicked need to separate him from flesh me because of what he'd done last time. I rushed in again but he blinked out and returned. His vibe was very casual, like we were playing a game he enjoyed because he could cheat at it. We went back and forth rushing and blinking a few more times but it went on long enough for me to lose interest.

We floated on either side of the bed then, looking at flesh me like adoring ghost parents.

So very peaceful, Aeternus said. I searched his voice for threatening implications. I watched his body for clues to whatever violence he was planning, though clues are not my thing and I knew I'd probably never see one in time.

Then flesh me, who must have heard some of our ghost commotion, awoke. Yawned. Opened his eyes.

"Hey," he said, sitting up, "it's Nolear Fa."

Stay away from him, I warned flesh me, *keep far away from him, understand?*

The last time those two met, Aeternus was mind-controlling him. I was pretty sure flesh me was free of that now, but then I'm pretty sure about a lot of crazy shit and most of it turns out to be wrong. Flesh me himself narrowed his eyes and turned and looked at Aeternus with what I knew he thought was suspicion, but which really was the look of someone in a cave blinded by a flashlight.

He understood my warning, however. He leaned back slightly and asked, "How can I stay away if he blinks? Won't he just blink anywhere I go? Even in the bathroom?"

It was a fantastic question. I was proud of him.

There's nothing to fear, little man, Aeternus said to flesh me. *Look.*

Before either of me could do a thing Aeternus raised his arms and thrust them through flesh me's shoulder with no resistance. Like my flesh was made of air.

Flesh me looked at the fingers sticking from his chest. "Hey," he said, without a lot of concern. His personal peril instincts had fallen off a cliff. At a minimum he should be screaming, and probably running in circles.

He has a living body, Aeternus said, pointing out the obvious for me, I guess because he'd met me before. *I couldn't harm him even if I wanted to. I'm only a ghost.*

Oh, you're a ghost? I ghosted out, stalling, scanning the room, trying to trigger some what's-next genius, which, when it came, was pretty disappointing.

Well bullshit! I shouted. The genius I'd chosen was just my regular obstinance. *I don't believe you. What are you really? I'm a ghost and I touch him. Ghosts touch him all the time.*

The plan I still held hope for was I'd reclaim flesh me, find Caroline, and take my ghost girlfriend out to watch me get my body drunk, like a normal couple. It was going to be great. But I was too nervous to jump back into him right now. Maybe Aeternus still had mind-control skills.

Aeternus slid his arm from flesh me's shoulder.

But you are not a ghost, Aeternus protested, softly. *I am—but you are not.*

Agree to disagree. I know what I am. Only too well. This was a lie of course but I was still just pursuing obstinance and looking for my next move.

At that point, he made an, "ah-*ha*" hole with his lips and nodded.

You know so little, he told me. *But I will teach you. We can start with this. You, Asher, are a spirit. Not a ghost.*

Spirit, ghost, tomato, tomato, no difference I can see.

The difference is enormous, he intoned, ignoring me. *The difference between a spirit, a shade, and a ghost is enough to end a world. Or begin one.*

Why are you even here? I demanded. I get short-tempered at intoning. It's my only pet peeve. *And hey, wait—back up. Just … wait a minute. You're moving, so someone heard your story … someone sent you on ghost vacation.*

Ghost vacation?

Hey, focus. I was there when you died. I saw it. So someone must have touched your object. And it wasn't me.

Oh, ghost vacation. You are charming! So direct. Like a puppy.

Is there someone else out there like me?

To be clear—you are asking about the endowment. Yes? In your way?

What I'm asking is, who heard your story and sent you off to Club Afterworld?

That process, the transition to a ghost—that is called the endowment.

I'm going to call it the ghost story thing. The ghost story thing.

No. You are a spirit. I am a ghost. Before they are endowed, the rest are shades.

I'll just say ghost story thing.

I don't know why I roll this way. It was just more obstinance in place of any plan. It might have been more obstinance than Aeternus had ever seen in his life. He took a moment to wonder at me with an expression every teacher who ever saw me wore, that said, *So much potential, but <u>why</u> does he have to be in my class?*

At last, Aeternus shook his head and gave an encouraging smile.

There is much you must learn, he said. He'd made up his mind right there. *I will teach you.*

I decline. Answer the question. Who's out there touching ghosts? Are there more Inmortalis?

None but you. Though I, technically, am the ghost of an Inmortalis.

He said it like a Saturday morning cartoon clue, slow and deliberate. Also like a person baiting a trap then carefully stepping backward. I made the obvious connection. Because of my personal history.

You did the story thing on <u>yourself</u>, didn't you? I asked. *As you died? Is that it?*

Aren't you magnificent! You are a stallion—wild, magnificent, unbroken.

Answer.

Is that what you'd like, Asher? An answer?

Oh my god. I cast my mind back. *I think so yeah but … what was my question again?*

You asked if I endowed myself. No doubt thinking of Caroline. You see how well I know you? You hope to stand beside her. To die, and become a ghost, and touch her. Am I right?

I was sorry Aeternus had guessed my hope about Caroline. Caroline was by this time the obsessive, generative impulse for everything I did, which was super unhealthy I knew, but that's also how I roll, sort of to the extremes. On the one hand, I knew Aeternus to be a threat. He could use Caroline against me somehow. On the other hand *somehow* after he'd died he'd become a walk-around ghost. And I desperately wanted to know how to become a walk-around ghost after I died. Because yes. Then I could walk around with Caroline.

So are you saying you, as a ghost, could send my ghost on vacation if I died? I asked.

Oh Asher. If you and I are going to embark on this journey, we should start the right way. The process you are asking about is known as endowment. You may ask me about endowment. Say it.

He waited and I did too. We were going to do a waiting game I saw. But I felt like I could wait forever if it meant not giving him the satisfaction of saying his word, which just shows you how badly I know myself.

Fine, endowment, I said pretty quickly. *Are you happy? So who endowed you?*

He made an expression that gave me a sinking feeling because I'm so sensitive to a lecture. I'm sensitive enough that I can usually avoid one by pretending I forgot what room it was in or by showing up drunk. But where could I go now? He had me at a lecture disadvantage, something they'd been trying to do since first grade. He was a wizard. Though not, as Phil liked to say, a real one, I hoped.

Consciousness is nothing but an emergent phenomenon, he said inscrutably, the way they start all the lectures. *All living organisms must solve problems: where can food be found? What should be done with threats? How can the most reproduction be achieved? You see?*

I see it's a lecture.

Consciousness, with which we identify—which we think of as our very selves—is merely the tool functioning organisms use to solve these problems. In fact, solving these problems is the only purpose consciousness serves. It creates solutions to problems.

Problems. Purpose of consciousness. Now who endowed you on vacation?

This was a trick I'd had success with in the past, pretending to pay attention and then changing the subject. Aeternus only smiled.

The problem-solving process has three stages, he continued. *Do you know them?*

Oh my god, I complained. *Seriously? This is like one of those cooking shows that are really about self-realization with no cooking.*

Yes. Here are the three stages of problem-solving, he rolled on as if I hadn't just complained about cooking shows. *Stage one—select the problem that must be solved. Stage two—imagine the solution. Stage three —execute the solution and solve the problem. It sounds simple, doesn't it? But much can go wrong.*

Let me stop you there, I said. *I don't know what this has to do with anything, and I—*

Do you want to know who endowed me?

I thought I did. Before you started talking.

Then learn. Learn from me.

After a moment I shrugged inside my brain and I put on my learning expression which, since I'm a ghost, looked like my other expression. Aeternus was very intent. He really, really wanted me to learn something. Thank god none of my elementary school teachers had been like this.

The three stages, he repeated. *Identify a problem, imagine a solution, execute the solution. Consciousness is inseparable from these stages. Consciousness is itself, thus, divided into three parts.*

I groaned. If I had a drink for every lecture where they divided the world into parts I'd be in a coma and all my suffering would be over.

You are doing very well, Asher. These are large, strange concepts to take in all at once.

You're large and strange.

Yes. He looked me over like maybe he'd miscalculated. But he had too much self-confidence to take an idea like that very seriously.

So here is the essential lesson: the three parts of consciousness. They are, one, the conscience, two, the imagination, and three, the will. With the conscience we identify a problem, with the imagination we create a solution, and with our will we execute a solution. Do you see where all this is headed?

No. What am I, psychic?

He looked me over.

You, Asher, are coming apart. It is the curse, affecting your native instability. Your pieces are separating. He pointed to flesh me, who looked fascinated but lost. *You have a body, you have your spirit and the Gray. Only I can teach you to synthesize them. And you must come together. Before it is too late.*

That's a fantastic offer. I'll give it serious consideration and then turn it down later. I've been coming apart for so many years I frankly couldn't give a shit. God damn it. Who endowed you?

The moment had come. Would he help, I wondered? Or was this just another railroad I'd find myself taking over a cliff?

As you surmised, he nodded at last. *I endowed myself. Every Inmortalis has the ability to endow himself at the moment of death.*

But you were Nidor, not Inmortalis. You couldn't see ghosts.

As we died—you remember? Such sweet release—I took your Inmortalis body.

I'm not Inmortalis.

Oh, Asher, your obstinance is so pure. You are a wonder. But you are wrong. How or why it happened may forever be a mystery. But you are, in fact, the world's only living Inmortalis. As I am the world's only dead Inmortalis. I am the only one who can help you navigate what is to come. I can teach you what you need to know. Let me teach you.

You can teach me this ... endowment? For when I die?

That? That is instinct. You will not be able to help yourself when you die. Unless you are broken into pieces. Then—

But I could feel a plan forming and I stopped listening. Such a simple plan. A Caroline plan where she and I could be together in as many ways as this world would still allow. Maybe hold hands. A plan that would solve all my problems. Maybe there'd been something to this lecture after all.

The end is almost upon us, Aeternus warned. *You are breaking. You need me.*

Sometime during the lecture and our ghost arguments, flesh me had left the bedroom, apparently to make himself some toast, because now he returned holding toast. And I thought, he can't be holding toast. Not with ... fingers? But he was.

His fists were gone. Or hidden inside his hands, or whatever happens to fists, I'll leave that to philosophers—but in their place, he sported ten flexible fingers and an expression of pride and bewilderment. His new ability—oh my god, there's always some new ability it's *exhausting*—was, apparently, he could navigate the world with opposable thumbs. He was twisting the hand holding the toast as he came back into the bedroom in amazement. He looked at me and smiled.

"They just started doing that," he said, and some toast fell from his mouth because his fingers had grown dexterous but his chewing skills were well behind what you'd want in a person his age.

I have a plan to get together with Caroline, I told him. *Are you ready?*

He nodded as he chewed, and said, "Also Phil says there's a police problem."

Also what? When'd you talk to Phil?

"Just now when he knocked. I opened the door with fingers! He said the police are coming here."

Here? Why here?

"Investigating a gun or something."

Hennessy's gun?

He shrugged. "Phil heard it on his Bradley Family walkie."

It was hard to keep up. First it's toast, now he's answering the door and bringing me important information. It got easier and easier thinking of him as a completely separate person. And since I'll unfailingly take the easier path I could see myself eventually writing him off as a total stranger and wanting nothing to do with him.

I presume the police are coming for the corpse, Aeternus told us.

Who is ... what corpse is this now? I asked. I'd spent too much time thinking about my plan to die and come back all flexible, and now I was behind in my real life. Flesh me pointed down the hall, marveling as he held one finger extended.

"The policeman corpse in the living room," he explained.

This was news to me—as almost everything almost always is—because when I'd left the penthouse this morning there had been no corpses. I whirled to Aeternus.

Did you kill someone?

He did *amused disdain* for me while he raised an eyebrow, *no.* It was bartender-quality disdain. I turned to flesh me to hear the explanation which he had decided to count off on his new fingers, just from sheer finger delight.

"One, a policeman died in the living room. Two, he's in there dead on a stool. Three, his ghost is there too but I didn't touch it but I wanted to. I told Phil about the dead policeman when I answered the door with my fingers and Phil said the policeman was downstairs asking everyone if you'd been seen with a gun. Five, I said you didn't have a gun. Five, Phil said he *knew* that about you, so he sent the policeman to the penthouse to look. I asked Phil to come in and have toast but he said he's not supposed to come in because he'll die."

If Phil knows people die in here why'd he send the policeman in? I demanded.

"To look for the gun, hello? Have you been listening?"

This conversation with myself, like all of them, was a waste of my time. More and more now I saw what people had been complaining about all those years. It's barely worth the energy required to listen to me.

I blinked into my sunken living room. There, the mural of the Undying Land spiraled a matrix of ultraviolet *light* and time and madness off the wall. Normally you'd say it dominated the space but it was currently competing with a glowing crowd of ghosts, comprised of everyone who'd died underground in Aeternus's quorum, or who'd died after that of old age on benches and in restaurants and all the other people who'd died in Skysill Beach recently—which was a *lot of people*—all shimmering in one room.

Bright afternoon warmth came in off the balcony, and the light of Earth's sun, and the Higher *light* off the mural all mixed in that living room air and it was, for a moment, pure glory. If you liked that kind of spectacle. I had no time for the scene because of the cop body on my footstool. The ghost of that body floated near the corpse. As flesh me came to stand at my side, all the ghosts in the room rotated toward him.

I was surprised—apparently Hennessy actually *had* sent people looking for this gun. I'd assumed it was a random cop threat to get a bribe or whatever—because seriously what's the big deal? A cop lost his gun? They have a *thousand* guns. They probably lose guns all the time on purpose just to get an upgrade. But I saw that Hen, for real, wanted this one back. Maybe it was his favorite gun or the gun his mother gave him for his first birthday. I'd have to ask him next time he arrested me.

"They have name tags," flesh me announced, pointing at the body. "His tag is Officer Smith." He was hoping I'd be impressed with his ability to read. I have no idea why my opinion meant so much to him.

We have to get this body out of here, I shouted, unimpressed. *Fast.*

"Why?" flesh me asked.

Are you kidding? They can't find him here. Grab him. Let's get him moved!

I'd already been through this with Victors so it was a plan with a good track record. But we lacked Victors' wheelchair, so the body would have to be carried out on someone's shoulder or something. Maybe wrapped in a carpet. The corpse was cop big, too heavy for flesh me alone.

Go get Phyllis, I told him. He shook his head.

"Phil said all the psychics left the building somewhere."

All of them? When was this?

"Phil said he didn't know."

You and Phil had quite the chat when you answered that door.

"Phil's pretty interesting."

No, he's not, now what are we going to do with this body? I was trying to keep us on track and focused. Me, keeping a conversation on track. What kind of world were we living in?

"How about *Gray* you?" flesh me said. "He's strong. He could throw Officer Smith off the balcony."

No, I said. Because then I saw the real problem. *We can't just hide this body. Shit.*

Shit exactly, Aeternus said. He saw the problem too. He had the billionaire ability, to internalize an entire disaster with a single glance. I thought out loud for flesh me's benefit.

There are cops coming to the penthouse. They know he came here.

They'll come in and see the mural and die. After that, they'll send more cops. More and more.

"Like lemmings," flesh me gasped.

But Asher, you are Inmortalis, Aeternus reminded me, his voice quiet, but somehow urgent. I wished he'd stop calling me Inmortalis, but I was distracted by lemmings and didn't protest.

This is a problem you were born to solve, he insisted. *You have the solution within you. You need only call the power forth.*

Look, I snarled, because I guess I thought I had all the time in the world to argue and complain, *why don't you just keep your opinions to yourself? Because your opinions mean fuck all to me! Time ended <u>because of you</u>. You're fucking psychotic. I do not trust you.*

But we are the same.

Don't do that.

Both addicts.

The surest way to get an addict's complete attention is, you talk about being an addict. It's all we're really qualified to discuss. More than anything else we love a chance to dissect addiction and rehash the addictive lifestyle. Particularly those of us who have recovered, like me, who miss it all. He sucked me in with his addict admission.

Ghost eater. Couldn't stop. Self-destructive. It tracked. The substance changes but the need is the same glass in your veins. Mechanics, psychics, teachers, generals—addiction's everywhere. And it makes you do everything you do. It changes the stakes. Flattens them out.

Aeternus floated before me with an expression I wouldn't call penitent since his face simply didn't have that shape, but something close. A kind of arrogant humility, something only he could manufacture. Like he wanted to help, but he didn't know how that worked. Like he was sorry.

He offered his transparent hands, fingers spread, palms up.

More police are coming, he said. *They will die. It will not stop. And only one person can head them off. Only one person can attest that the premises are free from suspicion.*

It was like a riddle with no answer. The kind I can't resist. *Who?* I asked.

Officer Smith himself.

"He's dead," flesh me reminded us.

Officer Smith's body must meet them in the lobby and announce that he's searched the building, found it free of weapons, and that the search can shift elsewhere.

He was trying to get me to do something, and not something normal or easy to understand. In a lot of ways, it was like one of Amy's vague, ridiculous plans. He floated closer, his voice insistent.

You must animate the corpse. Animate Officer Smith.

For a moment the only noise was air blowing, soft through vents, and the sound of ten million pounds of weightless deadly *light* crashing off the wall into the side of my face. I knew I was being led out onto the middle of a lake of thin ice. I hated how reasonable he sounded. Distantly, then, I heard a siren approaching.

So I asked, *What is this, some Inmortalis thing?*

He nodded.

You have such power, he said quietly, *power you do not understand. Let me show you. I want to help. You think me a monster. But the world is not that simple. I have done things. I must atone.*

I didn't trust him, though I did feel like I knew him. He was self-reflective in a way only one-time users like myself are likely to recognize. The self-reflection that comes after your dealers all leave town or go to jail and you have no other options. It's not a trustworthy stage of recovery. But I had to do something. I couldn't let a succession of dead cops fill the penthouse. It would be super inconvenient.

The inconvenience decided me. Sometimes I wish I was different.

So what do I do? I asked.

Come. Hurry. Orient your spirit so it rests within the corpse. Do not touch the shades.

My spirit? Shades? What are you talking about?

He widened his eyes at my lack of comprehension or interest or memory and at my other missing things. Then, pointing to himself, he said, *ghost*. Pointing at me he said, *spirit*. Pointing at the hundreds of floating, one arm out with a bag of chips spectators, he said, *shades*.

"I don't get it," flesh me said.

But I did. I felt like Stephan Hawking suddenly. Insight. This was what I'd been asking for—they *did* have names. Fully mobile—that was a *ghost*. Transparent but connected to a living body like me, that was a *spirit*. And after your flesh died while you were frozen waiting to go on vacation—*shade*.

The sirens were louder.

Aeternus insisted again, *Position your spirit within the corpse. Touch no shades. Then orient so you are floating face down above it, touching it with your arm extended.*

So that's what I did. I floated into the middle of Smith's flesh chest, nervous that I was going to break something. But it was only a corpse and what's the worst that could happen to it? All anyone ever did was burn them or bury them before they rotted. Corpses hardly mattered. It's the ghost that counts. I was pretty sure. I raised myself so I was floating, looking down at him.

Closer. Yes. Now, Aeternus said, eyeing me critically, *each Inmortalis has a personal key, a symbol, a word, a song—some key you turn to unlock your spirit from their flesh. What is yours? Quickly!*

His tone was sharp. Fast. Too eager. But it totally helped me focus.

I cross my eyes, I said.

Something left his face then, or something showed up, just for a second. Or maybe I'm crazy. Or both things are true. After that his intonation modulated, his voice got heavy and rote, and he said, *Then cross your eyes, young Inmortalis, and take your birthright.*

Don't call it that.

Cross your eyes. This corpse is yours. The Sea of Renewal awaits.

I'm as sensitive to a ceremony as I am to a lecture and this had started giving off distinctly ceremonial vibes. The sirens wailed to stop outside the building. All I'd wanted to do was find Caroline and go to the bar and here I was in the middle of a ceremony, raising a corpse to impersonate a police officer. I have no idea how this shit always happens. But now the whole ceremonial tone had me spooked. I'm all over the map, I know that.

I mean, I stalled, *why is animating corpses even a thing? Isn't that fucking weird?*

His face took on a look that could have been religious rapture, it could have been junkie dreamtime, in my experience there's very little difference.

Every corpse required an Inmortalis in the Undying Land.

Because?

Because in the Undying Land, before Ti'eirl trapped us in this world, a corpse was poison to the living. Any living person who touched a corpse instantly died themselves.

And again ... isn't that a super weird system?

That is but the tip of the iceberg.

"The police are in the lobby," flesh me said, staring down through a window.

I know when circumstances have trapped me, which is *always.* I put Aeternus and poison corpses out of my mind, like I can, and I crossed my eyes. I can only stall for so long. Not even that long. I lack patience.

When I crossed my eyes a *dominion* cloud came up out of me, or down through me, or in around me—whichever is the one that hurts most. I got the bad pain, like the first days of the body merge, the lava-razors down spinal bones pain, which sent me ghost screaming. Though flesh me felt nothing this time, only watched and wiggled his fingers. He was out of the loop.

The corpse began jerking, like electrodes catching fire. Supernatural electrodes.

Some force sucked me into superimposition with that dead flesh. Like a regular ghost merge, but with a dead body. *Dominion* squeezed both bodies together. I began feeling unfamiliar limbs, thick as tree trunks, and thin, hard, unfamiliar lips, and a tongue on teeth that were not mine. I felt an entire body. Then I was inside.

I found myself folded over facing down on top of a footstool. I had arms and legs and a torso, but none of them technically alive. I had a name—Darvin Smith. As I thought of my name, a cascade of information overwhelmed me. It was everything that made Darvin Smith himself. His childhood. His regrets. His love of the Chargers. His address and his religion and how he ate, dressed, talked, and pissed. It was a lot. He hated dogs and liberals. He was kind of a fucking asshole. He was me.

What the what? I complained, and then instead of ghosting the words, the open mouth I had said, "What the *what?*" out of the face with the eyes I blinked in confusion. Merry Christmas. A brand-new body. Not new. Lightly used.

Can you stand? Aeternus asked, urgent. His voice sounded distant and tinny inside the ears I had.

"Can I *stand?*" Darvin's mouth kept complaining out my words. "*What?* What did you do to me?"

Aeternus not only sounded like an underwater recording, he also looked wavery. All the ghosts—and the shades—crowded in that room looked the same. They looked like weak milk spilled in the air. Exactly the way ghosts always get described in books. Not that I read.

You've done it, Aeternus's voice wavered down the ear canals to the brain I had. He looked very satisfied with his work. I wondered what he'd done that was so hard. *You may experience some sensory distortions.*

"No kidding," I moaned through Darvin's mouth, "this feels wrong."

It is not. You are Inmortalis. You may animate any corpse. Stand it and go downstairs.

"I ..."

Flesh me, fogging up the window looking at the street, said,

"Two of them just came inside." At least flesh me looked and sounded normal.

Darvin Smith groaned. Of all the things that'd ever happened to me, this body swap was the most intimate and disgusting. Like wearing someone else's clothes while they're still in them. Or something. You were just touching things in here that obviously shouldn't be touched. I swear to god it's always something.

I had to look out through Darvin's eyes, and he had shitty eyes. They hardly saw anything. He needed glasses. There were prescription sunglasses hooked to his shirt—that fact arose in our mind as I turned our brain to thoughts of our eyesight. They were dark Terminator shades. I put them on. A hundred other facts arose in our brain. His vanity. His unspeakable fear of weakness. His father's face. Dead man thoughts, circling a dead man brain. They came breathless, desperate to be recognized. It was more thinking than I was used to and it made me sick.

Also, he had a horrible taste in his mouth. Like a dead animal. Which, maybe that was just him tasting his own tongue. His glasses had focused the room for me, but the ghosts remained transparent white sheets, waving in the air.

"This is not great *at all*," Darvin's mouth said. "When does this thinking stop?"

It does not. This corpse is yours. Its feelings. Its thoughts. Its every ability, born or learned. Anything this corpse could do in life you can do.

Aeternus flickered out of sight for a second, then returned. *They are in the elevator now.*

Officer Smith's linebacker legs got up under him. I straightened his torso off the footstool and put him on his feet. It was the same as working my regular body if my limbs were the wrong length and shape and strength and in the wrong places. I swayed, blinking my shitty eyes to gain my balance. Then lurched around toward the hall. Flesh me gave Darvin me a thumbs up. Not because he felt confident or hopeful, he just loved being able to stick up one thumb.

We creaked as we walked, from sheer cop leather overload.

Under his uniform, he wore a bulletproof vest and it made me claustrophobic and I wanted to take it off. But *we all wear vests*, came the thought. Hostile shooters. The town's gone batshit crazy. We had to stay safe—though in the end, the vest had not offered the kind of safety officer Darvin needed—protection from art.

When I got him to the door I fumbled it open. His fingers were so *wide,* my god, did people really have fingers this wide? Like spoons. How do you get anything out of your pocket? His muscles twitched at a very different tempo than my usual ones. The door slammed open super-fast. I leaned him out and started him for the elevator, crushing and kicking gift baskets with enormous booted feet. Then my eyes saw Phil standing to the side. Phil watched Darvin pass him in the hall like Darvin was a one-cop parade.

"Phil," Darvin's side mouth greeted him. Phil had a watery ghost form coming out his back. Other than that he looked normal. He was surprised Darvin knew his name.

"Hello, Officer Smith," he said.

"Let me ask you something Phil—where'd all the psychics go?"

"To a burial," Phil said and started walking along, attached like a remora to a shark, as Darvin trundled forward.

"Who died?" Darvin asked with his mouth.

"A lady named Caroline," Phil said, very sad. "She was a real psychic, not a TV one. She psychically found my luggage one time before a cruise. It was in my closet. May she rest in peace."

"Where's this burial?"

"Who knows? I mean who knows officer? Maybe the psychic graveyard."

"They have a graveyard for psychics?"

"Probably. Dogs have them. Did you find any guns?"

"There're no guns."

"Are you going back to your station house?"

"Phil, I don't know where I'm going," Darvin's mouth said, distracted and annoyed by Phil's many questions because even the dead have limits.

"You don't know where you're going? Well then go on a fabulous *Hawaiian vacation!*" Phil suggested, like Darvin had won a prize. "Prices have never been lower, and—"

Then the elevator opened and two cops jumped out with guns drawn and Phil stopped and put his hands up.

"Smith!" yelled one of the cops at Darvin. This was a lady cop, the one with the distracting dot in her eye who had previously arrested me in the lobby, back when I'd been Asher Gale. Through Darvin's shitty eyes she appeared worried, and her partner, the cop with extra-long fingernails, looked worried too. But both lowered their guns as Darvin forged bullishly down the hall. Both had ghosts emerging through their backs—no not ghosts. Spirits?

"Fawcett," Darvin's mouth said the name of the lady cop as it rose to his brain box. Desperately I parsed the stream of cop names and relationships that spun up to me, along with the various investigations and bribes and tragedies we were all concluding or pursuing or ignoring. How did they keep track of all the bribes? I was getting confused. It made me tip over slightly. You ask one simple question —what's the lady cop called?—and you're flooded with trivia. Darvin's foot hit a box of decorative candles. We almost went tumbling.

"*Fuck is this shit?*" I found myself using the Darvin mouth to shout. It was a pretty natural feeling, actually. Once you had these bodies moving you could let them navigate on autopilot a little to shout things, if you loosened your hold slightly. Facts kept coming, making me dizzy. Darvin kicked the box of candles against the wall because *angry*. From behind Darvin came Phil, hands still up, letting out a whimper.

"Skysill's Best Artisanal Candles," he said. "First floor. They're *delicate ...*"

"Shut it," Darvin turned and pointed to Phil's mouth. Phil paled and nodded, sealing his lips. The other cops, who'd been watching Darvin uncertainly, were suddenly relieved. They changed the instant they saw Darvin shouting arbitrary orders and threatening citizens. It's the cop recognition code. I'd cracked it.

"There's nothing here," I said, hooking Darvin's thumb over his shoulder like I'd seen Hennessy do. They get a lot of mileage out of a thumb, these cops, and I saw why. There's a seductive finality to the gesture. No going back. Fuck you.

"Dispatch said code 30," said the lady cop, who was named Theresa Fawcett, who Darvin had always wanted to ask to a Charger's game but who was a Rams fan, which was too high a hurdle for either of them to clear.

Maurice, the fingernail cop, asked, "You have trouble with him?" He hooked a thumb at Phil, who trembled.

"Hell no," Darvin snorted. "Radio problems is all." He put one massive hand on either of their shoulders to urge a turn toward the elevator. "There is nothing here though, nothing is here to see. This entire building is clean. I searched, no guns, no sign of Asher Gale. The sooner we are gone the happier I will be."

The other two shrugged and put their guns away and while we stood waiting for the elevator I sifted all the information in the brain I had. All the useless cop dates and law enforcement ideas, searching for what cop language to use steering suspicion away from Asher Gale. If I had to animate this corpse I thought I should try to get my money's worth.

"Oh," Darvin's mouth said, as the doors opened and we three cops stepped in, "Asher Gale is no longer a *person of interest* in any crimes. He's a person of ... disinterest. Now, let us put that case behind us. The entire police force can now leave Asher in peace."

The lady cop looked up with a smirk. "Yeah, well, Hennessy's got a hardon for that little tweaker and he's not leaving anyone in peace."

Darvin shook his head. "My information says Gale is not a tweaker. Though he is deeply confused and sadly disappointed with what has become of his life."

We reached the lobby and Darvin led the other cops out. I could hardly believe all this was working. Just like Aeternus had predicted. They'd accepted me. I was like a sheep in wolf's clothing. It was weirdly thrilling. It felt like I'd joined a kind of top-tier fraternity where everyone had guns. Here we were, just a trio of hard-working cops all laughing at Hennessy losing his gun. Who loses a gun to a tweaker? So funny.

The lobby was filled with cots and strewn bedding and piled personal goods salvaged from the ruins of Three Paths, but no people. The psychics were all off on their burial adventure.

"So what's this, overflow housing?" asked Theresa, scanning under the beds then looking at Darvin. "I thought those were the sites at the pier?"

"I hear *these* are from a mental facility," Maurice said.

"It truly feels that way," Darvin nodded. "You would be amazed."

"Do they have permits?" Theresa asked. "Smells pretty ripe."

"Let's get the city in here," Maurice said. He looked up at the ceiling. "They could be all through the building. Has anybody talked to the owner?"

Darvin gave them a push toward the lobby doors, which were still barricaded behind a large desk. It had not been removed, not by the Bradley family, not by law enforcement, not by criminal mobs or this influx of psychics. It was one of life's great puzzles, a half-obstructed door behind a desk was the perfect entrance for the Bradley.

"I say," Darvin said, pushing them toward the desk, "we leave the group here alone. These people are enfeebled but harmless, leave them and soon they will die, and it will not be our problem. Soon we *all* will die, in fact, maybe sooner than we think, though this may not be a subject I normally wax philosophic on, but they say death changes everyone. You know where you, we, should really send a team is Aliso Canyon, those addicts need food and methadone and—oh! Right. I have just remembered the location of Hennessy's missing gun."

"What?" Theresa asked, clambering over the desk and out.

When we three cops stood on the sidewalk, Darvin told them, "One of my ... that word we use ... *sources*. One of my sources says Hennessy's gun can be found up Aliso Canyon. Near the caves where the canyon people do their dancing. Someone should look there."

"Hen's going to shit himself if that's true," Theresa said. She was eyeing Darvin. "You okay? You don't look too good."

"I feel fine. No wait. I have had indigestion since this morning and shooting pain in my left arm."

"Smith, you idiot, you're having a heart attack!"

"My heart is fine—I am walking and talking."

"Go back to the station."

"I am perfectly healthy, though if my corpse is found later remember this conversation."

We three cops all laughed. Darvin laughed hardest. Then we parted cop ways. Theresa and Maurice went to investigate Aliso Canyon and Darvin watched them drive off.

Now what, I wondered, in Darvin's brain box?

The sun had slipped past noon, midway to the horizon. Using nerves I did not own I felt cool wind come off the water. Darvin's mouth tasted like a toilet bowl. For a moment I was tempted to go get drunk and wash the whole tangled mess away down Darvin's thick throat. But I was coming to the conclusion that the Charles was off the table for today. I sighed my corpse and found the effect restful.

PCH ran in front of me, bisecting the gallery district. I watched a single car pass. A lone car, where there should be hundreds. I recognized the driver, a painter. He glanced Darvin's direction warily while stopped at the signal, then eased off, leaving an empty highway. Where were the tourists? Supposedly Aeternus was dead. His masterminding the world, emptying towns for his quorum, that was all over. Shouldn't we have tourists back?

After Caroline died I'd locked myself in the penthouse and refused to interact with the world for weeks, because everyone deals with death differently, and my way was dysfunctional. So I hadn't been keeping track of events in Skysill. All the timelines had gone squishy, but hadn't it only been this morning I'd met the Monarchs at the Bayside for brunch? Or when had that been? There'd been brunch, then I'd released—endowed—Caroline. Then had come the endless sunset and the sun going out. Then the sun traveling back to start over. So what day was this?

Hey Darvin, I had Darvin think to himself. *Did we see the sun go out in the sky at any time today or ever?*

The brain box sent up a very thin stream of information, mostly concerning a partial eclipse he'd witnessed as a boy which had bored him.

Hey Darvin, I tried, *where are all the tourists? And what about all the people who are getting old and dying?*

That was too many questions at one time and I was stupefied, momentarily, as a roar of trivia swirled up, but as it settled I was able to pick out the gist: for a time the Skysill police and other civil services had been overwhelmed by a plague of people dying of old age, despite not being old. Plenty of his brothers and sisters on the force had fallen this way. The morgues had been besieged. The funeral homes overflowing. The city had been forced to burn corpses on the beach. Which, I thought—*what?* How did I not hear about this? How long had all this taken?

His raw brain pictures were beyond gruesome, but the impressions Darvin carried about them were very ... casual. The horror I'd have expected, the denial, the defeat, at minimum the confusion, were absent. Maybe it was a cop thing, or it could have been a dead brain thing, but I had a different theory—it was a thing the curse was doing. It was this world we were stuck in. A world of death, trapped between the Undying Land and the old world. If you could even call it the old world. We were sealed under the spell of this half-lifted curse in a place where life itself was unwelcome. Death hung from the clouds. It rose from the waves. Death was the canvas this world was painted on.

And then I saw in Darvin's dead-brain thought stream that the old-age deaths had stopped some days ago. Though again there seemed to be a timeline discrepancy because it had been just this morning, or yesterday morning depending on how you were counting, that I'd seen fresh corpses on the beach and dead people at bus stops as I went to the Bayside for a Monarch brunch. So, like Caroline said. Time didn't work the way it used to.

And in the end, the only people who'd insta-aged and died had been outsiders. So maybe that made a difference. Because who cared about people from outside? We were a small town full of small-town graft and psychosis and though we depended on tourists and newcomers for paychecks, we ultimately didn't trust them. From what I gathered, everyone born in Skysill had lived. It was like we existed in a bubble, separate from the rest of the world.

I liked none of these thoughts. Liked them not at all. And I wanted out of the brain that was shoveling them at me. But as soon as I vacated this body, it would fall back over dead, so I needed a good place for Officer Smith to have his heart attack. I hesitated just leaving the body on the sidewalk. Where do cops go to die?

Finally, I took Darvin to his police car. It was parked down the street in a red zone. He reached his fat fingers into his pocket for his keys, and it wasn't hard because he turned out to have fat pockets, and then I had him unlock the door and climb in, settling slowly into his seat the way bears enter their winter dens. The car creaked. I put him behind the wheel and shut his door, and let all his motion stop. No breathing. No blinking. No heart beating. He just sat.

Here in the car, surrounded by his guns and face scanning software and zip ties was a proper final resting place for Officer Darvin Smith. I saw gum wrappers in the center console. He'd been a gum chewer. I put a stick in his mouth, and we chewed a few bites, just to freshen his breath before I made two fists and squeezed. I squirted backward, up, and out into the air above the car.

Feeling nothing now, the way you do up here, was pretty fantastic, though I was disappointed about the way performing all these Inmortalis tricks had so quickly become so humdrum. I could see myself doing these tricks again, without hesitating. I owned them. Now I floated over the siren lights for a moment, looking down at the street then up at the sky, grateful that my eyes were no longer shitty, spending a few seconds soaking up all the failing afternoon *light* of Skysill Beach.

But I didn't linger. Darvin's deadman babble about bodies in Skysill had reminded me about Caroline. She had a dead body—and the psychics were, even now, off somewhere burying it in the ground. Since she'd gone to join the Monarchs, the odds were good she'd tagged along for the funeral, unable to get their attention. I wasn't a hundred percent on the protocol but I assumed your boyfriend was supposed to go to the burial of your dead body so he could give you moral support. Not that moral support's my thing.

I blinked back up to the penthouse to collect flesh me.

CHAPTER

FIVE

A scene of cozy paranormal domesticity both comforting and revolting—though how that's possible I do not know—greeted me when I reappeared among couches in my penthouse full of recycled sunlight. On one wall blazed the mural, a luminous haze of ghost *light*. Before it on a footstool, flesh me sat, idle as a boy watching a magic TV. He'd found string, I thought maybe a shoelace, and had all ten fingers twisted and whorled there like a cat with yarn.

Behind him, also facing the mural, floated Aeternus. He'd thrust both hands down my flesh back up to his forearms. In my mind I still called it my back, but did I really own that back anymore? It was starting to feel like a rental. Like shared office space I used when I had to work.

Aeternus flexed ghost fingers in whoever's chest cavity it was, idly kneading something, studying the mural. Officer Darvin's ghost —his shade—floated with the other shades, all of them watching flesh me get a ghost massage.

Don't put your hands in there, I said. Aeternus didn't stop.

Flesh me, get up, come here, I told flesh me.

"I'm doing a cat's cradle," he said and did not get up. I wanted to sigh but alas.

Put the string down and let's go, we're leaving.

"Where to?" he asked without putting anything down.

Caroline's funeral or burial or whatever.

"Will it be sad?"

I doubt it.

Neither of them had moved. Aeternus went on gripping around inside my body. He didn't really seem to notice he was doing it. He appeared mesmerized by the mural.

You, I said to him. *Hey! You built Skysill, did you put a psychic cemetery someplace?*

As if I hadn't even spoken—which, technically, I hadn't—he continued gazing into my wall, and without turning he said, *This is extraordinary work. In the Undying Land, you would have been a leading light. Your vision is like nothing ever seen. I am almost jealous.*

I almost give a shit. I'm trying to find Caroline. Where do they bury the fortune tellers?

Oh, my child. Really? Compelled by that impossibility, even now? He sighed and shook his head. He was back to his habit of turning our conversations into performances where I stared at him. *Have I taught you nothing?*

So far no.

He wasn't even looking. He couldn't tear his eyes off the mural.

It is a masterpiece beyond description.

Let's call the Louvre. In the meantime yes or no—is there a cemetery?

Yes, there is. Tell me this—could you create something like this again?

Why would I want to? It's like ghost catnip. Look at them. They're in the way..

They are drawn because of your ... oh, could it be, Aeternus wondered, finally turning his gaze to me, *that you painted this without comprehending what you'd done?*

That sounds like me. Hey, did I mention, I need to get to Caroline's thing, can you help?

No, Asher, death and time are the two poles. The boundaries of existence. Even Agape, the mother sense itself, was bounded by death and time. The poles should be unknowable, yet you have <u>painted</u> one of them. This is one of only two limits defining reality. Mount Obitus. The seat of Death. Where Inmortalis drew their power.

I now saw that Aeternus was on his own schedule and was never going to give me directions. Or maybe he would if I waited long enough, but patience, for me, is like sobriety—I have a low tolerance. It was time to go. If I hadn't lacked opposable fingers I would've snapped because I felt like flesh me would really respond to a snap.

Flesh me! Come boy. Funeral's on. Come.

Flesh me stood, fingers still knotted in string. Aeternus watched us.

I know where the burial is, he told me. *But there is something you need to know about Caroline first.*

The world's full of things I need to know, and I'm tired of the games. God damn it—get rid of the string so you can grab on!

Flesh me tried shaking his hands free and Aeternus took the opportunity to point deep into the mural, where distant fields spread for leagues in ruins I may or may not have painted, depending on your definition of "I."

Caroline is not what you think she is, he warned.

What is this, divide-and-conquer? Leave her out of it I'm telling you.

Listen to me. Before the curse destroyed it, the Undying Land lay divided perfectly in two. It was about to be more lectures, I saw—and flesh me still struggling with his finger bondage. This is why it's hard for me to get anything done. Nothing's in my control. Then Aeternus started in, using his Gettysburg address voice, and it was hard to ignore because Abraham Lincoln is my favorite president.

On one side of the Undying Land were the kingdoms of Time—the homelands of ghosts. On the other side lay the kingdoms of Death, the homelands of people. The ghosts in the kingdoms of Time were tended by the Viaticus. And the people in the kingdoms of Death were tended by Inmortalis ...

Flesh me was very distracting, and the lecture petered out as Aeternus watched him. Flesh me had almost literally interrupted the Gettysburg address trying to untie his finger knots.

Is he always like this? Aeternus wondered.

Except when he's sleeping, I said, sadly.

"This curse makes my fingers twisty," flesh me said in wonder. "I want to hear your story about Caroline."

I dislike getting fascinated by Aeternus's lectures or anyone else's lectures. I have my pride, and I like to use some of it before I fall. So now I could pretend it was only finger string keeping me here, instead of a story about Viaticus ghosts and Inmortalis people, possibly involving Caroline.

Ti'eirl's curse created this world, Aeternus continued, *your world. And the Inmortalis and their keystones became the Five Families. This much you know. But the curse also transformed the Viaticus and placed them here. Ti'eirl herself was transformed. All the Viaticus were transformed. They became the psychics.*

You see, Asher? In the Undying Land, Viaticus and Inmortalis were bound to opposite boundaries within the kingdoms of Death and Time. Fundamentally opposed. These are polarized forces, Asher.

You're saying Caroline's Viaticus.

All the psychics are.

You're saying there's a thing where ... Viaticus and Inmortalis are polarized?

The universe is built upon opposites. Beginnings and endings. The light and the dark. Viaticus, Inmortalis. The boundaries cannot ever touch. If they meet, they cancel. The two of you are doomed. Caught between time and death. Star crossed forever.

Why should I believe you? I asked after an empty moment.

Why would I lie? I want only to guide you to the truth.

I don't know why. but you obviously have an agenda. I'm just ...

Flesh me had by now wrestled the string from his fingers and stood, looking from Aeternus to me like the sole witness to the tennis match of the century. I wanted to scoop him up and fly us off without another word because it would be dramatic and dismissive, but I still didn't know where I was going. And I admit it, I wanted to see if there was any more to Aeternus's tale. In case, against all odds, there was a happy ending in there. Though deep down I knew what kind of ending he was selling.

The universal forces of death and time cannot come together, he said, looking sad. *You have separate fates, Asher, though you can still save her. I can give you that power.*

Because you're really just thinking of me.

I am thinking of all of us. With enough power, what you did with this mural you can do everywhere. You will never regret it. His seemed to light with some memory, which is a very literal thing to say about a ghost, so literal it's meaningless. Still true, though. His eyes focused a thousand miles off and his voice was thick, as he said, *The taste of them Asher. The essence. It fills you. The power. I developed techniques, I taught my followers. I will teach you. I will teach you to eat them.*

And by them, you mean...?

Ghosts. Of course. It is your destiny.

So that's a really intriguing offer. Eating ghosts is not at all creepy or disgusting. Let's put a pin in that and why don't you say where the cemetery is then let's never talk about it again.

You will need me. You will see.

If nothing else, Aeternus can tell when a conversation ends, maybe from watching so many worlds end. He gave me the graveyard info, I thanked him for nothing because that's the way I am, and I sped off with flesh me so fast I almost ghosted us through the sliding doors without opening them. If flesh me hadn't screamed he'd have been cut to ribbons. So now he was better at glass doors than me. It was humbling.

Off the balcony I barreled down the coast through grapefruit sunset light peeling off the waves, slanting across all the sandal emporiums and curio shops of Skysill Beach. And I found myself thinking out loud to flesh me. If he was good at doors, maybe he had other surprising wisdom to offer. Who knew what he knew? Maybe he was a lawyer. It'd be cost-effective having a lawyer in the family.

What I wonder is, why's Aeternus working this hard to educate me?

"He must be desperate," flesh me shouted into the wind after thinking for a moment, "it's impossible to educate you."

Right? Why's he so eager to teach me to eat ghosts?

"Maybe you look hungry."

But seriously. I think he wants me fully Inmortalis. Am I imagining that?

"Or he wants to be best friends."

I see. Okay. You mastered glass doors but the rest of it's still a mystery, isn't it?

"I miss my string."

We'll get you more, I ghosted, then flew on in silence. I made no mention of all the things I myself missed. Why complicate his life with those? Flying him to this funeral was already a complication. It was going to confuse him, Caroline's body going into the ground while Caroline's ghost and I carried on flirtatious banter. If it hadn't been for Aeternus I might have left him in the penthouse, but the eternal ghost—who for the first time in history actually was a ghost —had an agenda. I did not trust him unsupervised in a room with my body.

The psychic district appeared below us, stretching from the beach up to the base of the foothills. Gaudy fortune teller shops sat among quaint adobe cottages and coastal bungalows, and all the streets lined with trees. All painted sunset gold. I turned my back on the sun and headed inland, watching flesh me's shadow dance over the roofs below. The cemetery was supposed to be up near the foothills, but I'd never been to a cemetery and wasn't sure I'd recognize it.

In the end, I just followed the cars. The psychic district was more or less abandoned, but from above I spied a pencil-line road running up into a lonely grove of elms where dozens of cars had parked. I'd come to Seaview Memories, the psychic graveyard. I swooped us down.

Through a gate, among the trees, people were gathered. It was quite a crowd. It was probably every psychic who hadn't died in Aeternus's quorum. As I dropped I saw the spirits emerging from each of them, giving the whole grave-filled scene an unwelcome Higher glow that mixed with sunset light to make me nauseous.

Phylis stood reading from a book, Jorge beside her with a staff, with the rest of the crowd facing them in a crescent, an open grave and a casket in the middle. Caroline's.

Floating nearby I saw Caroline's ghost.

The considerate thing to do was to *not* flamboyantly drop my flesh from the sky to land beside the open grave, so I didn't. I wanted to impress Caroline with how considerate I can be because you never stop wanting to impress your girlfriend. That's how you know she's your girlfriend. Instead I landed us at the cemetery entrance, before a gated path.

They Walk in Peace, suggested a sign, and below that a graveyard subtitle, *time's journey never-ending.* The gate was warm with peach sunset. When I sent flesh me up the trail toward the grave he cast a long shadow until he disappeared into the trees. I drifted along after him until the crowd came into view, and I started recognizing psychics. I saw Li Wei and a gaggle of his head knockers. I also saw Amelia. She wore large, dark sunglasses. She had a *light* shape coming out of her back just like all the rest. I ghosted on, over gravestones and plaques, looking for Caroline.

At the boundary where the fence held back the wild, I found her. Here among the earliest plots, at the very top of the grounds, she floated, reading a weathered headstone, bathed in deep red sunlight.

None of her psychic friends could see her. They had no idea she was attending. She looked lonely. One thing you can easily do when you're a ghost is sneak up on another ghost accidentally, which is what I did when I ghosted to a stop beside her. She gasped, then shook her head.

Is that normal? she asked. *Getting startled by a ghost when you're a ghost?*

Ghosts are always surprising each other. We're amazing. How's your funeral?

Good. I wanted to invite you but didn't have your address.

Any time you need me, just whistle.

To be honest ... it's all making me feel a little insubstantial.

Let's get out of here. You want to go to my bar?

She turned to the half circle of psychics where Nikita now gave a speech scornful of death and cemeteries.

It's just starting to hit me, she said. *I'm gone.*

Flesh me can give them a message any time you want.

That'll be helpful at some point. Right now ... I just have to get used to it.

She turned back to the headstone. I ghosted closer to read; *Luis Hüseynov, 1753 - 1831.* Above the words were three small carved thrones. Caroline pointed at the grave.

That's the first Monarch of the Path Behind who was ever buried in Skysill. The greatest seer of his century. But he's gone. They all are. What happened to the ghosts of all the people here?

Here she was, looking the way she never does, lost and a little confused, asking for my help with some of the big questions that come up for a ghost, and I had no idea what to tell her. Necromantic knowledge is supposed to be my field of expertise. It was frustrating. I decided to make it all about me because that's a subject I'm familiar with.

At first, I thought it was just me, I said, *like I called these ghosts into existence by seeing a dead body. In which case, this guy, the seer of his century, just died without a ghost. Because think about it: humans have been dying all over the world for millions of years or whatever but ghosts only started the day I saw my first dead body. Right? And after that ghosts happened to all the bodies I saw. Which was a surprising number. But now I don't know.* I gestured at the psychics standing around their hole wearing their Higher doppelgängers. *Those things started appearing, and now I wonder if ghosts haven't always been inside us.*

Caroline looked, and frowned

What things started appearing Ash?

These ... the spirits? The things coming out of everyone's back.

They're new? I figured was seeing them because I'm a ghost now.

No, they started today when I lit the sun on fire, or—oh! Hey, how about the sun going out, was that weird? Did you see that? You didn't see it? Like, still in the sky but completely black? Maybe this morning or sometime?

She laughed, and a kind of marvelous Higher sparkle washed off her face when she said, *No I did not see the sun go out. Ah Ash. I love having no idea what you'll say next and how crazy you sound, even though I know you're not. You're the best.*

Maybe I am crazy.

No, because I've been in your brain—you're just real excitable. Now what's this about the sun?

Flesh me appeared through the trees then, coming over gravesites without the respect for the dead I'd started him off with, and I had to admit his way was better. He flapped his fingers in his face as he came, like they were twin duckbills having a conversation. He was coming fast and kept looking over his shoulder. I had something to talk to Caroline about and I didn't want flesh me to hear. He'd take it the wrong way.

So I saw Aeternus earlier, I started, super casual, *and he told me what happens to this frozen spirit body of mine when my flesh body over there dies, and it's pretty awesome.*

It was a loaded up sentence. I like to start with as much information at one time as I can, so people can pick and choose what interests them. Caroline was interested in one thing only.

Aeternus is alive? she asked. She did not sound happy.

No nothing like that. Maybe a little like that. He talks and looks around but he's totally dead. He's what you are. He's a ghost.

Instantly she realized the implications. She's so fast. *Who released him?*

That's the thing—he did it himself. All Inmortalis can. So I can. I can die and join you.

Aeternus told you this? she asked, puzzled at my credulity, which is often my problem. I've heard flesh me talk. I know how unlikely my stories can sound.

Aeternus said it yes, but why would he lie? I said. *He's got nothing to gain. Right?*

So you trust him? she asked. *The madman who ended the world?*

All I know is, I know I didn't release him. The instant when he died he <u>was</u> my body—Inmortalis—and he had all the powers I had, and I might not exactly trust him but he showed me another Inmortalis thing where I move corpses around. He's for real.

You move corpses?

Yeah, they get in the way. It's actually pretty useful. Anyway. It's great news, right? I can die. And we can be ... we can touch. We can be normal.

<u>He</u> can die you mean, she said as flesh me hurried up to us, snapping his fingers. *What's he think about it?*

He doesn't care. He takes it as it comes.

So if you die, can you still release other ghosts?

No. That's a flesh thing.

But you can't abandon them all. There's a place all of us need to go. I keep thinking about the ocean ...

Well, what are <u>you and I</u> supposed to do then? I complained. I could tell that I felt petulant and misunderstood because that's the way I sounded. Sometimes that's the only way I know.

I don't know what we do, she admitted, *I just—*

"Holy *cow*," flesh me yelled as he reached us, turning to look behind him. "Does this seem like the longest sunset you ever saw in your *life?*"

And I thought ... wait. Long sunset—yes I thought this *did* seem like a hugely extended sunset. Another one. Had this sun been setting for hours? Was I just getting used to it? Could that be possible? Of course the alternative ... my ghost stomach clenched, something that apparently happens now. And I shot myself into the air, above the trees, to survey the sea and the sun, still hanging just above the horizon.

Caroline rose with me.

What is it, Ash? she asked.

I don't like this, I said slowly. *The last time this happened—*

And that's as far as I got. Because it happened again.

Sudden as a candle pinch, all the light and heat from the sun stopped. Just stopped. One second our star hung blasting nuclear fire, and the next it was nothing but a cold black sky ball.

Behind that. stars flickered—fewer stars, I thought, then I remembered. I hung where I was, unable to move, and watched as those stars still shining began blinking out.

Beside me floated Caroline, barely visible in dimming star shine, her girl shape blurring, the Higher splendor of her fading, expression frozen, motionless high above the graveyard.

I went drifting again, my movement unrelated to momentum or gravity or known laws of nature. The universe was stirring me, spiraling, down to oblivion. Caroline drifted out of my vision, the cemetery swung in, and I was psychics at a gravesite, unmoving, and then flesh me himself. And he did move, though slowly. He crouched to the ground, one hand down in grave dirt.

And I thought, this is it? This is how it ends? The broken Path, an endless sunset, the sun goes out, and off we fade? Unless I stop it?

Cross them, I commanded flesh me down below. Because what else could I do?

He pinched his eyes, all furious energy, and on his own, he clenched his fists. Like a homecoming, I felt myself sucked downward. I left Caroline in the sky above me. I plunged.

We began our merge.

And I braced but felt no heat. No pain or pressure. And no *dominion* cloud. What now? We squeezed, but the *light* didn't flow. I kept us separate, kept the circuit open, helpless but still hoping, but the sky continued blackening, the trees, the dirt, the psychics, all of it ceased existing by increments of nothing, and no light came to refire it all, and then far away—not in distance, not in time, but far away—something cracked open. Like a giant dam breaking. A dangerously enormous dam.

A flood ripped through me.

I wept from it. I could do nothing but just let go. The pain was outside known ranges of agony. It was a feeling no person had been designed for, it was out of all tolerance. All you could do was let go. Then find out where you went next.

Out into the world. I expanded, riding the forward edge of a *light* flood erupting through me, filling the world from the inside, from core to mental. *Dominion* lit it up and raced me toward the surface. Screaming. Screaming an unstoppable song beyond agony. I hit the crust of the world and recognized it through twisted anguish— recognized it from last time but it was in much worse shape.

Ghosts were everywhere—not ghosts. *Shades.* Frozen spectral shapes, hands outstretched, and all of them fading. And there were monsters everywhere, the planet was thick with figura, who raged among the shades and held them down, in packs the way big cats hunt, and the figura seemed to be ... *endowing* them. And only after endowing a shade did they consume the resulting ghost. What this meant I did not know. I was too busy screaming.

Then, again, I heard the voice. It was stronger. It called my name, and in the distance, I saw a figure ... someone familiar. I felt like I'd lost all reality connections. That the bleakness and pain had pushed me over an edge. The figure I saw was my mother.

She didn't see me. She called and called, her voice a whisper in the maelstrom of grotesqueries. Was this my planet? Was this Earth? Whatever world I was seeing, whatever version of Earth I was psychic visioning, it contained a version of my mom.

And then she was gone. And the pipeline I'd become, the funnel with cosmic *light* tearing through it, groaned and stretched, so wide I knew it would crack. It stretched me open in unimaginable ways and thinned me as punishment for ever doing or wanting to do *anything*, punishment beyond belief. And through me, like water into a glass, *dominion* filled the world.

The *light* of it rose to lick at the sun, snapping sparks around it. To catch it on fire. But at the last moment, the cold disk refused. Through desperate pain, I urged it—catch! Please catch ... please stop this ... and finally, one ember fell, or rose, hot enough, to reignite our sun.

It roared to bloody sunset glory and spread arterial light over beaches, up buildings, across the coastal hills ringing Skysill Beach. I watched this happen from the bottom of a crater of soft graveyard earth. I found myself curled there, still screaming. And as I screamed the sun rose *backward*, up off the horizon, in a blur it rose backward into an increasingly blue sky.

From sundown through noon it went, to settle over the eastern hills where you'd find it around midmorning if this were regular reality. The place it restarted to last time.

And then everything was normal.

I'd merged. I was exhausted. There was dirt on my face. I couldn't raise my head. I'd been hollowed. Like someone took pipe cleaner to me and left only shocking emptiness behind. Avoiding that feeling was the precise reason I'd decided to become an alcoholic, but here it was, unavoidable.

Caroline's ghost appeared above my hole.

Ash, are you okay? she called. She swooped down to hover beside me. It was nice to have the company.

Oh baby, what is all this? she whispered, turning ghost eyes around the pit. *What just happened to you?*

"I'm ... sunset ... *gaghh*," I told her. She bent closer.

Was it Aeternus? she asked. *Did he do this to you? What's ... where did the hole come from?*

"Every time the sun goes out ... " I told her, struggling to sit up. She reached to help, but her hand passed through my flesh. Just like

Aeternus's had. Because ghosts followed different rules than shades or spirits. Of course.

I popped ghost me up and floated beside her. Everything felt much better then. Flesh me lay groaning in the dirt, almost insensible, but ghost me felt pretty normal, which is to say, I felt nothing. Actually, I did feel a little guilty. Leaving him down there seemed mean. But the pain was debilitating and one of us needed to think straight. Not that any of us had a great track record there.

This is better, I ghosted to Caroline. She still looked concerned.

What in the world happened? One second we're floating in the sky, the next you're gone, and I find you buried. And ... did you say something about the sun?

Wait, did you not see the sun go out? Just now? It turned black in the sky ... the actual fire of the sun stopped. Didn't you see that?

She answered carefully, slowly, like you answer a mental patient you also happen to be dating.

No. Please tell me about the sun. You saw it ... ?

Okay but listen, I'm not crazy. I mean I am crazy, of course, but this really happened. We were here burying you, and the sun was setting. It was setting for the longest time—remember?— never going down?—then it went out. Is it not ringing any bells?

She shook her head. But she was fascinated. Because how could you not be?

Well it went out. Then it caught fire again. Dominion did it. Then the sun went backward. It stopped up there where it is, and now it's morning again.

It's been morning the whole ... Phyllis and Jorge got here at sunrise, the rest came after breakfast. The sun won't set until tonight.

"I wouldn't bet on that. Listen—when did I hear your ghost story? The morning we went to the closure and heard the figura, remember? When was that?"

That was yesterday. Ash. Are you okay? Did you hit your head?

"My head's been better. So everything seems normal? Sunsets and sunrises?"

She nodded. It was sad, her being forced to question my version of reality, since up to this point we'd mostly had shared realities. Sitting on that swing inside our brains together really made almost any reality seem normal because if even one other person shares your picture of the world, it's enough to live a normal life. I knew what I'd seen, however. And I knew what I'd done. We had a problem with the sun.

That's when we heard screaming from over the lip of my crater.

As one, we rose and found the psychic mourners shrieking, pointing at each other, and fleeing all directions.

I think they can see ... Caroline said. *They see their ghosts.*

It was true. The psychics in the graveyard clearly saw the luminous forms emerging from everyone around them. It terrified them. I didn't like it either, because these spirit forms had emerged further and that was not the direction I liked seeing them move. The head of each spirit now rose completely out of, and behind, its flesh skull. The shoulders had mostly appeared too, to lean up and away, like a dolphin leaping from the water, leaving the legs and torso still buried.

Only three people out there were *not* screaming and running: Jorge, Phyllis, and Amelia. They still had expressions of slightly astonished terror and in Amelia's case irritation, but were savvy enough to realize there's no running from something that's attached to you. A percentage of the psychics had been borderline crazy already and this made it worse. Wie Lie, for instance. He was spinning in place, reaching to his back.

Amelia had her glasses off, scanning white eyes everywhere for a culprit. Phyllis and Jorge were bellowing orders, *everyone stop, people god damn it you're going to get hurt,* though the power of the Monarchs had been exceeded by the power of supernatural terror. You'd think psychics would be immune to supernatural terror but no. They scattered like forest animals before a fire.

Caroline and I ghosted toward the trio and they fell silent. Watching?

"Caroline?" Phylis asked, literally rubbing her eyes, getting graveyard dirt on her face.

"Ash?" Amelia whispered, right at ghost me in the air. *"Ash? Are you dead now?"*

"*You,*" Phyllis turned to rage into my ghost face, "what'd you do *this time?*"

Nothing, I snapped. *the sun stopped, every time it stops things get worse.*

"Caroline … " Jorge asked, transfixed, "Are you a ghost?"

You can see me? she asked. Her relief was very clear. *Can you see and hear me?*

"I can," he said in wonder. "Like our worlds are coming together."

Or starting to completely break apart, I suggested.

"Ash," Amelia asked, now beginning to cry, "oh, Asher, how did you die?"

I'm not dead, my body's in that hole, probably fine.

Phyllis looked awkwardly over her shoulder at her spirit rider. "What are these things? Why are we seeing this?"

Those things are spirits, I said, *and how am I supposed to know?*

"Tell us what you do know," Jorge insisted. He was split between our conversation and his scattering psychics but chose to gather facts. Some people are born self-disciplined, and others are born like me. "Are they dangerous?"

I don't think so I said. *After you die … these are the things that are left. They leave your body behind as shades. Frozen with an arm out. And I have no idea why you suddenly see them so don't ask. All I can say is … welcome to my world, people. Hey, did you guys see the sun go out?*

Amelia had gone to look into my hole. Her milk bowl eyes still somehow served her as organs of sight. She'd lost weight. Her hair had grown out from her warfare skinhead look. You could see she was exhausted. Like she hadn't slept in days. Though technically that was true of everyone.

She came back to stare at ghost me and put her hand on my arm, but it fell through. Even without pupils, she managed to look surprised. "I don't understand," she whispered. "What's happening? Why?"

I don't know, I told her. *Ames ... I think I saw Mom.*

"We need to get these people out of here before something else happens," Phylis shouted.

I'll take everyone in Behind. Caroline said. *Let's circle them back to the Bradley Building,*

Her voice, always so organized, suddenly had a giddy lilt— because she had something productive to do. She had her psychics back. She was the kind of person who liked having things to do. I'm the other kind, but it was nice to see her feeling better.

Talk later, she told me. Then she was away up the path in pursuit of Wi Lie, while Jorge and Phylis sped back toward the cars chasing psychics, leaving Amelia and me alone. Amy had her glasses back on.

"Oh baby brother," she said, shaking her head. But whatever accusation or sad observation or sarcastic question she'd been planning died in her throat as she seemed to have a sudden thought.

"Does everyone in the world have a spirit you can see now?" she asked.

How should I know? I asked reasonably. *Who am I, Edgar Cayce?*

"Who is—oh my god, never mind. Just tell me this: if Veronica has one of these spirits coming out of her, that means there's still hope, right?"

I have no idea, Amy, listen, <u>seriously</u>, I ... I think I saw Mom.

"Mom's dead," she said, voice flat. "Dad's dead. Aeternus killed them. Stop living in the past. You have to grow up."

Her voice was cold. There was a time not so long ago that hearing me say anything about our parents would have kicked off a hopeful tiptoe dance between us as she tried to draw me out. She thought the tragedy of our missing parents was the key to healing all my mental problems. Now, apparently, she didn't give a fuck about my mental problems. It had to happen eventually.

"And charge your phone," she shouted as she turned away. "I've been trying to call you for *days*."

You don't know—my phone could be <u>lost</u>*,* I ghost shouted, though it was in my pocket uncharged. But it *could* be lost. She didn't know.

She screamed in rage and went running after Phylis down the path toward the parked cars. I'd grown so used to *fabrica* all appearing and disappearing in balls of *light* that seeing her run like a normal person was almost shocking. It was another reminder. There wasn't enough *light* left to go around.

I was left floating in silence in the middle of a beautifully wooded cemetery, listening to birds and wind stirring leaves, and far away the beaching waves. The eternal soundtrack of life in a seaside town. For maybe five seconds, I experienced a moment of numb peace. Like you get just before you pass out in a bathroom.

Then I heard groans from the crater. We'd all forgotten flesh me. I floated back, to find him scrabbling weakly at one side, trying to crawl out. It wasn't that steep, but he was absolutely destroyed. When he saw me he settled back to the bottom, relieved. All he'd wanted was some company.

Okay, well, I said, hovering down, *you ready to go?*

He nodded. He stretched a muddy hand to grab my ghost neck, trembling as he tried to pull himself up. It wasn't clear he had the energy for a ghost ride.

Do you think you can hold on? I asked. He shrugged. *How are you feeling?*

He shrugged again, and his eyes fluttered. He was trying to be brave, I thought, pretending he could manage. But in actuality, he was endangering us if he didn't have the strength to hold on to me in the air. I wondered how bad he really felt.

Cross them, I said, wishing again that I could sigh. *And grab ... grab a handful of dirt I guess.*

And then as easy as putting on my favorite jacket I slid inside him. He was a disaster. Weak as a kitten and trembling. But the thing I noticed was the merge itself—there was no pain, no pressure, no *dominion.* Nothing glowed. No *light* balls going down my arm, no duplicating items—did that mean I no longer needed to carry around a key blob? To test, I merged in and out a few times. It was effortless and painless. Like taking off and putting on a slipper. We were now either completely broken or finally on the road to being regular.

But my flesh body was going to need to recover his strength before he, or I, could be trusted to hang on as I flew us back. So I sat beside Caroline's casket and let the morning sun fall on my head. I had a new appreciation for morning sunlight. I felt personally responsible for it.

High in the sky, the sun appeared to be doing normal sun things now. It wasn't flickering or fading. It appeared healthy. If a planet's sun went out, what would happen? And if all the suns in some universe went out ... I didn't even know what to ask. The answers were out of my league. I'm no astrophysicist. All I knew was, the curse kept trying to end the world, and I kept stopping it. How long that could go on I did not know.

I held my hand to the sky as a measuring tool, like they teach in survivalist cults like the Boy Scouts, and I thought the sun might be moving faster than normal as it rose toward noon. It was time to go.

So up I climbed from my hole, clawing and panting. Over the lip I rolled, covered with dirt, and there I saw a ghost. One of Wi Lie's shaved-head chickadees, dressed in white robes as she'd been in life, holding a fireplace poker and floating near Caroline's casket. The field was clear of living psychics. They'd all abandoned the body. It was just more confirmation of my theory that the body mattered not at all.

The shaved lady faced me. Unmoving in the air. I wondered how she'd died. Maybe she'd fallen into a grave. Or she'd been crushed in the psychic stampede or had a heart attack. She watched me pant and wipe dirt off my legs and it took a moment, but then I realized.

This floating shade had not caused me to pop a ghost.

For the first time since ghosts became a thing I saw one, hovering, facing me as they do, a seemingly normal supernatural being except that she hadn't popped me. I hadn't ghosted. Like the rest of the world was getting stranger, while I became more normal. I sincerely hoped that was not true since I had no experience with normal. The idea made me feel sick and vulnerable.

The cemetery was suddenly the last place I wanted to be. But flesh me lacked the energy to cling while I flew us away. So I had to walk away. The fireplace poker lady watched me stumble down the graveyard path toward the exit, feeling increasingly normal and out of my depth.

CHAPTER

SIX

I staggered out the gate of the Seaview Memories burial ground and stopped. The question was where to go at that point. I felt like I'd been everywhere, and none of those places ever helped. Eventually, I decided to go back to the Bradley Building. It had somehow become the hub around which the entire remaining universe revolved. Skysill Beach was like a funnel, and you went round and round, dropping all the time, and finally ended up in the Bradley Building eating something Phil gave you. Why fight it? Plus that's where Caroline was going.

I almost asked the *Gray* to come help walk me home, I was that tired. But it just didn't seem safe. I hated to admit that Amelia was right, but it was true, my phone would have come in very handy at that point. I took it from my pocket and gazed at it blankly. After a minute I tried turning it on. I found that my phone *was* fully charged. Hello, *Amelia*. It had just been turned off for a few days. She thinks she knows everything. I got myself a ride share.

When I slipped into the little hatchback a few minutes later I saw that the driver had a full-sized spirit head sticking up through her neckrest. The spirit face was completely exposed and it turned exactly as the driver turned, checking traffic and toggling her GPS without expression.

She knew the head was there. She kept looking at it in the rearview mirror. After a few minutes, I noticed her checking me out, huddled in the back shedding cemetery mud on her upholstery. My own spirit was tucked away inside my brain or wherever, Inmortalis style. She seemed puzzled.

"Where's your thing?" she finally asked. "Today everybody got a thing." She pointed to her spirit head, a little suspicious of me. They always are.

"I have one," I told her, "but mine has a mind of its own. Let me ask you something. Why are you even working?"

"What do you mean?"

"I mean like you said, everybody has one of these coming out of them today. You can all actually *see* them now ... why aren't you freaking out? I mean doesn't it— doesn't *everything*—seem unbelievably strange? Yet here you are, driving this ride share."

"Yeah, it's been weird today," she agreed, "but I have to work. I don't have health insurance."

"I don't know how much that's going to matter."

"I know, right? The healthcare system's screwed. I'm also saving for a trip to Paris."

"Some people say the world's ending."

"People are crazy. You can have a water if you want."

I was actually very thirsty and I took her water. Obviously she'd been changed by the curse. It was changing everything all at once. The entire world was possibly dying, but like that frog in that boiling water story, the curse was numbing people, so they didn't even notice. The curse was changing the very definition of *normal.* Instead of nearing their final hours in blind panic and despair people were approaching it slogging through gig economy jobs and worrying about doctor bills. Hoping against hope, maybe. Whatever that even means.

After that, we rode in silence. I kept falling asleep and snapping back awake, afraid the sun had gone out, like one of those nightmares where they make you responsible for the continuation of reality but you're really tired and have a lot of other things to worry about.

Over and over I heard my mom's voice. Just in my mind this time, not the cataclysm where I'd hallucinated her earlier. Amelia thought Katerina was dead. But then Amelia thought my phone wasn't charged, so she had no idea. I pictured Katerina out there among those figura, calling me. Was I supposed to know what it meant?

We reached the Bradley. I gave the driver a five-hundred-dollar tip and told her to take the rest of the day off and see a doctor, and maybe hurry, then climbed out of the car, over the desk, and into the lobby. Only a few psychics had made it back so far. I looked around but didn't see Caroline. I did see Nikita, hunched near the ficus. When she thought no one was looking, she pulled a bottle from a backpack, swallowed from it, and slipped it back into hiding.

She pretended she didn't see me when I sat beside her, and I pretended I could wait there forever. Finally, she sighed, bent with a grunt, and pulled up her bottle.

"You have pretzels?" she asked without any hope. I shook my head and drank, and she continued, "There is grave dirt on you. Maybe you will shake off outside."

"I doubt it," I told her. She nodded. I asked, "Have you seen Caroline?"

"The ghost? No. She went collecting hyena psychics down city streets." She watched me drink. She shook her head. "In my opinion, you should fall sleep."

"Well, if I'm asleep when the sun goes out, everything's fucked."

"Yes. Fine."

"You remember when you gave a reading about my mom?"

"I do. All accidentally fake."

"I know, but you probably got a strong sense of her at least. Right?"

"Nothing."

"Okay, but listen, do you think it's possible she's still alive?"

"Anything is possible," she decided. "Dogs could invent time travel."

"True. These talks with you really put things in perspective."

She nodded. "That is my gift. Also a terrible burden."

I drank more from her bottle while she watched in alarm. She took it back before I was done. After a moment I shook my head.

"I'm not even sure what I'm supposed to *do* now," I admitted.

She snorted. "Why do you think you are supposed to do anything?"

"I can't just give up. Is that what you think I should do?"

"I think you smell like zombies," she told me. "If you shower, your mother will still be dead or not dead but you will spread fewer plague lice."

A shower was an appealing idea. I told her goodbye. In the end, I shook the dirt off in the elevator. When I got out on the penthouse level I had my phone in my fist, just to be safe, but the hallway of supernatural visitors—who all rotated toward me—did not make me ghost pop. So it really was true. I was free. Or less free than ever.

The shades were so thick that walking the hallway was like flying through a fog bank, with which I do have some familiarity. The idea of a shower drew me on. But then, in the living room, I found Aeternus. He stood with a huge crowd of shades. The shades all looked at me. Aeternus faced the mural. He might not have moved since I'd gone to the cemetery.

So I popped a ghost and sent flesh me off to shower on his own. The shades in the living room looked less full of *light*. The energy was different since the last sunset. Now, even pressed together with all their *light* combined, this crowd had faded. The mural, too, glowed just a little less wildly.

Did you really kill my mom? was how I started my interrogation, because of my subtlety.

He watched the mural. *No. As I told you, she and your father killed each other. Somehow.*

Then why do I keep seeing her? Hearing her call me?

He shrugged. He was at least as obsessed with the mural as all the other ghosts. When he spoke, his voice was mesmerizing and soft.

It is the song of the Forgiving Sea that calls me here. Perhaps it calls Katerina. Even though I myself will never see it, still it calls. Then he turned to me. *It calls Caroline. I do know that. It calls her very powerfully.*

I heard the shower go on. I heard flesh me begin to sing a song about a turtle.

Okay, so what's this so-called 'Forgiving Sea?' I asked, a little too casual, also because of subtlety. The soft, unwelcome bells of realization had begun to ring. They are irritating.

Aeternus returned to study the painting. I looked into it myself for any evidence of water, but all I saw was land, dry, broken, shattered, in a space so vast no painting should have been able to encompass it. There was not a sign of a Sea to be found.

This painting. Aeternus said, *I've never seen its equal, and Asher, believe me, I have seen <u>everything</u>. What you've created is a window into a land, a land you yourself summoned to life so that your window could lead somewhere. You have recreated the Undying Land itself. Doomed but complete. With your art, you've taken a twist in the fabric of the many worlds.*

Nice, so—again—what's the Forgiving Sea? Are you saying it's in there?

Far away. On the other side of the Undying Land at the foot of Mount Tempus. The Forgiving Sea waits to take ghosts, singing.

So tell me this, I said, polite in my way, *how come you ghosts like this Sea so much?*

You mean why does Caroline like it? Why does she crave those waters? Why must even a Viaticus, such as she, return?

No why must anybody? Let's leave her out of this.

I will teach you about the Forgiving Sea if that's what you'd like.

Why's it always a lesson with you people?

There are many things I can teach you. Listen now.

When his lesson started, I finally understood how all those lectures I'd hated in the past had just been bad lectures, because a lecture from Aeternus was like a waterfall of amazement. With his thick hair flowing, in his loin cloth like an underwear model, he started painting pictures with words. He showed how it was supposed to be done.

Imagine the life cycle of a ghost, he dramatized it with his hands. *Imagine you are a ghost. We find you embodied in living flesh. You are a spirit, bound to a body, though you are much older than your body—your essence has cycled through untold flesh lives. Every experience you have in this body is imprinted within you as the body ages. When the body becomes a corpse, you carry these experiences forward.*

After you leave your corpse, you change—from a spirit, you become a shade. Now you must venture out of your body, mute, deaf, burdened by the weight of your body's experiences. Every emotional, physical, and metaphysical act from your most recent life, every sorrow and every joy, is the terrible weight you carry. This interlude, while you are a shade, is called the Remembrance. Every cycle you have lived, every flesh body you ever sparked to life and imprinted, is accessible in this stage. It is said that all shades are screaming inside, from the horror of those memories, but shades are frozen and we will never know. Once you are endowed, those pains become a deep ache. You must be cleansed.

When at last you are endowed and become a ghost again, and have agency, you enter your expressive form. Now you can finally seek the Sea you have so yearned for as a shade. The first thing any newly endowed ghost will always do is dive—plunge!—to bathe in those waters.

Because can you imagine, Asher, if all those lifetimes of fleshly experience accumulated? If the burden of a life was never lifted? The madness would grow with every new body, it would become unbearable. But the waters of the Forgiving Sea wash the burdens of life away, the sorrows, the loves, the pains and ecstasies, so you can begin again. That is the promise that draws us to this mural.

It was a long lecture, but it felt short, like watching an action movie. Where did the time go? He really knew what he was doing.

So what happens to a ghost who takes this bath? I asked. *What's a ghost remember?*

A ghost such as Caroline?

Can we leave her out of it and just tell me, do they tend to come back okay, or what happens?

A ghost is never the same. They are clean and at peace.

So ... what are you all waiting for? I shouted at the ghosts and shades everywhere. *Go get your bath.*

None can enter this mural without your permission.

It looked like a golden opportunity to clear a bit of space, so I could think straight.

Listen up, I said to them, *I'm giving all of you permission to leave. Go bathe—you know you want to. Go wash it off. You're welcome.*

All they did was nothing, like they'd already been doing.

They must be endowed, Asher. Only a ghost can enter the Sea. Not a shade.

I'm not endowing this room of ghosts. I tried that once and lost an entire day.

There are techniques. Let me teach you.

Wait a minute—you're a ghost, I told him. *You're saying you yearn to be cleansed?*

He nodded, slowly. *In the Undying Land, I would naturally have sought the Forgiving waters already. Here I must contend with your barrier. I can do nothing without your permission.* He waited with an expression that expected nothing. A blank. He couldn't possibly think I'd give him permission to go wash his burdens away. Could he?

It's like a get out of jail card for you, I said, slowly. *All the shit you pulled all through your life and you'll just wash it away? I guess they let basically anybody get cleansed. Is this supposed to be justice?*

Oh. Justice. You are so young, Asher. Justice. I have suffered because of what I have done. For millions of years. In ways you cannot even conceive. Would it be justice if you knew how much I have already paid? Well know this then—if you offered me permission to pass, I would refuse. Once a ghost enters this portal, they will never return. This journey goes but one way. So I will remain in this world, and seek what forgiveness I can find, atoning for my sins. I do not want permission to pass through into the Undying Land.

I know reverse psychology when I see it, and I was super sure he was doing reverse psychology. Pretty sure. It was confusing. Usually *none* of the psychologies work on me, reverse or the other directions, because I'm immune to psychology, but I found myself triple-thinking his motives. Somehow I'd become his jailer, and also his judge, and maybe his bailiff.

The shower stopped. Flesh me was still singing the song about a turtle. It might be the only song he knows. Outside, high noon sun lay pale upon all our sand. It reminded me of my biggest problem. The one Nikita wanted me to give up on, or take a shower before solving.

Here's a question, I said, *Your memory goes back—how far? The beginning of the world?*

That far, yes, and farther still. I recall the entirety of our history, not only in this world but of life in the Undying Land. The world of our birth. Our native world.

In all that time, how often did the sun go out? Not like an eclipse. Like water on a campfire.

The Undying Land had no sun.

How about Earth? The sun goes out and there's only a few stars. What is that?

I do not know. Why are you asking this?

I ghost pivoted to point my stuck out arm toward the beach, toward the sun now beginning a gentle descent in the direction of the horizon. Even as I watched.

There's a fucking problem with the sun, I said.

What does that mean?

See how fast it's moving? He looked, but he didn't see. *Well, take my word for it. The rest of you don't see it but it flies through the sky. Then it goes out. Everything freezes. Then I relight it and it's morning again. What am I supposed to do about that? Why's it happening?*

It came out pretty petulant. I recognize that. But Aeternus took stock, and I saw him have an unwelcome thought. Something about me?

It is the curse, he said, after a moment. *The curse of Ti'eirl. It is grown too old ... it was never intended to last this long. No curse <u>ever</u> has existed this long. The curse itself ... is failing.*

How do we fix it?

There is nothing <u>we</u> can do—but you, you could stop this. All you need is power. Let me teach you! If it has come to this, if the very sun of this world is flickering out of time, then we must move quickly. Let me teach you.

God damnit, we talked about this.

You cannot imagine ... it is incalculable power. An artist with your gifts could control the foundations of creation You could remake the all worlds. This is your birthright. Let me show you.

I'm not eating any fucking ghosts.

Then all of us are doomed. Are you prepared for that? It is one thing to doom me—I accept whatever fate I am destined to meet. But would you doom every thinking being in the all worlds?

I wanted to point out it was *him* who'd doomed us and it was pretty ballsy laying the blame on me, but then flesh me wandered out of the bedroom.

"Amelia's calling," he said, yawning and holding our phone out.

What am I supposed—I can't talk on a phone. Just ignore it.

"I already answered."

Why? Stop answering my phone—is she listening right now? He nodded. *What does she want?*

"She's crying too hard, you can't really understand."

Oh, for fuck sake you—cross them.

He did. Instantly I was in him, clean and feeling quite a bit better, with the taste of crackers and cheese in my mouth because apparently he'd been snacking, holding a phone out in the air in front of me. All without a cloud of *dominion,* or pain, or any struggle. Why did that leave me feeling so conflicted?

"What?" I said to the phone. "I'm busy. What?"

"I just told you, please, what does it mean?"

"What does *what* mean? You'll have to repeat that entire conversation, I wasn't there."

"*Veronica!* Why does everyone have a ghost coming out, but not her?"

"What's she have?"

"*Nothing! I already told you this!* There's nothing there. Does that mean … she really is dead? I don't know what to do, please come help her."

"Me? Help … Amy I … I'm … " But there she was, crying. Because of a relationship. Like always, her heart was broken, and like every single time, it's me who has to listen, hold her hand through the postmortem, it's gruesome. But I couldn't just abandon her. Could I?

"What do you want me to do?" I complained.

"We're at the Mermaid house. Come see her. Please come."

"Fine. Just for a minute."

"Come now."

"Oh my god Amelia, I said I'm coming, I'll come over."

"Don't get distracted like you—"

"Distracted by what? The end of the world? The sun going out? Animating corpses? What's to distract me? You people are driving me crazy!"

I hung up. It wasn't my finest hour, but then, none of them are. I felt full of flesh cortisone. Everything was better in ghost me. If only he could talk on the phone I'd never leave. I stared at Aeternus, who was watching me closely.

"What'd you do to Veronica at the quorum?" I asked.

I did nothing. Astonishingly. Through eons uncounted, only she has beaten me.

"She's basically dead. That's beating you?"

She escaped. No one had ever escaped a direct genetic instruction of mine. She must somehow have prepared for it. She somehow triggered her own False Death.

"False Death? What's that?"

Your sister will know. You should go to her, Asher. Tell her how you have doomed her.

"This *you're dooming the world* thing's going to get old *really fast*. You're the one who doomed us—and you know how you did it? Eating ghosts. So. If you're not here when I come back, I'll live through my disappointment."

Gathering flesh me I hit the air above the balcony. Without even realizing it I just ghosted and he jumped aboard. The transition from body to body took zero thought or planning, it was like passing a sandwich from one hand to the other. And we were airborne. Just a ghost and his flesh monkey.

With the horizon on our right, going south down the coast, you could see sunset coming much too fast, because morning had flown by and noon was gone and now it was three or four in the afternoon already. I told flesh me to hold tight and I lit the supernatural after-burners. It was pretty punishing for him. The wind rippled his face like those pilot g-force videos. But I wanted to get to the Mermaid safe house where Amelia had Veronica's pseudo corpse stored and get this over with.

The disaster was so on-brand for both of them. For all of us, I had to admit. For Veronica, whose brand had already been so pale and corpsey, and for us Gales who are cursed in love, with polarized parents and badly managed relationships we can't seem to work, and now Amy had a girlfriend in a coma, and I had a girlfriend who was dead.

Caroline was the one I wanted, but she was the one I couldn't touch. And because I couldn't touch her, she was drifting away. I couldn't help feeling that.

So, I said to flesh me, because thinking about Caroline made me anxious, and I get talkative when I'm anxious, *I guess once they go through the mural they never come back.*

"I know, it's *great*," he yelled into the wind. "It's easy to understand!"

Inside that mural is the Sea, you know. The one Caroline hears where she wants to wash, so she's not tormented about murder.

"She's going to be so happy you found it."

So I should tell her, you think, and send her through the mural?

"I don't think. Do I?"

I mean I agree, obviously I'm going to tell her.

"If you love something set it free. If it's meant for you it'll come back."

Not through a one-way mural though.

"Sometimes they don't come back, that's true. At least she'll be happy. You can go in after her."

But think about this. That's a Sea to wash the burdens of life away. And I swear to god I try but I'm aware some people find me burdensome, plus almost everything that happens to the two of us ... it's all just burdens. Murders, traumas, the only choices being bad choices, pain. Sadness. Who wouldn't want to get rid of all that? But that's more than half our relationship. I don't know what parts she'd even keep.

"You guys had sex on a train once, that was nice."

Aeternus says there's just an imprint left, an imprint of the life you left behind. I don't want to be her imprint. Not after all this.

"Okay. You're right. Don't tell her about the Sea. Keep her with us."

But that's just so selfish! She's suffering.

"I see what you mean. I guess you do have to tell her."

Even though I'll lose her?

"I don't want to lose her. Don't tell her."

Talking to you's like talking to myself but even less useful.

"I know, I feel the same way."

Below us, a little elbow of promontory appeared where they'd named all the streets after famous mermaids. I slowed us and pointed into a dive. Waves broke on the point, and the air was full of wet salt. I saw it bead on flesh me. The sun, lower all the time, stretched shadows between the houses. It was an insular little cape of mermaids and shadows. A place for CEOs to raise perfect fantasy children. Or to put up post-apocalypse safe houses.

The safe house Amelia waited inside clung to cliff rock amid lookalike neighbors, a row of houses facing down the entire western ocean. I dropped us onto Mermaid Court. Mermaid Court was deserted. No cars, no shifting drapes, no one to call private security.

Hurry, I told flesh me.

I ghosted through the front door into Amy's house and hung in the entryway, impatient. A moment later came his knock. Then the doorbell rang. Flesh me, still dazzled by his fingers, taking any opportunity to stick them places.

Stop ringing, I told him, *just come in.*

As he pushed the door open I eyed the layout and remembered how the house was set up—like a hedge maze of illogical post and beam staircases and glass walkways in place of normal floors and walls. You needed a guide.

Once flesh me was inside I had him scream, "Amy, I'm here—*are we doing this or what?*" And then, on his own, he added, "I'm sorry if that sounds loud and mean."

"Wait a minute," I heard her call from deep in the glass bowels.

"Okay," flesh me shouted, on his own, while he used one of his fingers to flip a light on and off. A few moments later Amy appeared at the top of an extra set of stairs. And did not look good. Which sort of applied to all of us at this point, but Amy was in real trouble.

I'd wanted to talk to her about seeing Katerina, but I gave that idea up when I saw her eyes. Still pure alabaster marbles, they were now full of hangover bloodshot. It's a brutal combination. There'd be no talking to those eyes, shadowed in bruise rings, in a face pale as acid wash. She looked so unhealthy even I was concerned, and I never notice shit like that. Katerina would have to wait.

A spirit-form grew from Amy's back and it didn't help her look. It turned its Amy-face everywhere she pointed her flesh head. She looked like she'd lost even more weight. Since I'd seen her in the graveyard a few hours earlier. That was concerning. Or it hadn't happened—except—if time was playing crazy tricks why not weight? Why not everything? Maybe vodka didn't get you drunk anymore—there was a bar where I could find out, but every time I started a catastrophe or a new ghost stopped me.

Amelia looked back and forth from my flesh to my shade, unhappy.

"Which one is you?" she asked. "Do you *have* to be two at once?"

"We need to hurry," I had flesh me tell her. "Sunset's coming, who knows how long. I need to find Caroline after this. What's up with Veronica?"

Flesh me was pulling himself up the stairs as he spoke, using the rail and experimenting with his grip. I hovered and watched, but Amy focused on my ghost. She could tell flesh me was not the commander.

You can hear me, right? I ghosted at her.

"Yes," she breathed. "It's so weird."

"I like holding your door handle," flesh me told her, and stopped on her landing.

Ignore him, I ghosted. I hadn't moved because I hoped my obligations here could be discharged with a pithy remark or some advice. I just have a low breakup tolerance, because of her history. It's always something. Her hookups are never good, but I long ago stopped pointing it out because I have better ways to waste my time. She was never going to learn. It's irritating.

So what's going on, why am I here? I urged.

"She… " Amy said. " … I think you're the only person who can help."

I hope that's not true. Do you need advice or what? Hurry.

"It's not advice! It's ghosts, Asher. You know about ghosts. Come on."

She took the initiative then and went back the way she'd come.

Without the initiative, I'm basically lost, so I followed her. Apparently this was going to take more than advice. Flesh me followed third, grappling the pointless banisters gliding to all sides. Up and down Amy led us, and we ended up below ground level. The windows were left behind. I'd lost track of how we got there. There was a hall with a bank vault door, and concrete passages in the cliff which might have surprised the Mermaid HOA, or maybe all the executives had tunnels like these. It was an end-days hideaway, with food and weapons and boxed supplies in careful order. And all it demonstrated was how precarious preparations like these are. You have to hope you're afraid of the right disaster. Veronica had prepped for the end of democracy, but none of this was going to help with the end of time.

We saw no one. The absence was conspicuous—it was a space designed for many occupants. Amy took us through a swinging door and into a brightly lit space, high-ceilinged, painted white. In the center, within a ring of quarantine drapes, was a hospital bed, and a figure under a sheet pulled up to the shoulders. Readouts glowed on instruments organized in racks, everything sterile. Like a TV set of a fully functional operating theater.

"We were supposed to wear a mask, but everyone's gone, and I stopped a while ago," Amy said, easing up beside the bed and looking down. I ghosted up beside her.

It was Veronica of course.

CHAPTER

SEVEN

She lay on her back. Eyes closed. And though normally on TV you hear sounds in a room like this, like beeping and pumping and humming, I heard nothing. Tubes and wires ran from various parts of Veronica to monitors displaying flat lines and zeros. She looked asleep, but in the way a corpse would sleep. Dead, but could wake up at any moment and tell you her dream. This was how they'd found her. How she'd been since the quorum. Amy turned to watch ghost me.

If I told her I had no idea what I was there for, I knew she'd just roll her eyes complaining I don't pay attention, since not paying attention is my main habit. I do it because most of the time people are just saying things they're going to say again anyway, so why bother? People say the same things over and over and over.

On the other side of the bed, flesh me had taken a stethoscope from a tray and was listening to his own heart, looking very concerned as he twisted tubes and made thinking faces. Like now he had fingers so he was considering a career as a surgeon.

"Well?" Amy demanded, pointing at Veronica.

Well what? I asked. *I have no idea why I'm here.*

She rolled her eyes. "Asher, pay attention! She doesn't have a ghost thing. Look!"

Ohhh, I said. Yes. Veronica's body did not have a spirit coming out of her back. I ghosted under the bed—no. No spirit.

"Shouldn't she have a ghost?" Amy asked. "Everybody else does."

Her voice was rough with phlegm from days of not sleeping.

Technically, I told her, *those are spirits. They turn to ghosts later.*

All the fight just suddenly drained out of her. "So she's really dead? But why is her body frozen like this, day after day?"

What did the doctors say?

It wasn't pleasant to watch Amy think back. She came close to crying. Just painful to watch when someone has no pupils. She wasn't giving up, but she was getting close.

"The staff that didn't leave right away got old and died," she finally said. "For the first few days they were trying to get her transferred ... no one ever came. After all that time her body hasn't changed."

Have you ever heard of something called ... a false death?

"You mean ... *the* False Death?"

What is it?

"How do you know about that?"

From Aeternus. He said Veronica triggered her own False Death? He was pretty impressed.

"Aeternus? When was that?"

Today. He's a ghost. He's annoying as shit.

"You've seen him?"

He's basically staying at my house.

"What? *Why?*"

That's where they all go.

"But he's the one who did all this! To Veronica! To us!"

Put that down! I ghosted at flesh me, who now fingered up a scalpel, and he startled when he heard me and dropped the razor on the floor. It did not impale his foot.

Stand over there, I exasperated, pointing to Veronica's head with my mind powers. *Don't touch anything in here!*

He slunk into position. Amy ignored him.

"What does Aeternus want with you?" she asked.

Who knows, Amy, he's crazy. He wants to pass on his Inmortalis knowledge because he feels bad for ending the world. He's insane. What's the False Death?

Watching Veronica's deathless face she said, "... I don't ... there's so much I don't know about her people, about the *fabrica*—oh—"

Her face went a little shocked. Because of my curiosity problems, I asked, *What?*

"When Willametta put Veronica on trial, they wondered if it would come to the False Death. They said that. Now I remember. You've seen *fabrica* duel, right?"

In my mind, I nodded.

"Well," she continued, "a *fabrica* can't kill another *fabrica* with *light*. But when your Ball of Seven is drained you pass out, and someone else can ... take more of your *light*. You don't wake up until they replace it. That's the False Death. But Veronica ... "

Aeternus said she escaped him. Like she did this to herself. Against his wishes.

"She was totally under his control. We both were."

She planned ... can you set a timer or something to sparkle in the future?

"A triggered *eminence*."

Maybe she set a trigger. Is that possible?

"But what was the trigger? I didn't see anything. He sent her at me with a knife. To kill me."

Then that's it—that was the trigger—your safety. Because of Seamus, the last thing she could have wanted was another ... she sacrificed herself. I mean it's ... pretty badass.

"Then where's her spirit?" Amy demanded. "If she's not dead?"

I did not want to be the one to say the obvious, that if she had no spirit she might as well be dead, and I was glad I waited when, from behind us, flesh me spoke.

"Is *this* it you guys?" he asked.

He had one hand just an inch above her forehead and he peered around at something on top of her head. We watched him lower his hand to her brow, moving so slow it was hard to stop him. Then he lifted it, then he dropped it again.

Stop that, I remembered to say.

But he didn't. He patted her like a starfish in a touch tank, fascinated. When I blinked to the top of the bed I saw it too: every time he touched her, a thin tendril of *dominion* lit up, stretching up from the crown of her head and fading in a few feet to nothing. It disappeared whenever he raised his hand.

"It's tickly," he said.

Maybe that's her spirit, I said, pointing to the stretched *light* filament. And then, in a mental flash, I saw it all. It's my least favorite way to see. I prefer *through a haze,* or *in the distance.* You can ignore those. This was too obvious to ignore.

"It wants to suck me in," flesh me said. "But it can't, because it really wants to suck *you* in. Like when we restart the sun. You know, you flow out? This will take you to her."

"Ash," Amy breathed, "can you? Can you save her?"

No, I said, because it's my first impulse.

"You might be able to," flesh me said.

"Do you know what he's talking about?" Amy asked. "Flow out? What's that mean?"

It means it's always something. Every time.

"It means he can do it," flesh me told her.

"Is it dangerous?" she asked. Now she didn't know which direction to look, me or him.

"Volcanoes are dangerous," flesh me shrugged. "He's Inmortalis."

Quiet, I told him, frustrated that every move I made was pushing me further down the Inmortalis path. For some reason I found myself blaming Aeternus. He'd already taught me too much. He was the one who brought up the False Death to begin with. He wanted me to assume his Inmortalis crown. Or whatever they used. Staffs?

Let's get it over with, I decided. Because sunset. And standing around weighing consequences bores me. Plus Veronica had saved my sister's life by doing this, and I owed her for that.

Cross them, I told flesh me. *Let's move this along.*

He was only too happy to let me in. We superimposed in a flash, and I held us a hair's breadth apart. He'd left us posed over Veronica's body with my palm an inch from her forehead. I felt no warmth at all there. But something was pulling my hand down. Some kind of magnetic circuit.

I took a deep breath. Just for the novelty.

"Be careful Ash," Amelia said.

"Careful's my middle name," I said, as I like to. I don't know why.

Then I palmed Veronica's forehead and felt it instantly. The tickle. I recognized the feeling, like a tiny version of what happened when *dominion* carried me into the Earth. This was just a seep, like water through a straw, coming through me and passing into Veronica and exiting out of her to somewhere ... that wasn't the world.

By now I'd honed the act of riding a *dominion* torrent, so it was almost a science. Not that I believe in science, at this point. This wasn't anything like a torrent, so I felt confident as I let it begin to pull me, even though confidence—as I tell myself over and over—is a sign I'm misunderstanding my situation.

When I released myself into it, the force of the current took me. My mind, or whatever I have, was sucked down my arm like a leaf down a gutter. Irresistible. It occurred to me then to wonder, how was I going to get back? And where was this stream going to take me? But it was too late for any answers to help.

I poured into Veronica's body and out through her head, following the thread of *light,* and darkness closed around me, and I knew I was in trouble. All my confidence faded, but again, too late.

I recognized the empty place, where there are no spirit bodies or flesh bodies or living things of any kind allowed. The void. I'd been trapped here when I'd locked myself out of my ghost and flesh. This was the place nothing should be. A zero-sum denominator of cold-dark-endlessness, a place that made *things* into *nothings.*

It was not a place for consciousness. To all sides, I felt it. A light-less realm opposed to consciousness. I knew I should go back, to where Amy was waiting, and count myself lucky if I was able to do it. The consequences of venturing into this void might be terrible. Any idiot could see that. But if addicts of my caliber have a defining skill, it's the ability to ignore the consequences. I lunged on.

Veronica's body vanished below or behind me. An almost solid, totally dark nothingness closed around me. I flashed onward, riding a thinning strand of *light* piercing the dark. A lifeline. Or the opposite of that. Leading me somewhere bad.

Ephemeral pieces were now peeling off me—early memories, random ideas, experiences—torn away by a void that pressed so tight it was a wind. A wind of absence. And I felt it was no big deal since I hardly ever used those ideas and experiences and memories. But the void was grinding down. Like dermabrasion of the soul. And I knew there'd be nothing left of me if it went on long, and fought the ugly appeal of that idea.

Onward through void medium I forced myself. It thickened and the way grew harder, while the tendril of *light* stretched far into the dark. The void wind now was a roar, the pressure on my face intense, and through it all I heard an open, endless, peaking scream.

Void wind pressure slowed me. I was desperate to follow the fila-ment of *light,* though inching forward was battling hurricane forces, ripping thought, ripping awareness, and then … ahead I saw … Veronica. Or the thing that had once been her.

The gale tore, confusing my mind, shredding my knowledge of where to move and what to think, though because of my expertise drinking I could proceed without that knowledge. I forced my way. I forced my way to her. There at the very border, where thought could go no further, I stopped.

She was tilted forward like a figurehead on a battered ship. She wasn't a shade. She wasn't a spirit. She was a convulsing, agonized ghost. A false ghost—her body wasn't dead. A false ghost battling endless black nothingness knifing through her.

Her distorted mouth hung open—to scream I guess—but her eyes were pressed shut against the streaming nonexistence. She was fed by her trickle of *dominion*, the ghost *light* stretching back in sickening ripples, connecting to her body. But here we were as far from bodies as reality would let us go. My limited window was closing. I'd have to return. To stay was to cease.

But Veronica was here for the duration unless I could help. How?

I heard her voice shriek out of the void, waver, fade, [... WHA ... T ... WH ... O ...]

I forced my voice through the wind, not knowing if she'd hear me, [VERONICA! IT'S ASHER!]

[... SSSS ... HOULDN'T BE HHHH .. ERE ... GOOOO! ...]

Her ghost, or proto-ghost, whatever it was, thrashed and rolled its eyes like a fish on a hook, her eyes passing me like I wasn't there. The screaming stopped when she spoke. When she stopped speaking, it began again.

[VERONICA COME BACK] I shouted. Because of obviousness.

Then, for a moment, her eyes found me. Her face stabilized. I heard her clear.

[YOU ... WILL DIE ... HERE ...] she told me.

[GO BACK TO YOUR BODY] I yelled above the roar.

[I ... CANNOT ... EVER RETURN]

[I'LL HELP. WHAT CAN I DO?]

[... OOO ... NLY ...] she said, [OOO ... NLY ... KILL ME]

It's just the extremes with these people. To get what they want they have to end the world, or poison all hope. They can't just get rescued like a normal person.

[LET'S NOT DO THAT. AMY WOULD BE MAD. LET'S *REVERSE* THIS ...]

[... ONLY THE FABRICA WHO CALLED THIS LIGHT ... REVERSES IT ...]

[BUT THAT'S YOU RIGHT? YOU DID THIS TO YOURSELF SO HE COULDN'T MAKE YOU HURT AMY. YOU PREPARED ... NOW CALL IT *OFF*. AND WE'LL LEAVE. I DON'T LIKE IT HERE.]

[... ONLY IN FLESH CAN A FABRICA GATHER LIGHT ...]

Suddenly I saw her problem. It was one of those word problems they use to stump people on math tests; the *fabrica* who started the False Death was the only one who could end it. And that *fabrica* needed a body which could counter cross its eyes. Which in her case was the impossible step. Her body was out of reach.

[OKAY WELL WHAT DO WE DO?] I called, desperate.

[... ASHER ... AGONY ... YOU MUST LEAVE ... FIRST ... KILL ME ...]

[I'M HERE TO HELP YOU!]

[... END ... ENDLESS PAIN ...]

[NO]

[FFF ... REE ME ... PLEASE ... OR THIS ENDLESS ...]

And her mouth went dark again, wide like a horror tunnel, and her eyes goggled off to the void. And I had a desperate idea—I'd go back, control her flesh the Inmortalis way, like Officer Smith, and call her home. But that idea died—Inmortalis only do that trick with dead bodies. Veronica's body wasn't dead. And by the time it was, it'd be too late.

Because of how my brain sometimes slips from subject to subject, I had a flash of amazement, there in the void, and I wondered to myself, *do things like this happen to other people?* You never hear about anything like this on social media, some person who has to pick between killing his sister's girlfriend or leaving his sister's girlfriend to endless suffering.

It's probably just me. It's so depressing.

[HOW EVEN ...] I complained. [... EXACTLY WHAT ARE YOU ASKING?]

[... CU .. T... ME ... FFFF ... REE ...]

She strained to pull the *dominion* thread. Her screams echoed in my brain and the howling wind was obliterating my thoughts and it was just terrible there. I couldn't leave her. There was only one choice. Amy would be pissed. I clung to the hope that killing her wasn't the end. Hopefully she became a shade. At some point, I could endow her and she and Amy could pick up where they left off, bickering and making each other unhappy. It wasn't going to be paradise, but it'd be better than this.

Or maybe I was killing her for real.

How do you even cut a tendril of *light?* Had I done anything like that before?

It was getting hard to remember the things I'd done. All the facts of me were spreading, evaporating into absence. But this tendril looked so thin. So vulnerable. Like a pulsing vein, uncovered.

I dropped my hand to block it. I felt pressure on my palm. Just for a moment.

And then, so easily, it vanished. Far, far away, I felt her body begin to die.

Her screaming ceased. Her ghost form spread into a fog, to dissipate around me. It wasn't what I'd been expecting. Though what had I been expecting? Sparkles, I thought. Instead, she was ... fading ...

[... TTTT ... HANK YOU ...]

Her body finished dying, and surrounded by implacable anti-life, her mutant spirit began fading into the abyss. Fading and ceasing. Not as a shade. Not as a ghost. Not as anything. It happened *fast.*

As she thinned into background radiation and nothingness I heard her voice, one last time.

[... IT'S UP TO ... YOU NOW ...] I heard.

And she was gone.

She hadn't even left a last message for Amelia. I swear, my sister can really pick them.

EIGHT

The first thing I did when I snapped back into my flesh was suck a huge gasping breath and fall on the floor. But even as I was doing it I was squinting around the little medical nook hoping I'd see a ghost. A new ghost. But I saw no ghosts.

Amy bent beside me, offering me all the comfort a wild, pupil-less madwoman can give to her void-emptied brother, saying my name and shaking me like a ketchup bottle. She went through the complete Asher Gale diagnostic procedure, even though it was all outdated. She checked my fists, checked my temperature, asked me questions to test for human empathy. Finally I got surly, so she stood and left me on the floor, satisfied I was normal.

From there she went to Veronica on the bed above me. She couldn't look away.

The thing I most wanted was not to see what Amelia couldn't look away from. But I stood and looked. It seemed like the wrong time to insist on what I wanted. And there I beheld Veronica's body, mummified. Cheeks tight, eyes sunk into dark holes. Her pale skin had darkened and turned brittle and tightened. She was just bones wrapped in cellophane. Like she'd died months ago—which she had —and been stored in a smokehouse. Which I doubted.

"What ... Veronica ... " Amelia said to herself. Then to me, she said, "What's this?"

"I found her ... there's a void ... " I said. "Veronica ... "

"Veronica *what*?"

"She asked me to free her. Because she wasn't going to get another chance."

"Free her?"

"She was trapped, Ames. I'm sorry. She was trapped." I peered around the quarantine space. "I hoped there'd be a ghost ... "

"What *happened* to her?" Her voice was clipped. She titled her bloodshot, hardboiled eyes at me. It was super horrible. Slack. Like a doll face but with missing irises.

"I don't know exactly what happened," I admitted. "But I did what she asked me to."

"Did you talk to her?"

"The pain she was ... it was bad ... "

I tried, but some pain you can't explain. Some pain isn't vulnerable to the language arts. You have to see it or feel it. And even if I'd had the words, would I have given them to Amelia? I don't know what good it would have done. I knew less and less as the seconds passed and Amy watched me. The terrible truth was that in the end, I hadn't done what I did for Veronica—I'd done it for myself. If I'd left her, convulsing, echo-screaming for eternity, I might never have slept again. So now I had to live with this, instead. With some pains, the only analgesic is time. Also alcohol.

"No," Amy growled suddenly. Her voice was intense but strangely flat. She reminded me a little of the *Gray*. "No. This isn't ... this ... god damn him."

"Him who?"

"Aeternus!"

She grabbed my arm and pulled, and I stumbled after her, weak because it'd been a long time since I'd had anything to eat. The spirit cresting from her back looked back at me whenever Amy did. I tried to ignore them both. She steered us all out of the operating room, back past the ammunition and the freeze-dried peas where I grabbed a box of protein bars, prying it open as she moved me. She slammed us back out the bank vault door and up a vanity staircase or two until we emerged in an ocean-view billionaire living room.

There she shoved me into one of the couches. "Wait there!" she yelled and spun away on some Amelia errand. I barely heard her. The box had been sealed for the apocalypse, but I'd finally broken it open and started eating bars in huge mouthfuls.

The whole experience of killing my sister's girlfriend had left me a very dry mouth, so it took a few minutes to generate saliva and swallow. What I'd done shouldn't have bothered me or surprised me, seeing as I was a death guy—or, as Aeternus and flesh me would have it, Inmortalis. It might have been just hunger that left me so absolutely hollowed out.

When Amelia returned, my brain had regained the processing power to notice the sun angling through the windows—the day nearing its end. Was it possible? Sunset already? There were so many things to keep track of now. Suddenly I understood all those people setting timers and reminders on their phones. I needed a reminder set for this time every day: *FIVE MINUTES and you may need to reignite the sun.*

Amy stood before me. In her hands, she held a cage cup. She must have taken it from Three Paths, after the quorum disaster.

"What's that for?" I asked, unhappy to see it.

"Fill it," she snarled. She shoved it at me.

"You're crazy," I told her. She looked crazy. "That shit's *horrible* for you! Have you seen your eyes, have you ... Aeternus said it, it turns your brain to—"

"I don't give a fuck what Aeternus says—fuck Aeternus! Look at everything he's done. He killed our parents. He broke time. Now—"

her breath caught, a quick gasp, then control again, "now he kills Veronica—*I'm not letting him get away with it!* Fill this! I'm going to fucking *kill him!*"

My sister can get unbalanced after one of her relationships ends. Though it'd never been this bad. I thought I'd try reasoning with her since I lacked a dart gun with tranquilizers.

"Okay, listen," I suggested. She narrowed her eyes. "It's a ... not good idea."

"Don't you want him *dead?*" she demanded

"I mean ... for one thing, he *is* dead. You can't kill him more than that. Unless you eat him, I guess. Which—don't."

"Give me a battery! You don't know what I'm capable of!"

"I mean I kind of *do,* Amy. You used to babysit me, remember? But it doesn't matter! Killing a ghost with *light is* like killing a fish with water. That's what they breathe."

"I have a *bleed* root. Do you know what that means? If I have *light,* I can rip anything to pieces. Anything."

"Well, I can't do it. That doesn't happen anymore. There's no *dominion* left. I don't fill objects when I merge. Amy, listen, you need to get someplace safe."

"Safer than a *safe house?*"

"Really soon the sun's going to set. And believe me, that's a bigger problem than Aeternus. *Believe* me."

She looked like she had her own idea of what big problems we had, despite my track record of basically *always being right* about big problems. Those are my specialties. She didn't care. Her breathing was all over the place. She was listing to one side, shaking her head. She put her vacant eyes on me and bore down. Oh my god, it was so horrible.

"Where's Roman Sutherland?" she snarled.

"Why are you asking me?"

"Is he dead? Have you seen his ghost? Is he alive or dead?"

"I haven't seen his *shade,* if that's what you mean. He's not in my living room but that means nothing. Amy, I'm serious, you need to find someplace safe."

She scanned me, her eyes filled with disappointment instead of pupils. It's amazing how I bring disappointment out of people. Apparently, I'm just not what any of them ever expects. Then she turned away down one of the staircases.

"What do you want with Roman?" I called. She'd probably need to be rescued again. I wanted to know where to find her

"He's old school *fabrica*. He'll know everything about Veronica's False Death. Get me a battery, Asher. If I can't kill Aeternus maybe there's still something I can do for her."

"No, *I can't get you a* ... she's not ... you're—"

But before any of my sentences could be served, Amy stormed off. I knew even if she found Roman he wouldn't be able to help her. Aeternus was untouchable, and Veronica was gone forever. The void had erased her.

Other than dry mouth, which I'd already resolved, I felt but a small hollowness when I thought of Veronica. I'd been conditioned to view death as trivial because it's so easy to condition me. Death was inconvenient but not that big a deal. But Veronica had been edited out of reality, she'd been evaporated, I suspected forever, and it seemed like *that* should feel like a bigger deal. I could only hope I'd done the right thing. Though that hardly ever happens.

A few protein bars later I revived enough to swallow my lack of feeling and climb to my feet. I popped a ghost and guided flesh me through the Jumanji house. Along the way, he grabbed the cage cup and practiced finger work on it. He's like a toddler. Once outside I spent a moment misgiving the speed with which the sun was falling. Part of me wanted to remain there among the captive mermaids, exploring my misgivings and all the other feelings I was having and not having, in order to postpone the inevitable. But you can't postpone a sunset. Before the sun set again there were directions I had to give to Caroline. I felt like a death crossing guard, waving people through.

So back up the coast, we flew, the sun sinking in smoldering orange on our left, hoping Caroline had finished chasing hyena brains. It felt like all I'd done today—all I'd done for the last several days which were all today—was fly back and forth from the Bradley Building. Just the same thing over and over. This time I landed and had my body burst through the doors, over the desk, into the lobby, and found the lobby empty.

Nikita's bottle lay on its side on the floor. It was empty too. I wondered ... were the psychics away at another burial? Did I need to head back down the coast *again* to Seaview Memories?

"Hello?" I screamed through my mouth. It was irritating. You couldn't keep track of these people.

Then I saw the square dance couple crouched in the corner near the ficus, eating from a tin of fruit salad in syrup, which Phil said was what the Bradley Family had been reduced to. There was no fruit in any stores. The elderly couple caught flesh me looking and silently, knowingly, pointed up. I got flesh and ghost into the elevator.

On the fourth floor, the doors opened and my instinct was rush out, but I saw a corpse in the hall near a ransacked basket of cracker boxes and overcame my instinct. For once. My instincts aren't even that strong, it shouldn't be as hard as it is. A shade floated above the body.

I actually let the doors close again and stood inside looking at my polished metal reflection. More dead bodies at the penthouse. Was it ever going to end? Yes, I remembered. Of course, it's going to end. Sooner than people realize. So I opened up again and went to examine the corpse.

It was the dead body of Li Wei. His shade, wearing a goatee and pajamas, held out an old-fashioned watch on a chain. Which, pretty on the nose for a psychic, Li Wei. But then he'd never been the subtlest. If he hadn't liked you he shoved a pistol in your face.

His corpse, when I remembered to look at it, was decades older than the last time I'd seen him. Ti'eirl's curse had aged him out of this life. I hadn't seen this happen to any psychics yet. Why Li Wei?

Was the curse culling the weak? His brain had been damaged touching the broken Path so he'd probably had no chance. I wondered if any other psychics had succumbed like this. Were we all heading that way?

I was hearing voices from the penthouse, I realized. My front door was open. Someone was in my living room, which meant they were either dead or psychic. I dashed us to the door and found my entrance hall full of soothsayers, all with shades breaching their backs.

Abruptly they all stopped talking. Not because of me. They were straining to hear something in the living room.

I gave flesh me clear instructions to batter his way to the living room through the crowd, then ghosted through the wall. Maybe somebody in there had a new crystal ball, and they were giving a presentation? Maybe Caroline was there. I tried to remember the decision we'd reached—the Sea of Forgiveness was right there behind the mural and I might or might not be about to send her through to find it—and then I remembered we hadn't reached any decisions. Those are not our specialties.

The living room was quiet chaos, with flesh bodies and emerging spirits and crowds of floating shades all overlapping among the couches and footstools. I rammed ghost me in, bouncing shades to the sides, passing through everyone else. It was super claustrophobic but psychics don't care. They like it. The more packed Three Paths had gotten the happier they'd been.

At the head of the assembly, facing away from us at the mural, stood Jorge and Phylis, a spirit on each back. They had their hands pressed to the painting, while it exhaled Highers and *dominion* like spa steam to fill the room. Their eyes were closed. They were mumbling, while the path walkers waited. I had no idea what was happening and I didn't care.

I saw Caroline hovering near the balcony doors. I was not happy to see Samantha floating right beside her. Samantha, always the harbinger of some oncoming doom or reminding me of my failed promises. The more I found out about how this shit worked, the worse her problem looked. She was stuck like she was forever.

Caroline wore an expression of longing, and Samantha expressed nothing. From the hallway, I heard a few yelps, which meant flesh me was still coming, though I'd have known anyway from the way the shades in the room were facing.

Ladies, I said to them as I ghosted up. Caroline smiled—a smile with sad corners—then her gaze swung back to the mural to watch Jorge and Phylis.

What'd I miss? I asked, like I was coming in late to a movie. I was being super charming. I wondered if anyone noticed. *Catch me up.*

They're sifting for clues, Caroline told me. *For a way to break this curse.*

Flesh me shoved free of the crowd then, to stand at the living room steps. And only at that point did I see he still had the useless cage cup. Once he got something in his hands these days, he liked to carry it a while to get the most use from his fingers.

Caroline had only looked away from the mural for a second. I assumed because the song of the Forgiving Sea was calling. She had that kind of look. Distracted by eternity, or whatever.

Is it bad? I asked. She knew what I meant. Just like I knew that, yes, it was bad. But that's how most normal conversations go. People just saying things everyone already knows.

It is what it is, she said after a moment. *Like I'm wearing a coat made of rocks, weighing me down ...*

I wish I could take that weight for you, I told her. I would have done it happily. *I'd trade places in a heartbeat if it would help.*

Well you're real sweet, but that's not how it works. We all have to live our consequences. I accept it.

Remember that movie Trading Places? It worked that way for them.

Are you thinking of Freaky Friday?

That one, I said. *Probably. I'm not really a movie person. Hey I have some exciting news for you.*

How come you don't sound excited?

That's just my stupid emotions. I ... look I know where your Sea is. And I can get you there. And once you bathe ... all your weight will be gone. I can get you through this mural. That's where you'll find it.

She pivoted to stare. She'd forgotten the Monarchs, and all the shades, and her ghostly problems and the overcrowded psychic heat of the room. All she saw was me.

Did you see this in a vision? she asked.

It's heard it, according to Aeternus, but it's obviously true. I know this ocean. I've seen ghosts dive into it after I release them.

Wait, this is according to <u>Aeternus</u>?

Yeah. But the thing about it, though, it's a one-way trip. Once you're in you don't come back. And ... you might forget about me after you wash off. Which I only add in full disclosure. Not to influence your decision.

Her face slowly transformed. It was at the same time wonderful to see, and also terrible. Because of what it meant. The mere thought of washing clean was such a powerful force for her. But she wasn't entirely swept away.

What makes you think he's telling the truth? she asked.

He's a ghost. What's he got to gain?

After all those years, she whispered. *I was so young. Is it true? I can finally put it behind me?*

She bit her lips together and her beautiful face twisted, like someone who wants to cry but can't because they're a ghost.

All I have to do is give you permission, I told her. *And away you go.*

It's like a dream. Do you—.

Before she could finish, Jorge and Phylis both fell back from the wall, shuddering, and an excited buzz rose among the psychics. They crowded forward around the two. I noticed many of them whispering questions to their neighbors, so I gathered the whole *ask no questions* thing had been thrown out the window.

"Back, you, quiet!" I heard Nikita shout, then saw her pushing worried-looking psychics away from the Monarchs. Nikita's age and scorn had elevated her to something resembling authority. Caroline flew from me to hang watching Jorge and Phylis. Both of them looked ashen-faced and totally spent.

"You—yes ferret brain *you—step back*," Nikita shouted at someone with a ferret brain.

Nikita cleared a channel of soothsayers so Jorge and Phylis could go lay on a couch. Whatever Path they'd just come back from, it hadn't been an easy trip. I wondered, having seen them in action, if there'd been battles. The psychics started shouting questions.

"Give them *silence,* " Nikita insisted. She got everyone quieted by pinching and jabbing. She was like a sheepdog for psychics. In the expectant silence, Jorge and Phylis stood. I could tell it was going to be a presentation, close cousin to the lecture, but found myself interested to hear whatever explanation they might give for my living room full of psychics.

"For one thing, I can confirm," Jorge started, clearing his throat. "The Path is accessible from here."

At that, a murmur of psychic chatter rose. Phylis chopped it off.

"*Quiet,*" she commanded, her voice warming up. They quieted. She nodded to Jorge. Caroline floated behind them. The flesh psychics sat up straight. It was almost formal, this arrangement of Monarchs. Like, a pose for issuing edicts. After a moment Jorge continued, billionaire cool.

"The Path is weak, but it's there. That's the good news. We're not cut off."

The crowd couldn't help themselves, they started chattering. Phylis interrupted.

"That's the *good* news," she said. "The bad news is there are figura everywhere. *Everywhere.* They're coming in groups. Five, ten together, lurking in a vision ... " she trailed off. She hadn't recovered from her adventure.

"Is the Path safe to travel?" a man called. Nikita flicked her fingers at him but was herself too interested in the answer to do more.

"No," Jorge said. "Closure House is sealed shut. We can't walk, so we can't fight them. All we have are visions."

Phylis picked up Jorge's thread. "We were attacked constantly," she said, "by figura who weren't even disguised, roaming the Path in their native form."

"What's that even *look* like?' asked someone.

Giant, ugly, and hungry, Caroline said.

"What she said," Phylis agreed with a thumb hook at Caroline. Like cops do. And then I started seeing the similarities. In another life, she and Hennessy might have been great friends. "It isn't safe for any of you out there. But at least we're still connected."

"However," Jorge said, as the hubbub threatened to grow again, "we managed to revisit the vision of the curse. And we have an idea."

While Jorge went on, I saw Caroline and Phylis whispering comments to each other and then glancing in my direction. She and Phylis had a thing. In fact, these three Monarchs went together like puzzle pieces. I felt an unexpected jealousy. I did not enjoy it. I vowed to be extra nice to Phylis to prove how emotionally stable a boyfriend I could be, instead of the needy kind I'm sometimes mistaken for.

"Ti'eirl is the key," Jorge continued. "The moment *that* world became *this* world we saw the ghosts of Undying Land, *all of them,* transferred here, just as the people were. Including Ti'eirl. She's here somewhere. Here in our world."

"All we have to do is find this ghost," Phylis said, "and we turn this shit around."

Now all three Monarchs were looking at me.

"And once she's found, she must be killed," Jorge said. "The curse can only be lifted if both Nolear Fa and Ti'eirl are dead. It is our only chance. She must die."

Riiiight, I said, really pleasantly. *How come everybody's looking at <u>me</u>?*

"Look shithead, right now the curse's half lifted," Phylis snapped. "The Path's almost gone. Once it's not touching this world, psychics are fucked. You know this—you know it better than anyone!"

I don't know it, I told them. *That's the whole point of me, I don't know anything! Okay I know one thing—if you find her, how are you going to kill her? That's not something I know. It's a question.*

"We can't kill her," Jorge said.

"*You* have to," Phylis said.

What, I asked, politely, *the fuck are you talking about?*

"You killed Nolear Fa," Jorge said.

But I didn't, I protested. *Samantha did.*

I pointed at her. She'd been very passive lately, zero flickering in with clues and messages. I wouldn't get any help there.

Plus Aeternus—Nolear Fa—wasn't a ghost when I, or whoever, killed him, I continued. *There's no way you <u>can</u> kill a ghost. Everybody wants to kill them—well, you and Amy, but it's impossible, which is the whole point of ghosts. They go on and on. Flesh bodies die but ghosts recycle forever.*

The psychics watched Samantha. Some of them were toying with outrage, but it didn't get far. Confusion robbed them of energy. Maybe they were hangry. They looked gaunt.

You need a different plan, I told them. *Even if Ti'eirl is here, somewhere on Earth, how are you going to <u>find</u> her?*

After a silent moment, in which they saw all the problems, they were about to give up their plan. When, "The aunties can find her," Nikita said, into the unhappy silence. "The aunties will know."

"Nikita stop—" Phylis started, but Jorge put one hand up, emperor eyes focused on Nikita.

"Wait," he said. "Think about it. Twilight House has always insisted on their ghosts."

"Ts," Nikita said, shrugging, "in the old country we know. Ghosts, we have been saying. Ghosts everywhere, somewhere out there. The Aunties could find Ti'eirl. Hundred percent."

They all looked at me. It was very uncomfortable.

What's this Twilight House? I asked. They weren't going to include me unless I really jammed myself in. Sure, they wanted me out killing ghosts, channeling *light,* whatever else, but they didn't like to confuse me with too much information.

"Three Paths is one of a handful of Closures in the world," Jorge began in a lecture voice. Because oh my god, it's always a lecture. That's the reason you should never ask questions. It's the first thing they teach you in school, don't ask any questions.

"Twilight House is also a Closure. In cycles past, the Monarch thrones have rested at Twilight House, though not in thousands of years. It is a deep well of psychic knowledge. The Twilight scholars have always maintained … a conviction in ghosts."

"Scholars," Nikita scoffed, "they are aunties. Very mean. Many wolves ate their families. They are unhappy."

So these unhappy aunties, I said, picturing them, *they're the ones who'll find Ti'eirl? How? Ghost compass?*

"Probably no," Nikita shrugged. "Their vultures, probably."

Vultures can find Ti'eirl?

"Possibly. Then you kill her. Pish-posh apple sauce. This will work."

Pish-posh apple sauce? But you <u>can't</u> kill a ghost!

At which point a voice thundered through the room. Because of course. It's always something.

I know how to kill Ti'eirl! boomed Aeternus.

And down through my stylishly high ceiling he floated. Many psychics gasped. Apparently their capacity for surprise had not been exhausted by the end of time or the deaths of so many tourists. Some people are just endlessly surprisable. I'll admit he was startling, with his new-age outfit and his flowing hair made of *light*—he had a knack for the grand entrance, you had to give him that. He settled to the floor. The psychics cleared out of the way. They didn't want to touch him.

"Who the fuck is that?" Phylis said.

Aeternus, Caroline guessed. She looked at me. In my mind I nodded. None of the people in that room, or anywhere on the planet for millennia except for me, had seen this figure in the flesh. Through all that time, he'd been invisibly pulling the levers, shaping the world, grinding his plan. Now that they could see him, something about the way he carried himself made an impression—he seemed like someone's boss.

He rotated in place with his arms out, to give everyone a look at his loincloth, and stopped, facing me.

You see, Asher? You need what I can teach you.

"What," Phylis muttered, "is going on? Why is he here?"

Aeternus smiled. He looked rueful.

Once I was your master, he explained to Phylis. *Now I am as you see me. Humbled. A penitent. And the only one who can give Asher what you need. If he will only ask.*

We don't <u>want</u> *your help,* Caroline spoke up. She bent to say a word to the other Monarchs, very quiet. Aeternus watched.

I understand, he nodded. *But as you have seen, the only way to save this world and every world attached to it is to kill Ti'eirl. Only then can the curse be lifted.*

"And you can kill her?" Phylis asked.

I cannot. But I can teach Asher. As I once taught all the Inmortalis.

Not going to happen, I ghosted.

Jorge figured it out. He's one of those genius Monarchs you hear about.

"You're Nolear Fa," Jorge realized. "You *started* the ghost war ... by eating ghosts. Eating ghosts is how we kill Ti'eirl. We eat her?"

Not we, Aeternus shook his head. *Only an Inmortalis can learn that skill. Only Asher.*

But Asher, I explained, *says no. Is anyone listening?*

Then what will you do? Aeternus asked, speaking as much to the psychics as to me. *This is your only hope. If you refuse your birthright, you doom this world.*

The whole room, which just moments before had been swinging my way, now swung away from me. Fickle fucking psychics.

I tell you what I'm going to do, I said, so the psychics perked back up. *Nikita can take us to these aunties to find Ti'eirl, and when we find her*

I'll talk to her. How about talking? Is that too civilized for you? Come on, Nikita, let's go.

"Where?"

Where the aunties are. Take me to Twilight House. Quick. Sunset's coming.

She flicked her fingers. "To get there is weeks. Many airplanes, a train, llama rides. So yes, we should start now."

Okay, I said, *I'll fly there. Where is it?*

"*Eh,*" she shrugged, "who knows? I left as a girl. It is hidden. You must take special trains."

Can we call them?

"Messages come in by bird."

Is this place real?

"Very real. I remember it like yesterday. Though very, very long ago."

Have <u>any</u> of you been there?

No one raised their hand. This was room of people who'd pretty much never left Skysill Beach, or long ago lost the desire to do so. Even the Monarchs had been subject to Aeternus's biochemical control.

I have been there, Aeternus said to me, after the silence got dramatic. *I will take you.*

"You've been to Twilight House?" Phylis asked, suspicious.

Child. There is not a place on Earth I have not been, through the millennia. Do not doubt it. Everything here, everything around you, your cities, your languages, your technologies and wars, the very ideas you think—all of it is my creation. You are my creations. I have visited Twilight House many times since I created it. I can take you there, Asher.

I don't trust this at all. Why he's this helpful? Caroline demanded. The other two Monarchs were still making up their minds.

If you cannot trust my regret, my honest remorse, then trust my self-interest. If this world fails, we all are doomed. I am caught, like the rest of you, in a black spiral.

Through the balcony window, I noticed the clouds breaking into sunset streamers. They were bloody rags stretched through the sky. We had a sunset problem, less than an hour away, maybe just five minutes away with how clocks worked these days.

Let's go, I told him. *You fly, I'll follow.*

Fly? No. We will blink together. I can take you in a single step.

How's that work?

Take my hand.

I hoped that by *take my hand* he meant shove my uselessly frozen outstretched arm into his side, because after a mistrustful moment that's what I did, since that's all I *could* do. He positioned himself the way he thought he looked best, then put his hand in my palm.

Instantly through that connection surged a black, magnetic force, flowing from his body to grip me. Pull me. He was blinking us somewhere. It felt like being tied to a supernatural train engine. My blind impulse was to resist—all I have are the blind ones, I know that—so I dug in and refused to be moved, sealing myself down somehow, and we both were surprised to discover that I'm a pretty supernatural train engine in my own right. He couldn't shift me.

First, he gave me a look of surprise. Then he smiled. I felt the force vanish, and he released my hand.

That's not going to work, Caroline said. She'd taken an instinctive dislike to Aeternus, now that she'd had a chance to watch him in action. She had fantastic instincts. *We <u>know</u> that won't work—if you're touching, you can't blink.*

But you can. Linked ghosts can dislocate—blink—if one is stronger than the other, or one cedes control to the other. Asher must give me control. Of his location. So I can take us to Twilight House.

They were all looking at her now. Apparently she was the one deciding for me. I'd never felt myself in better hands.

I don't like it, she said.

Me neither, I said. *But we have to find Ti'eirl. What choice is there?*

I'm coming with you.

Aeternus shook his head. *I can only bring one.*

I'll be careful, I assured her.

That's just not your strength, though, is it?

I will protect him, Aeternus said, reaching for my hand. *Will you come with me now?*

I nodded. In my mind. Which no one saw. So I nudged myself back into his grip. In for a penny, in for a pound. That's what they say.

Good, he said. *The world beyond Skysill Beach is not what it once was. Prepare yourself.*

Then my living room of ghosts vanished.

CHAPTER

NINE

I found myself a thousand feet in the air, a wide glass of Pacific Ocean rimming off in front of me, and the Southern California coast, dim with shadow, below. I kind of screamed.

Aeternus held my arm. The sun we faced lay close to the horizon and squeezed out brownish light, without heat. A dead, colorless sunset from a dying sun. And somewhere, like a whisper, I heard ... the voice ... my name?

What is this, I complained. *Where's Twilight House?*

Though it is a fool's errand, I will take you, he assured me. *If you still want to go, that is, after you have truly seen what it is you face.*

Oh my god. Can we please just do the plan? For once? Let's go talk to the aunties.

Look below you.

God damn it. I tried blinking back to the penthouse but he was touching me, and he hadn't given me permission. So I tilted ghost me down, and far below saw Manders Point, and the sweep of shoreline that shaped the streets of Skysill Beach. I saw my home city, inch-deep in commercial splendor. It looked like a city in a bubble.

Within a wide ring centered on downtown, the city lazed in stan-

124

dard beach colors, with its streets and parks and standard coast horticulture. But *standard* existed only within a three-mile circle. The world beyond the city was blighted. Charcoaled. Darkened by apocalypse. And out to sea where the ring ended, the water was turgid, black, dead.

Up the coast near the edge of vision, where the light seemed to fail, there came movement—but from this height? What could I be seeing? Trains? Herds of elephants?

Figura?

What the hell's this? I demanded around. *Are you killing the planet?*

Aeternus was disappointed in the question. *This? This is the curse.*

What the—how come Skysill's … what's wrong out there?

His answer took a moment. First, he shook his ghost hair. It was pretty unconscious, how he posed, and that made it work even better. He floated in the air and mentally visited whatever sanctum held his important ideas. He was making me wait. He was like a chef presenting a fine meal.

You alone sustain Skysill Beach, he served at last. *Your work. The mural. Though even now the range of its effect grows smaller. The shadows creep closer.*

Me, sustaining Skysill, would be ironic since I never thought Skysill was that great. But something was going on. Maybe my subconscious really liked this town.

Make me understand, I complained.

Your mural is a portal to the Undying Land. Through it flow the final reserves of time still available to sustain the all worlds. You see? Time the medium, flowing through a fissure you opened, that connects you to a world which you yourself summoned from nothing! The Undying Land should not exist!

It's the kind of grandiose theory that works because there's just no way to check it, the favored style of cultists and politicians. Sometimes, though, the theories are just grandiose enough, and against your will you join the cult.

So what point is there showing me this?

The curse is dismantling this world. At the moment, you sustain this city in a separate pocket of time. This pocket is connected to the wider world, which is the only reason the Earth yet clings to existence. Your painting, against the curse at the end of the world. It is extraordinary. But it cannot last. You will fail.

I've been hearing that all my life..

Think, he said, mistaking me for someone else. *This world is sucking time through your mural from the all worlds. It is like a leak. When it runs out, existence will fail. Before that happens you must extend your mural. Take this world away. Let the rest of the universe implode, your family, your friends, the people you love will be safe. To do it you need power. That is what I want to show you. I can get you that power.*

I tried, but Aeternus wouldn't let me blink. He couldn't keep me from swimming from one of my bodies to the other though, so I jumped to flesh me, far below, and through flesh eyes saw the living room, flesh me surrounded by ghosts and facing balcony doors toward sunset clouds making stained glass of the sky. Pink and red and orange fell over our beaches. The kind of sunset I'd always taken for granted. No sign of blight, or charcoaled ruin. Skysill existed in a different world.

Slipping into ghost me again, the contrast was stark.

The farther from Skysill we travel the worse it will get, Aeternus told me. *You need power to stop this Asher—you need it now. It is almost too late.*

Him reminding me how late it was reminded me of my sunset timetable because my mind sometimes goes in loops like that.

Ominous warning received, I told him. *Now let's flicker to Twilight House. We have even less time than you even think.*

Asher, do you hear me? Twilight House is a wasted trip! You must do it now, while you have strength. Return with me to Skysill. Let me teach you to consume ghosts. With that power, you can enrobe the world in your mural. Save us, and become our source, like a god—I can teach you— simply let me!

You're the one wasting time! You're so super obsessed with this ghost thing but I'm not going to do it!

You cannot save them, ghosts are already being eaten—the figura consume them, and will consume them until they are stopped by the end of the all worlds, or by you.

Twilight House. Now.

A waste of what we lack. Time.

Now.

He sighed, which looked so satisfying. Then shrugged.

Then I will show you Twilight House. What remains of it.

He hadn't stopped touching me. He still had permission to blink me. So once again we jumped. Once again it was not what I expected. We appeared in darkness, enclosed, a patch of dim light glowing nearby. The dark was full of soft hollow echoes. I decided it was a cave, though I don't think I've ever been in one. The glow came from the cave mouth, and there was an ancient, portentous atmosphere around us. Like a place where Neanderthals had painted walls.

Aeternus tugged us toward the opening, and there we stopped, looking out at a sky of bludgeon-black. Dead grey clouds fell over mountains in rock ranges. The cave looked out the side of one of those mountains and far below, past blasted trees and shattered scree and poison, was a long, darkened valley.

We were not in Southern California, which I knew from obviousness. Probably not even America. It had to be the old country. It definitely looked old.

The sun hung low, in the same place in the sky as it had in Skysill, though blotted by clouds of dust and gas. And I'm no astrophysicist, but I thought if we'd translocated to another part of the globe, the sun should be in a different place. Was the sun somehow setting for everyone, everywhere? At the same time?

Out the cave door and silhouetted against the sky I saw winged shapes wheeling circles. Horribly familiar. They circled the valley. More filled the distant sky. All with dominion glowing on their chests. I watched one dive, wings back like a broken kite, and thought it would pull up, but it didn't slow at all, and it hit the ground and broke. Already dead before it struck. Another followed, and distantly I saw others. Earwig corpses, falling from the sky. Cursed.

This was Earth?

In the valley, sheltered under sheer bluffs in darkest murk, was a huge palace facade carved in a cliff base, a limestone relief of columns and doorways sculpted from the marrow of the rock, weathered by millennia. The palace was drawn so deep among the cliffs that the sun would never reach it. Not even back when the sun had been normal. It had to be Twilight House. Also obviousness.

At the other end of the valley was a town.

And once again I heard a whisper. *Asher...*

Do you hear that? I said to Aeternus. *That voice?*

But he wasn't interested in hearing my things, and instead pointed to the town, toppled in quarry stone piles, hardly a wall untouched. Just ... massive earthquakes? Why had we not felt them in Skysill?

And not a flesh body moved. Not one anywhere.

Instead, shades spun thick as leaves. Every one holding its object. And though *dominion* sustained them, it had none of its usual energy. It only eased over them, like syrup.

Among the shades monsters roamed. Hunting.

The town was filled with earwigs, crowded around a cleared square. They peered at something they'd captured. The sunlight was weak, I couldn't tell what they had, but I felt a sick suspicion. The crowd parted further then, and I saw in the *dominion* glow of their bristles that they'd cornered a shade.

Are we here? I demanded of Aeternus. *This is Twilight House?*

What is left of it.

This cave?

Aeternus ignored me. *The fabric of the many worlds is fraying. They flood in to eat. But they too are dying. The curse consumes everything. Everywhere.*

In the village a spiral of *dominion* was revolving around the shade, spinning and spreading through the square and over the figura. An endowment. Ghost vacation. The *light* spread past the edge of the village and into the sky. Then, as suddenly as it started, the *light* collapsed. It was a pinprick. The shade was gone.

But a ghost remained. Exactly what'd happened with Caroline. That was the new rule—shades turned to ghosts right in front of you, because they were trapped here. They needed my permission to get out.

With a roar, the figura fell on the ghost and a frenzied feeding so loud it reached our distant cave commenced—the screams were pack animal cries. It only lasted a moment. A burst of Higher color spread, like a balloon full of paint had popped, and the *light* of the ghost was gone.

The figura heaved back. Some fell on their sides, legs waving dreamy circles. Like they'd just had Thanksgiving dinner. And others turned, sluggish but already reaching for new shades.

Explain that, I demanded, *did the figura just release that shade?*

Did they ... ? Aeternus wondered, watching without expression. Like, super passive-aggressive. It was all mind games with him. Which—along with all the other kinds—is the kind of game I always lose.

My god. Did those earwigs just <u>endow</u> a shade? And then eat it?

Yes. And see how they swell with power. He pointed out a small group that glowed like landing lights. Even their wings simmered with dominion. They shook their massive backs, shuddering out creamy exultations like post-coital tyrannosaurs. Another shade was loaded into the square. It hung, helpless and unmoving while chitinous limbs positioned it.

This is what you wanted me to see? I demanded. *Monsters eating shades? What am I supposed to learn here?*

Not shades. Shades cannot be eaten, they are deadly poison. A shade must first be endowed, and the edible form revealed—the ghost. That is your first lesson. Never eat a shade.

Does any of this make you sick at all, or you're just that lost you don't see how fucked up it is?

This is a scene repeated in every corner of this world. If you refuse to stop it, which of us is sick?

This is your fucking fault, don't pin it on me!

Aeternus got a troubled look. I watched as he peered deep into his memory playpen, then turned beseeching eyes to me.

I did not want the ghost war, he said. *That was not my choice. I would like you to believe me.*

Let's leave Revisionist History for next semester, I said. *What's the plan here?*

Peering out and down and scanning the canyon leading to the Twilight House facade I saw it momentarily free of figura. Again I checked the sun. It hadn't moved. It moved on a completely arbitrary schedule. But it went only one direction.

Let's move, I announced.

But Aeternus's haunted eyes didn't leave me. I mean—ghost eyes, of course they're haunted, but this was more than usual. Sort of twisted and terrible.

It was the figura, he told me.

Oh my god. What was? What was the figura? Can we please go?

The figura caused the ghost war, he said. *They made me what I am.*

You're just an innocent pawn?

Oh, I bear my responsibilities. But it was the figura, they were the ones who branded me ... so I could eat ghosts. They did it out of greed and arrogance. If it had not been for them, none of this would have happened.

I had to admit, the similarities had crossed my mind. Nolear Fa— the ghost eater. And earwig bat monsters—also endowing and eating ghosts. Like the world was just a supernatural, all-you-can-eat ghost buffet. And here he was, playing the victim—like, who did he think he was talking to? Passing blame is something I've been doing all my life. I know that smell.

Got it. You're saying yes, you're a war criminal, but it's someone else's fault.

Some choices are made for us. Consumption is not native to the Inmortalis form. You must be branded by the figura, or taught by another Inmortalis who was, before you can eat.

For a moment I forgot how sunset was going to end the world. You really liked watching him tell these one-sided, myth-perpetuating stories. It's the cult leader razzmatazz.

They came to me in a moment of weakness, he confessed. *The figura seduced me. With their brand, they gave me an unquenchable craving. From that first taste ... the ghost war became inevitable.*

In the valley, the pack was screaming again and endowing another ghost and I wondered was I ever going to get out of this cave, or is this where the world ends for me, listening to an ancient ghost confess his boring secrets to escape his responsibilities? I tried blinking to the shadow palace in its gorge but Aeternus's touch locked me.

Now, I told him. *Aunties.*

He took his hand away, shrugging. *You will find the aunties of Twilight House dead. Let us leave this valley of carrion. Return with me to Skysill. Let me teach you.*

Just using intuition and common sense and the evidence of my eyes I suspected what he said about the aunties was true. The half-lifted curse had tipped our whole world into a shadowland where death pressed everything flat. I'd felt it happen when Mount Obitus vanished into the ground. Everyone was dead. The aunties were dead.

I don't need a living auntie, I said. *A shade will do. I'll endow her and chat. Goodbye.*

I blinked down into the avenue running up toward Twilight House, carved from the canyon stone floor. I appeared directly in front of an arched passage cut in the palace facade. It had maybe once featured thick wooden doors, but they lay splintered on the ground. Above that, an enormous clock face was carved, with Roman numerals but no hands to point the time. Just like the tower above Three Paths.

Dust and sand blew to fill every hollow. I knew there'd been no groundskeepers here for a while since groundskeepers would have cleaned up the human skeletons half buried in silt everywhere. These were the bones of people who had fallen as they walked. Long enough ago that not a shred of flesh remained.

Aeternus appeared beside me. He was unimpressed by the skeletons that had caught my attention. His gaze was fixed above, where the figura patrolled.

Hurry, he urged. *They cannot eat you but they would me, if they could catch me.*

They're not friends of yours? That's not your team, up there?

No figura has ever been my team. They made me dependent. Then turned me free.

Take me to the aunties.

He nodded, and with a nervous look above him, hurried under the arch. I followed. The passage inside was wide—a tunnel precision hewn straight into living stone that went on and on.

How old is this place? I asked.

Tens of thousands of years it has been here, in one form or another. Long ago the aunties of Twilight House discovered ways to manipulate time and make it serve them. They hollowed these walls themselves.

Our hallway branched into smaller hallways, past rooms which still had doors, past dry, cavernous spaces and small, wet grottos. It was creepy as a pharaoh's tomb, though it wasn't as dark as you'd expect. We moved in deadly silence, the way ghosts floating through space always do, while passing empty divots where lanterns might once have hung. But illumination still seeped from patches on the walls that gave off a subtle Higher ... something. Could it be *dominion?* These felt like emergency lights. Slapped up at the last minute.

What is that? I asked, pointing to one patch.

As I said. The aunties used time as a power source. Such ingenuity. What might they have accomplished, given another thirty thousand years?

How you have any kind of conversation with a person who thinks thirty thousand years ahead, I do not know. His plans ran on a fundamentally different scale than mine. I couldn't imagine having to live with myself for thirty thousand years, let alone manage a plan while I did. No wonder he was insane.

The dusty warren went on and on. He led me through it. The floor looked worn by millions of footfalls, and the walls smoothed at waist level by thousands of years of fingers. We passed skeletons everywhere. A few times we came upon fallen *figura*, decayed to chitin shields, blocking the hall, and we floated right through them. You get used to that kind of thing pretty fast.

Then he stopped. We had come to a chamber stained with *dominion* on the walls, like someone had blasted *light* around. Within was a group of fallen *figura*, just dried exoskeletons hollowed out. And around them humans bones lay, a hundred skeletons falling into skull dust. The psychics had lost a battle here. Or maybe the *figura* had lost, but the *figura* obviously won the war, since not a single shade remained. Eaten, I assumed.

Aeternus, gazing on the scene, wore an expression I hadn't seen before: pissed off. Like someone had disappointed him. Like he'd had a stake in this game and didn't like what he was going home with.

Dead friends of yours? I asked, prying with extreme subtly as I can.

I do not know anyone here, he said. *On either side.*

So these figura, I took a different tack, also from extreme subtlety, *came way down here just to eat shades? When they had all those villagers out there?*

The figura would have been drawn into Twilight House by these shades—psychics. Viaticus. Their natural enemies in the Undying Land. Consuming a Viaticus is ... most extraordinary.

What a minute, did you want to eat these psychic shades? I asked. A shot in the dark. The only kind I'm trained for.

To eat a shade is death. Remember. But in my thrall ... I have consumed Viaticus.

And now your thrall is over? You're cured?

He gave an impassive head tilt and said, *One is never cured. Only recovering. As you of all people know.*

Before I could deny it and complain about the people who thought they could tell what I knew, because those people are one of my pet peeves, a series of heavy thumps reverberated through the walls around us. Dust cascaded into the little cavern.

The screams of hunting figura echoed through the halls.

They know we've come, Aeternus said. *It is time, we have to leave.*

I'm going to find the aunties.

Dead, Asher. And you can see—consumed. There are no shades to endow here.

You don't know that for sure! Is there a throne room or something, like—

Listen, do you hear that—the figura are coming! he insisted, like that was all I needed to hear. Which it probably would have been, except I have the listening issues.

Leave if you want, I yelled, then spun further down the passage we'd been traveling. I heard Aeternus following, saying something in Latin that sounded like it might have meant *Though art a shit fucking idiot!*

But why should I worry about figura? I understood Aeternus being concerned since he was just figura snack food, which if it happened would totally be poetic justice, which is the only kind of justice I believe in. But I was a spirit. What could they do to a spirit? Can't eat me unless you endow me. Can't be endowed until my body dies back in Skysill. Plus if I saw something I didn't like, I'd blink into the sky or all the way back home. I was pretty confident, which is often my downfall. But this time I knew it would be different. Which is also my downfall.

Aeternus followed as I raced down the doomsday echo tunnel until it emptied into a vast, dark chamber. The ceiling curved to vanish in high shadow. Along the walls, dozens of halls opened or maybe ended, depending on which direction you were walking. Tiles covered the floor, like some kind of grand lobby connecting every part of the warren to every other.

From one tunnel, on the other side of the cavernous space, came a sudden flare of *dominion*. It cast ghost shadows up walls high as a stadium, and the stones rattled with thunderous blows.

Aeternus drifted to a stop ahead of me. What was he doing? Scouting? We should obviously take the passage with the noise and the billowing *dominion,* I thought, because where there's smoke there's fire. That's what they teach you in rehab. I darted after him. He was facing to the right, down a different passage, where a figure stood. A figure framed in flickering *light*. A human figure.

You, Aeternus said, or asked, pointing at the figure, *you ...*

All I saw at first was a woman. She rushed into the room. She didn't move like a ghost. Aeternus was edging away, back the way we'd come.

What ... he asked, looking back and forth between the woman and me, *what are you ...*

The woman. I'd seen her in visions. Dreams. Memories. I remembered her singing.

It was Katerina Gale. Time slowed when I saw her. Time had been doing a lot of things, though, and I hardly noticed. Was ... my mother here?

Another gout of *dominion* erupted from the first corridor and out rushed a dozen monstrosities, skidding into the black cavern to stop. These were not winged figura. These were like armored snakes, with spider legs and fangs big as shovels. Their black eyes were the size of manhole covers. They saw Katerina nearing me and screamed and launched themselves to cut her off.

And because of slowed down time I noticed all that in one second and dismissed it, to focus on my mother. Her dark hair was long, as in my dreams, as in Peter's death vision. She wore a patterned dress. With the snake-spiders charging, she began to run, dress flowing around long limbs. She looked confident she could reach me. She looked confident about everything.

Had Aeternus hidden her, instead of killing her? But Peter's vision had shown her dead. This was no ghost racing for me, I heard sharp breathes and saw her casting a shadow. She held my eyes, fierce, serious, and though she was glowing a little, she was every-thing I ... an aura of *dominion* around her edges and ... *glowing?* In a strangely familiar way ...

She reached me before the spider snakes and held up her hand and they just peeled around us, like they lost the Asher contest, and retargeted to Aeternus, a squealing stampede.

"Asher," she wept, heartbreaking, the thing I'd missed forever, "I've been searching, I'm so ... "

She touched my outstretched hand ghost hand.

" ... sorry," she finished.

Because, of course, she wasn't my mom, because my mom and dad were both dead and had been dead for twenty years. But my critical thinking skills were replaced by wishful thinking skills when they died. And now I'll believe anything, apparently.

Katerina became figura-shaped, the same way Tante Celine had transformed in the Undying Land. In an instant she grew fifty times, got a pincher mouth, chitinous claws gripping my ghost arm—she became a snarling, leather-winged earwig monstrosity, wings that were knotted with intricate black designs, like fields of tattoos. Or brands?

I tried blinking into the sky but couldn't, because of her touch. That was more wishful thinking. She tried yanking my arm but I declined to move, like a ghost fire hydrant. I saw the snake-spiders reach Aeternus.

Asher she— he cried, but then turned because he had bad problems of his own. The pack dove, arms extended, starving.

She will— he yelled one last time. His words cut off as he blinked from the room.

"Come with me!" shrieked the tattoo earwig who'd been my mom. My perfect mom. I just sealed myself in place. That was all I had. My obstinance. The moment Aeternus vanished, the spider-snakes whipped back toward us.

"Come with me *now*," the earwig demanded.

Let go! I screamed in ghost.

The spider snakes charged. What did I care? What could they do? What could any of them do? I wasn't a shade to be endowed or a ghost to be eaten. My flesh was out of reach.

My earwig raised one of many arms. At the end of that arm she brandished a metal rod. Maybe metal. Its tip glowed molten.

For one second she watched the onrushing pack. Then she raised the rod high and thrust it at my ghost chest. When it struck I *felt* it, pierce my supernatural body, felt it go through, felt pain and then numbness. The sensation of some radical trauma. Shock.

She'd branded me with a molten umbra eye.

The pack reached us. Through her touch I felt her blink, tearing at us. It was a massive wave. A thousand times what Aeternus had managed. I was distracted by the tattoo and weakened. It was too much to fight. And she took me. She took us away.

TEN

Better late than never I always say when I'm late, which is usually. The instant she blinked us I lodged a mental protest, and with all my disordered, oppositional, belated willpower, I interrupted our passage. My opposition is indomitable. It dominates everyone. Including me.

We aborted our blink and it felt like a bridge collapsing under us. We fell into reality again. High in the air, above the valley of carrion as Aeternus had named it. Below us, figura roamed and ate, and Twilight House hid in its cliff.

This was not where my earwig expected to find herself and her wings weren't stretched to fly. She started falling, grabbing me, screaming and unfurling ponderous leather sails while I hung, immobilized in space by her touch, steady as a lighthouse.

My chest flamed where her rod had gone in ... no. That wasn't my chest. Not my ghost chest anyway. That was *flesh* pain I felt. All the way back in Skysill flesh me had pain so off the charts it ripped me slipping back into a corner of his mind, and I saw the living room but had no control. I was a passenger. We fell to his knees gasping, collapsed to his side on the floor groaning, hands to chest. Li Wei was there, his ancient body tottering, bent over me, trying to help me loosen my shirt.

The earwig iron had pierced my ghost chest and gone all the way through to Skysill Beach and branded flesh me, was what seemed to have happened. I badly wanted to see, from my little corner of flesh mind; was there a mark on his chest? Did my flesh body wear the umbra eye? Is *that* what just happened?

Then I got yanked back to ghost me and the pain cleared. Ghost me, hovering over the valley of horrors, with earwig lady-claws grappling me, freezing me in space. As soon as she fell off I'd be cleared to blink. I hoped. Though who could keep track of all these fucking rules?

For a moment it seemed like she *would* fall. But like an air buoy, she kept clawing back up on me, slipping but getting huge wings spread and starting them up. She managed to right herself in the air. Then her many hands clamped me and she was hovering, expending a lot of energy, like a sailboat pretending to be a hummingbird. And after that, she started shrieking.

To the east a group of earwigs in flight soared around and started our way. Again my earwig lady tried to blink us, and it was almost overwhelming, like fighting to stand up in Niagara Falls, being torn and pressed on all sides. Again I managed to refuse.

"Do you want to die—what are you doing?" she screamed, the wind of her wings a roar. "Let go!"

No fucking way, I shouted, *and if you brand me again I'll ...* my threatening options were limited to absolutely nothing and I had to stop. It was humbling.

"If those catch you," she said of the rapidly approaching airplane monsters, "the tool I used will be as *nothing* to the torment you will suffer. There will be no escape. The weight of them will be too much, even for you Inmortalis. You will fall. It will end."

Don't say Inmortalis, I yelled back. *Wait—you're working with Aeternus! Is that what this is?*

"Who is Aeternus?" she demanded.

Aeternus! He's the—Nolear Fa!

"Working with *Nolear Fa?* Never!" The mass of wings and mouths and talons was nearing. "I despise him above all others. These drones approaching may be his allies, though. He has allies everywhere. Come, too much is at stake!"

The sky was dark with approaching wings, as figura from farther and farther bee-lined in. Some fell from the air, plunging dead to earth, and others took their place.

What did you do to my mother? I shouted.

She squeezed one wrecking ball insect eye up to me and the eyelid snapped and sounded like a giant camera. And she said, "I am sorry I took that form. I knew you would wait for her if you saw her. I needed to touch you. This is war. We are losing. I had no choice."

Did you know her?

"Through your visions. I have watched the Paths around you, the shades endowed, and I have walked their death visions. Celine. Peter. They both had visions of your mother. Figura hunt this way— you know this! Hurry, come!"

There was literally nothing I could do. And at the end of the day, I'm an impulsive person, especially when my mind wanders and the stakes are complicated. I'm an all-in guy at the poker table because smaller bets are too confusing. The thing that finally decided me here was wondering—if one branding iron had knocked flesh me down, what might a swarm of irons do to him?

I let her blink us.

We appeared back in almost total blackness. At first, I thought we'd blinked into the cave Aeternus started us in. There seemed to be an opening. There was echoing. Then an alien phosphorescence swelled up and in one second I saw this was a different cave completely. The sunlight coming in the opening was the wrong color sunlight. It was green. I was somewhere with a green sun. And the interior of this cave went on forever, thick with shifting earwig forms on cobweb bridges, wall-crawling horrors skittering and beating wings of skin. Hundreds of thousands of earwigs. A swarm. It looked like someplace they would live.

My tattoo earwig loomed above me. As the light swelled, an earwig mob gathered in the door behind her.

"*Inmortalis!*" they cried, surging forward. It was super terrifying. She was still touching me. I had no power and found myself in exactly the *out of the frying pan into the fire* kind of situation my impulsiveness often leads me to. There's just no way to prepare to be crushed by an earwig mob. I couldn't even close my eyes.

But my earwig spread her tattooed wings and blocked the others, shrieking, "Back! Do not touch him. Clear the chamber. He is fragile. He is the hope of the all worlds. *Clear the chamber!*"

Slowly the other nightmares crawled from the corner cave into the greater warren. It was all disorienting. Then it seemed like a curtain dropped, partitioning the hive away, so it was just me and my new favorite shape shifting insect kidnapper, alone in a private booth.

The green light through the outer opening made me sick to my stomach. That's not something that happens to a ghost, usually. But the rules were all breaking, so why would you need nerves or intestines to feel nausea?

I started complaining, since that's my North Star, *I have a lot of shit to do lady. Or whatever you are. Where is this? What do you want? Who are you?*

"I am the last queen of ... call me Cinesthellia," said the earwig. Her wings drooped. She sounded weak, though weak for a brontosaur earwig is almost meaningless.

I need to go. Why are we here?

For a moment I thought maybe she'd gone to sleep. She had insect inscrutability. Then she spoke, and it came out a little whispery.

"To finally find you, to save you ... with such twists are the fortunes of the many worlds decided. Perhaps all is not lost."

Most of it's lost. How's that for a twist? I have to go before the sun sets.

My ghost intestines lurched further up my chest as the earwig—Cinesthellia—changed her form once more. She folded like fleshy origami, *dominion* rising from her belly, and she once more became the person I'd have given almost anything to see. Katerina Gale. She still had one palm on my ghost arm. I knew it wasn't her. I could only stare.

"I'm going to let go of you, Inmortalis," she said. "But you will need a guide when you leave. Do not try to translocate on your own, it is dangerous. Do you understand?"

I didn't nod, because *ghost*. But she must have sensed me understanding, maybe with her antenna. Was I really going to leave now? When for the first time in decades I had my mother standing before me? My fake mother, I mean? I guess you take what you can get.

This is really what she looked like? I ghosted.

"This form is truth. The forms I take can be nothing but truth."

Katerina was perfect. A form sourced from my dreams. Lifted from a vision. And then she smiled softly and I—

Don't smile. Don't do that.

And she let me go. We both waited a moment, to see if I was going to run away.

"Good," she breathed, "I have but little ... " and she shifted back to monster form, then fell against the wall with a noise like broken wood chipper. One of her car-door eyes was closed, the other three were barely open. From her belly several bristles fell, no longer glowing. They bounced to the floor like drumsticks.

"Aging so ... " she gasped. "I am almost gone. I have but moments ... but I found you, finally, and now ... "

I thought I needed a guide? And now you're going to die? God damn it what's going on? When I get nervous I ask a lot of questions.

"You ... are the final Inmortalis," she said, and raised a claw as I started asking. "No, let me ... say what can be said while time remains."

The waves of *dominion* crackling through her bristles were dimming like a brownout power failure. More belly dowels dropped to the floor. Patches of her bare flesh oozing fluid appeared. She was for sure running on the last remains of something. Maybe time.

Fine, go, I said. Then I just listened. Sometimes I listen when I'm nervous, too, just not often or well. She gave her huge head a shake, like a person, which obviously she was in her own way.

"The all worlds are dying," she whispered. "The curse of Ti'eirl ... has begun ripping them apart. This curse should be done, but somehow, transitioning to a new world, Nolear Fa found a way not to die. And time passed. The curse grew ancient and began to decay. Then Nolear Fa died, and the Paths broke, and the curse is finally failing. But now, at last, I have found you. To finish it. Use my brand. Find Ti'eirl. Save us."

She stopped talking. I didn't know if it was my turn or what and I waited a minute to see if she'd died or was just taking a rest. These *my-turn / your-turn* scenarios are the worst.

When you say finish it, you lose me, I told her. Just stalling. I knew what she wanted. It's all anybody wants these days.

The flesh of her wings was thinning and sagging as I watched. In places it began to rip. It tore through fields of dark, scarred brands, with a sound like old rubber ripping. She cried out. Her voice weaker, she started back up talking.

"I've bestowed you a brand: consumption. You have but to accept it."

I do not accept it.

"You must. It is in you. When you are ready, press and hold your chest, the brand will rise to the surface. You feel it in you. We all do."

I don't feel anything, because hello I'm a ghost, and how come you're doing all this to save my world? What's in it for you figura?

"You ... painted a portal. You painted an open circuit that cannot be closed. And now, on one side, a dying world endlessly consumes *time* to keep itself alive, while on the other side, the many worlds wither as they are drained. All connected. Everything connected ... "

She convulsed and made a sound like a cough. More of her eyes closed. Her belly was almost bare, the floor before her littered with dark bristles. From behind the curtain drawn against the earwig hive, a wailing began. Like someone's queen was quickly passing away.

"It is in your hands," she told me. "Find Ti'eirl. Eat her. Free us from her curse."

No, I shouted, *You're the ones that fucked it up, you lured Aeternus in and made him a ghost eater—and I'm supposed to fix it? I'm supposed to—*

"No one *lured* Nolear Fa," she said, her voice momentarily rich with outrage. "He came to us! He offered—stop, say nothing, I have only seconds, hear me—Nolear Fa came to us. He begged to be given this brand. This was long ago. Many times many eons. The hive in that time made a grave error for which the many worlds have paid a thousand times a thousand. Because Nolear Fa offered that hive queen something she could not refuse. It was Nolear Fa who taught figura to endow shades. We took this knowledge as a brand and passed it forward. Shades were no longer poison. Shades became like livestock. A fully formed ghost is difficult prey, but as it is endowed, it is helpless. In return for endowment, that queen gave Nolear Fa the gift of consumption. He offered a thing that changed figura life forever. And for that, we turned him into a monster."

Even to me, a person lacking interest in or experience with morals and ethics, this move of Aeternus's appeared fucked up. He'd provided a guidebook for a very hungry species to eat as many ghosts as any of them wanted? Assuming it was true.

Why'd he do it? I said. *Why would he want to eat ghosts in the first place?*

"It is said ... he was driven to seek power by a broken heart."

Aeternus? Someone broke that heart? Hard to believe. Anyone I know?

"Ti'eirl, of course."

Aeternus ... you're saying Nolear Fa and Ti'eirl were ... involved?

"A most cursed coupling. One of the most powerful of all time. For eons they fought it. Or she did. A Viaticus and an Inmortalis, sitting on opposing thrones, grounded in opposite energies. Drawn together."

An Inmortalis and a Viaticus ,,, so these two were polarized?

There were so many things I suddenly wondered if I understood. All I wanted was a moment of silence to think it all through out loud, which is the only way it works for me. But Cinesthellia was dying, so I ceded the floor. Because politeness.

"Polarized. Their union would have destroyed not only themselves but many of their people, and much of their world. But Ti'eirl pulled herself free. It must have been torture. Nolear Fa lost himself, it is said. When he came to us some say he wanted revenge. Some say he hoped to create an artwork so magnificent, Ti'eirl would return to him. And then ... the ghost war. Ti'eirl's curse. Her greatest folly. She loved him to the end, you see. Her curse was, she would take his pain herself, and give him her clarity. She sought to trade places. But that is a thing ... all beings must live their consequences ... and to trade ... her curse remade the many worlds and brought us ... to ... "

The last of the *light* pulsed out of her. I ghosted forward. With a final groan, her body folded, and once more, if so briefly, she became Katerina. It stopped me. I rocked. My mom was crying.

"Now it is your time ... " she said.

Wait—

" ... and remember, you must tell him nothing about your brand. Do not trust him. He has plans ... within plans ... "

Wait! Hey!

But Cinesthellia the monster died. She retook her figura form, shuddered to pieces, and spread over the floor. It was as dramatic a death as I'd ever seen, which is saying something for me. It left me feeling things I didn't understand. Sorrow. Anger. Horror.

From behind the black curtain, the mourning howls rose to deafen me, and then it was torn away and across the basically melted body of their queen I faced a horde. Not a healthy one. The earwigs were all suffering the continue-living issues Cinesthellia had succumbed to. They staggered into the room, some hardly able to stand.

And I'm slow to react. I just am. It's one of my known character flaws. So before I thought to move, one of them touched me. Then they piled on.

I didn't do it! I ghosted as loud as I could, but my ghost voice was a drop in the sea of their torment. They'd lost their queen. They were losing their lives. Whether or not I was the responsible party I was the party within reach. I tried blinking away. I gave it everything. But this was Cinesthellia times a thousand. They had me.

And then ... sunset.

The green-tinted light went out. At the same moment, every figura in the place froze. The green light had been *sunlight,* I realized. This was sunset on an alien or alternate or multiversal world with a green sun. The new kind of sunset where the sun above you just dies.

And that meant Skysill was—I swam my consciousness into flesh me. It wasn't hard. I knew exactly where to find him, like when you put your hand in your mouth to feel a broken tooth. He was my flesh tooth. From within him, I saw a lightless living room filled with people caught in mid-sentence, with thoughtful or confused or angry expressions—they had all the expressions—and only flesh me able to move. I discovered that he'd decided to stare at Caroline. Her ghost expression was puzzled. She was pointing at the mural. She was beautiful. She was taking too much of his attention.

Go jump off the balcony, I told him, a plan he happily began executing. He doesn't care what you tell him, he's just happy when someone takes charge. Across the crowded living room, he went bouncing, like in those astronaut videos from that soundstage. He was light as a ghost, while I, the actual ghost, was weighted down by a pile of alien bugs.

I needed to merge. I needed it *now.*

Then the thinking part of me, which was honestly overmatched by circumstances but hadn't given up yet, got the idea to shout back across the universes or dimensions or whatever separated us, and say, *Cross them!* I imagined a string tying my far away flesh ears to my mouth, for convenience.

And he did it. He'd already jumped off the balcony. Now he was floating toward the beach. And while dropping through star glimmer, with the dark disk of a dead sun hung far above his head, he crossed his eyes like a lunatic.

In ghost me I felt a jerk, then was pulled straight through the motionless figura dogpiled on me. Out of the hive I arrowed into a scene very like the one in Skysill, a sky dotted with vanishing stars— not that many—and a cola black star radiating nothing above a planet darker than a mine shadow.

My merge picked up speed, spun me, and I flew without knowing the direction, with universal darkness to all sides flesh me dragging me back through a tunnel of worlds. Every sun unlit, each planet lifeless. A universe of these worlds.

Was I falling up? Being lifted down? I tried to orient. No sense of gravity or direction was left—like the last ten minutes before you pass out at the bar, thinking you *could* make it home but deciding not to try. Realms flashed to all sides, billboards on a cosmic freeway, and flesh me came closer.

I burst through the sky of my home world. I plunged, looking backward at missing constellations and emptiness. One question answered at least: traveling backward. It's great when I can answer a question, it gives me false hope, the only kind I'm comfortable with.

Wrestling around, I watched the ground expand. I plummeted toward flesh me. He crouched on the beach, near the boardwalk behind the Bradley, in position; knuckles down, knee bent, head titled like a football coach begging for victory. A second later we were touching.

Merging.

Dominion flowed. I felt myself sucking it from the mural.

Light coursed through me, down my arm and out, and spread into the ground. Pain followed, loosening the flesh and bowels and spine of me. The pain was a relief. A homecoming.

An evil historian friend I once had advised me I should *control the things I can, and let go of the rest.* And the thing I can consistently control is the source of my pain. Life's a thousand pains together, but you only feel one at a time. I choose what hurts. That's all people like me really want, deep down. That control. Happiness is unpredictable, and joy's a mystery. They come and go on their own. But pain has laws you understand. Cause and effect. That's what keeps people coming back to it. Although I wonder if that's true for everyone or just alcoholics, and people like me who used to be alcoholics but who haven't had a drink in *days*, it seems like.

Dominion drilled me under the crust, into the mantle, and from there spread me out and raised me, and I saw the world again, and I chose that pain. I let everything go but the pain and that made it all clear. Like flesh me said: I let it go, and it all came back.

Dominion forced me so wide I felt I was the world. I felt all its lives. Not that many. Skysill was now the only place where human animals persisted. The rest was shades, figura hunting them. Or hunting me. Or hunting Ti'eirl? What if, out of the eight billion shades roaming the world, the figura were to eat Ti'eirl, would that lift the curse?

But the figura were dying in droves. Falling from the sky, decomposing in mounds high as foothills. The few that were left gathered near Closures, and their drumbeat sounded—their wings, beating together, doom drums. They'd never eat a sliver of the ghost banquet now covering this world.

And around me was the pain of Skysill. My home town. Falling into darkness.

So with *dominion,* I fought the darkness back. I filled the world up, I levered *light* through my guts and out, into everything, until Skysill was full, and then the world was full, and then I stretched toward the sky for the sun. For just a moment I felt something new, a not-pain—I felt myself choke. Something caught in my throat ... something choking ... it wasn't my throat. Something closing, but not inside me.

The mural. The *dominion* spigot was ... closed.

I screamed like a powerlifter and reached, *reached-for-the-sun,* pulling all the *light* I could and snapping my fire fingers—but it wasn't enough. The universal well was at critical levels. There wasn't enough *dominion* out there to finish the job.

Except ... I had my own reservoir. Whatever *dominion* I carried in my blood. A reserve I'd never touched, that I've never thought about. A reserve I recognized, however—the source of every painting I'd ever created. The source of every artistic impulse I ever felt. It was the essential core of me as a creator.

I tapped that. Maybe I shouldn't have. I have my impulse issues.

And the sky lit up.

The sun burst to life.

Sunset became noon, the sun regressed back up across the sky, and then noon became morning. The same new day started over once again.

And every figura on the dying planet turned ... toward Skysill.

CHAPTER

ELEVEN

The beating wing drums of the figura faded, never entirely stopping as I felt the confines of my flesh body. Awakening. I found him curled on my side at the bottom of a pit of sand, in Hawaiian gear, in mid-morning sun. I fluttered sand off my eyes with my lashes, made an animal noise, then ran out of energy. I lay waiting for something clarifying to happen. It almost always will, I've found, or I could take a nap.

You should get up, something's wrong, said a voice I recognized as my own voice from above me. Who was talking to me up on the lip of this crater? Not flesh me, because I *was* him. I declined to look. I wanted no more wrong things. No more things.

But I felt a new hollowness in the world and a ripple shimmer in the air. A water-bed feeling. Something fragile and easy to puncture. Or already leaking. I sighed, my one comfort, while faintly, oh so faintly, the drums beat and the air waved in response.

Are you getting up? Someone with my voice asked again.

"What? What is it?" I said, finally looking. At my shade. Frozen in a pose. Pivoting to face his body down at me like someone checking under the hood of their broken dune buggy. Ghost me? That was ghost me. But I was embodied in flesh me so I should be locked up, unable to move, but I wasn't. Was ghost me talking? Did ghost me operate on his own now? Was he yet another separate version of me all on his own? How many versions would I have to keep track of?

Beside ghost me stood another figure, with the sun at his back, and I had to dial the contrast down to see ... the *Gray*. He'd taken his shirt off and wore a pair of slacks he'd found ... slacks with a utility belt and revolver ... he was dressed as half a policeman. I didn't want to know.

But wait ... *what?* The *Gray?*

"What's going on?" I asked, all casual. The *Gray* laughed. Ghost me ignored the question. I paddled sand—I had flesh hands, moving around, but who was I?—and I churned my legs but was too weak to escape my sand trap because I'd just used up some important percentage of myself getting the sun started. My reservoir. I wondered if I'd get that part back. Probably not. The universe has a pretty ironclad no refunds policy.

A hand grabbed my flesh wrist and then I found myself lifted, like an empty trash bag, by the *Gray*, who put me down none too gently on the slats of the beach walkway. Now facing the Bradley Building, I saw another figure heading my way, coming from under an awning. Someone shambling and unsteady.

Li Wei.

When he saw me he froze. He twisted his head like a gecko points its eyes. His own eyes were not moving predictable directions. But Li Wei was dead. Wasn't he? He looked like he should be. He looked two hundred years old.

"Hey—" I started asking, and then he fell. Collapsed, became a motionless corpse, and as he fell I saw ... something ... superimposed on him. The briefest trace, like a *dominion* strobe. Then it was just me, the seagulls, and me, and me.

The air around us rippled again. Far away we all heard the pounding. The drums and the faint, starving howls.

"So," I said to the *Gray* and ghost me, who were both listening to things in the distance. "This is super weird. Does anyone have any idea what's going on? Which one of us is the real one?"

You are, ghost me said.

The Gray pointed at me. Then he ran the fingers of his other hand over the hairs on his pointing arm. He shivered from pleasure and laughed. I was the real one? If I was the real one that meant we were in real trouble. Was I stuck in one body now? Suddenly it felt lonely.

"I'm going to try jumping in you," I said to ghost me. "What do you think?"

See what happens, he said. In his mind he shrugged.

So the part of me that was not my flesh, not the *Gray*, not a ghost —that part pushed, dove, went under, and emerged in my spirit body, which I found floating and looking back at flesh me, who was covered with sand and looked badly exhausted and very thirsty. His face was drained of color.

Nothing ever gets less complicated. I swapped back to flesh me to brush him off.

"What even is the *point* of this?" I demanded, flicking sand. Ghost me shrugged in his mind. The *Gray* laughed and lay back on the sand, getting a bit of apocalypse sun. Any normal person would be at least mildly concerned to find themselves literally split into different bodies, maybe even question their sanity. Totally question something. But questions get me nothing. All I could think was we were going to run out of fruit salad a lot faster this way.

It used to be, back in the beginning—by which I mean either not that long ago, or farther back in time than human minds can comprehend—when a stray ghost blinked in near me it came on the scene blasting a ball of *dominion* bright as a gas station fire. And then I'd pop. Sometimes I'd even hear a sound. But those days were gone.

Now, when Aeternus ghost-blinked in a few yards away, he just faded to visibility. I heard no noise. There was no *dominion* burst. It took a second for him to get fully formed. Then he hung amongst our little tryptic of Ashers like he'd just awakened from the best nap he ever had.

All of us turned to him, which he seemed to expect and give us plenty of time for. But there were too many Asher's on that beach and he looked surprised. He cut his entrance short and drifted to the *Gray,* who looked up from the sand in amusement. Aeternus toured him slowly, peering down, then turned to ghost me and finally came to flesh me. Where I was currently embodied.

And all any of us did was let him. That's his power. He makes the smallest gesture theatrical. He's so entertaining. Plus we were exhausted.

The curse has torn you farther apart, I see, he said to all three of us. *I warned you this was happening. At least you have made it back. I was afraid you would not return at all.*

"Yeah, no thanks to you," I snapped. "Thanks for all the help. I mean no thanks for it. You know what I'm saying."

What help could I give? Do you forget I am a ghost? A ghost among figura—if they had touched me I would have been lost. I am no Viaticus. I cannot fight them. He watched me now, with a strange intensity, different from his usual strange intensity. His lingered on my chest. *What did she tell you?* he asked. *The breeder?*

"The who now?"

The figura. The hive queen. What did she want with you?

He was talking about Cinesthellia, obviously. So he knew about hive queens ... right. Of course. My short, desperate conversation with Cinesthellia came flooding back and I remembered, Nolear Fa trading the endowment for the brand, Nolear Fa and Ti'eirl together. Of course Aeternus knew the hive queens—he went *way* back with them. And Cinesthellia said I shouldn't trust him. Big news. The question was should I trust her?

"The hive lady died," I told him, super casual. "She aged. The curse I guess. I merged back here. Just in time to restart the sun. Which—good morning and you're welcome by the way."

He wasn't charmed by my friendliness because it's not a tone I've practiced. He looked suspicious, like I knew things I wasn't saying. Sort of the opposite of what I usually do.

The figura are mortal enemies to all who come from the Undying Land, he reminded me, studying my face. *They have always been so. Hunting and eating us. They are covetous. Greedy. And long ago ... at a certain point in time, they began to covet more. Did she tell you?*

"Yeah, at our tea party. While the world was ending. Now we're pen pals."

The figura were a failing species, Aeternus insisted. *They reached too far. They were endangering not only themselves but the many worlds. I was sent to them, and they saw my weakness, and they branded me. Made me what I am, out of greed, to start the ghost war and bring the boundaries down and feast. They lied to me. To get what they wanted. What lies did she tell you?*

When he'd mentioned his brand, I felt mine. Deep inside I felt it—the umbra eye. Waiting, almost eager to be called to the surface. It didn't feel right in there. Like they'd operated and given me a pig heart. My body wanted to reject it. I heard Cinesthellia's hiss—*when you are ready, press and hold your brand, it will rise to the surface.*

Aeternus couldn't keep his eyes off my chest. So, feeling a little slutty, which was refreshing, I brushed my chest with my palm then unbuttoned my shirt like I had sand on my nipple. *No umbra eye* was the picture I wanted to paint. Just Asher and his nipple.

"Whatever she wanted," I said, "she's bug juice now."

Did you speak of Ti'eirl? he asked.

"Enough to get the impression they want her dead. Which reminds me ... how are we going to find her now that the aunties are gone?"

You will not. You were never going to find Ti'eirl.

According to the insect kidnapper who'd sheathed a mystic poker in my lungs Nolear Fa was an enemy—more than her, it was implied. But while *the enemy of my enemy is my friend* is a great concept for a bar fight, these allegiances were too murky. Who to trust? No one, of course. But who other than that, I meant?

I studied Aeternus thinking of the ways I could trick him into talking without also tricking myself into talking, which are ways that don't exist. Playing stupid's always an option though, and it seems authentic to people when I do it.

"Wait a minute," I snapped my fingers, "hey I mean, you knew Ti'eirl, right? You fought a war against her. You ate all her people. If anyone could find her you should be able to. Right?"

I didn't know if this was playing stupid, or just stupid. Did he hate Ti'eirl or love her? Or both?

He floated without moving or breathing—because *ghost*—for seconds, then gave a small nod.

I knew her. But what I knew of her ... will not help us.

"Hm, really? Any little thing, you know—what was she like?"

A warrior. Unparalleled. Fierce. But with ...

"With what? Garlic breath? Fierce, but with beautiful eyes? Did she have secret yearnings?"

Why such questions?

"Why? That's how this works. I've been doing it a while now, surprisingly—investigating—and how investigations go is, it's ridiculous, you wander asking stupid questions looking for a thing, then find a different thing you never thought of and start asking those questions—it's not efficient. I'm pretty good at it. Or lucky. I think the secret is to accidentally ask the right question. So I'm just wondering, do you have any idea where Ti'eirl can be found?"

No. I cannot help you find Ti'eirl on a planet of eight billion.

"Cannot? Or will not?"

You will not find Ti'eirl—there is no time! To save this world you must encompass it with your painting. That is the only path! And for that you need—

At that moment a scream issued from the penthouse, falling to us from the balcony doors.

Hadn't flesh me left the psychics up there?

I blinked to the balcony. Or tried to, but nothing happened, and I thought *shit, now I can't blink?* Then I thought, *shit, I see the problem—* I was in the wrong body for blinking. I had too many. It was going to be a problem.

"You," I called to ghost me, "get me up to the penthouse, hurry!"

I threw an arm around his neck and stepped on his toes and he rose like a rocket. It felt very precarious and filled me with new respect for flesh me—he'd been doing this for months. He hadn't seemed scared at all. He'd been confident in ghost me, but I had no such confidence and the five-second trip to the balcony was like riding a meteor. Then ghost me dropped us on the balcony.

The door was open but the shades were pressed too tight to see in. There were hundreds and hundreds. As they rotated to face me I slammed my ghost in and cleared a path. I hurried toward the source of the screams—a group of psychics huddled in the center of the room.

They had every right to scream, I thought.

The spirits breaching their backs and shoulders had emerged farther. They all arched upward and back, only hands and knees still imprisoned in flesh. Every spirit wore a mask of frozen, silent terror, mouth wide, teeth bared, eyes shocked. Ghost tendons straining up. They were the faces of spirits trying desperately to escape. Terrible to behold.

Apparently the psychics thought so too. The sight was too much to bear for some of them. You'd think a psychic would be harder to panic with the supernatural stuff—they cultivate a blasé, seen-everything vibe. But these psychics had seen more than they could take.

They rolled, swung at their own bodies, or sat moaning while other people's shades slipped through them. They were pointing and wailing, but there was no running from the horrifying creatures that now followed them everywhere. It was supernatural bedlam until Phylis began to bellow.

"All right people—everybody listen up—*do I have to start knocking heads?*"

Phylis also had a massive and harrowingly panicked version of herself towering out over her shoulders. You could tell it freaked her out, but her irritation was conquering her horror. She had world-class irritation.

"SHUT IT!" she shouted.

And finally, maybe their throats hurt, people stopped screaming. A few of them whimpered. I saw Jorge and Caroline consoling the worst cases. It was probably terrible for Caroline. It was like an institution in here. One of the places she'd been held as a little kid. But her expression was firm and confident. Not unfazed, but equal to the moment. Like a person who'd accidentally cut off her leg, but who also happened to be a famous leg reattachment surgeon. Not a problem she couldn't solve.

On the floor, among all the other signs of chaos and havoc, I saw new dead bodies. Psychics, some of whom I recognized, who'd insta-aged into corpses. One of these was Nikita, though the condition of her original body made it harder to tell if she'd insta-aged or passed away naturally in her sleep. Her shade floated near her corpse, holding a bag of chips.

"You!" Phylis was shouting. She did it a few more times, then I realized she was shouting at ghost me four feet away.

"*What?*" I demanded from flesh me. "I'm over here."

"Why are ... why do ... why are they like that now?" She was pointing over her shoulder at her silently screaming haunt.

"I assume because they know something we don't," I speculated.

The air rippled again, and far away the hollow, dire echo of drumming rose, a flood coming inexorably closer. Some of the more alert psychics screamed again. Most just sat or stood looking numb.

Ash! Caroline said, sweeping up beside me. *You made it.* She hugged my spirit, though I wasn't even in my spirit. I wouldn't have felt it either way. It hardly mattered.

"I'm over here," I told her, and she flew to me, and almost tried to hug me again, then remembered how hard I am to touch.

What'd they say at Twilight House? she asked. *Did you find Ti'eirl?*

"All the aunties are dead. Everyone's dead out there," I told them.

There was nothing to gain sugarcoating it. Plus I had my reputation for unnecessarily brutal honesty to maintain.

"Everyone?" asked Jorge. "You don't mean … "

"Every living person," I nodded. "The only people alive anywhere on Earth are in Skysill Beach. Out there it's a wasteland. In here … we're under a dome here, the mural's keeping us alive but out there … the Earth is done."

As if to confirm my point, another vibration-ripple hit the air. Some people fell over, disoriented by air that moved, like we were acid tripping on a tiny ship in a storm. The drums added desert island cannibalism to the mix. Like somewhere a roasting pit was being readied for us.

"Also the figura are coming," I told everyone.

"Here?" Phylis demanded. I nodded. "Why?"

"Because you people are delicious to them," I said.

Who is 'you people?' Caroline asked. *In this case?*

"It's confusing," I told her, "but I think the curse … the Inmortalis were the human priests and they became the Five Families after the curse. On the ghost side were Viaticus—call them ghost priests— and when the Inmortalis became the Families, the Viaticus became you people. You psychics. You're all Viaticus. And Ti'eirl tried trading places using a curse and everything broke, and Viaticus are just … delicious to figura. That's why they hunt you in visions. To eat your brains or whatever."

Jorge examined the shades, his worry growing. "If the figura are coming, these shades are helpless. They can't move."

"Not exactly helpless. A shade is actually deadly poison—eat a shade and you cease to exist, so I've been told. The figura have to endow them, then while the new ghost is shaking off the cobwebs … "

The discovery that you're the favorite snack for a species of supernatural monsters takes a moment to process, I saw. For everyone but Caroline.

What if you endow them first? Caroline asked. *Give them a chance to escape?*

I loved the way she assumed I'd be able to help. It was misguided but it was the kind of misguidance that stable, long-term relationships could be built on. I hated having to shake my head.

"No time for all these shades. I did a room of shades up here once and it took a whole day. We don't have a day."

"Why not?" Phylis demanded. "I'm not afraid of these shape shifters. We'll keep the figura back and you do all these shades. Then we *all* go out and find Ti'eirl and kill the bitch! I want us to stop sitting around! We have to act!"

"The figura aren't the problem," I told her. "I mean, yes there's a figura problem, but the real problem's the sun. It could set any second—I know it doesn't seem like it, you people don't remember it, but it's done it three times so far, where all the *light* goes out. It has to be restarted. Manually."

And then Aeternus, the shimmering, sociopathic, irritating gadfly, vaporized into view up near the ceiling and began to float down among us.

The solution is within you, Asher Gale, he pronounced. *You know what to do.*

I narrowed my eyes. I suddenly got it. I'd worked out his style. It was predictable as high tide. What he did was he waited, out of view, in silence, while a situation got increasingly impossible, then he appeared, dramatically, often near the ceiling, to offer exactly the help you did not want. It was starting to get a little boring. At least to me.

But the others were riveted. They lacked my immunity to psychopath drama. Before I could dismiss him, Jorge asked, "*What* solution is within Asher?"

Aeternus spread his hands to demonstrate good intentions. Then out they came. Good intentions everywhere. Talking to Jorge. Aiming straight at me.

You all know what I have done, he began. *You know my trans-gressions.*

"So that's what you call eating a species to extinction?" I asked. "A transgression?"

The very scale of my sins will be your salvation, he assured me. *I can teach you to endow many, many shades at once. In an instant. They do not all have to be eaten. You can save them from the figura.*

He turned to the rest of the room looking guileless and genuine, which I know was for my benefit. I mean I *thought* I knew that. The truth was it was getting harder to be completely suspicious of him. Everything he'd done for us had legitimately seemed like a person trying to help. Even pushing for me to learn ghost eating. All he kept trying to do was save himself, and make amends. Like he wanted to put his past behind him. Which I totally understood. It just wasn't going to happen.

Because my strict policy has always been, *fool me once and that's the last chance you ever get to fool me because I'm not a fucking idiot.* He'd fooled everyone else for a zillion years pretending to be an invisible ghost, planning to crash time and space into a wall. But me, he would not fool.

But everyone else hung on his every word.

To my great sorrow, he explained, *long ago I did endow and eat ... many ... there is no undoing those acts. But I stand before you chastened. I want to use what I learned for good. Or what could the point have been for all of that? Asher! Please. There are techniques I created. For mass endow-ments. You could endow all these shades at once. Save them and* <u>*still*</u> *prepare for the sunset. Let me help!*

"Is he telling the truth?" Phylis shouted. Oh my god the shouting. "A lot of the dead ones could fight if they could move like Caroline. Twilight House isn't the only House with tricks. We could fight! If we can't find Ti'eirl I want to go out fighting!"

Public opinion was going to turn against me, which I recognized because of how often it's happened in the past. From the assembled fortune tellers arose muttering, then isolated cheers, then every psychic eye in the room turned to me as they waited to hear me accept Aeternus's innocent, no strings attached offer to pass on the things he'd learned eating all the ghosts in the world that one time, back before he'd reformed.

"Well?" Jorge asked.

Don't do anything you don't want to do, Caroline told me.

"There's only one thing I want to do," I said. "But I can't. So I'll do a few things I don't want to, because I hope, before it's all over, I'll kiss you again. That's what I want."

That's sweet Ash but it can't be all on you! It's not fair. We can't trust him. There has to be another way!

This is his birthright, Aeternus assured Caroline. *I care about his well-being. I will see that Asher comes to no harm.*

I bet every ghost you ever slaughtered heard that story, she said, slowly, with venom.

You do not like me, little Viaticus?

I think you're slicker than owl shit. You don't care about him.

And you do? He gave her a look of pity and said, *Your paths will never touch. You and he are metaphysically opposed. Your union is cursed. But I am here. I have solutions. If we are to survive, you all must trust me.*

Usually, when people have these conversations about me while I'm still in the room I feel compelled to speak up. But watching Caroline ... I could've watched her forever. Phylis, however, couldn't.

"We're wasting time!" she shouted. She pointed at me. "You—do it!"

Again the air rippled, figura drums echoing off the foothills—the wings of uncounted starving predators rushing through time and space to consume us. And I admit, at that point, I ran out of energy to argue. What approach was I supposed to take? I couldn't keep the threats straight. Which was most important? Fighting figura? Resetting the sun? Endowing the shades, finding Ti'eirl, or...? I had no idea. I decided to deal with issues in the order they were forced down my throat, since I have a lifetime of practice swallowing that kind of shit.

I turned to Aeternus. "Fine. What do I do?"

And he did his thing, casting his mind into his storied past, surveying all his wisdom to select the proper pearl. It's a crowd-pleasing performance. The psychics ate it up. They looked very willing to trust him. When he found his pearl he nodded to me.

My problem in those days was one of scale, do you see? he asked. I thought I knew the problem he referred to, an eating problem he had, and it made me sick. Such huge mobs of ghosts to eat. So little time.

Near the end, he said, *shades were thick upon the land, the Viaticus growing ever more powerful. To continue my fight ... took unbearable sacrifice. But I taught myself techniques for mass endowment. I am not proud of what I've done. Though it is, in its simplicity, brilliant.*

"The funny thing," I said, "is you do sound pretty proud."

He had the audacity to look at the ground in what might have been shame, but I doubted it.

"Get on with it," I told him. "What are these quote-unquote *techniques?*"

The shades you wish to endow must first be submerged beneath the surface of the world. All these shades must be pressed down, as far as it is possible to push them. That is the first step. Are you ready?

"How the fuck do I move a bunch of shades?" I asked.

Search within, Inmortalis. That skill is native to you.

"There's nothing *within.* Believe me I've looked. Just tell me."

There is nothing I can tell. Shepherding is intrinsic to Inmortalis. Just do it.

"I thought you had a technique!" I protested.

A technique, yes, a formal method of applying skills to a problem.

"What are you a dictionary ghost? I'm saying I have no—"

Oh! interrupted my own voice, *Okay, I got it,*

Ghost me had no expression, but his voice sounded impressed, which would have been a danger sign if it had been me, but in his case who knows? The psychics in the room followed it all, rapt.

Aeternus was masterminding a production that none of them would ever forget: the Asher Gale show.

Ah—one of your pieces has the skill, Aeternus nodded, turning to ghost me. *Intriguing. Are you ready?*

No, I can't do this, only he can. Ghost me pivoted to flesh me, *Aeternus's right. I do know how you move ghosts around.*

"What do you mean *you* know? The ghost knows it? I don't think that helps me."

Yes, come inside, he urged. *It's all here. I have skills. Come get them for yourself.*

The room was silent. I was like a reality show where you wondered, how strange was Asher, really, and would he and his ghost ever work things out? Did either of them actually have a *skill?* No one could believe it might really come to *that.* Even I was amazed.

I took a breath and slipped into to ghost me.

And once embodied there, I found the skill. It was just waiting on the surface of my brain, like my personal assistant had left me a detailed note I somehow, magically, didn't even have to read. Knowledge filled me, which is a feeling I've never liked but what choice did I have? Aeternus was right, this part would be easy. It was real necromancer shit. Without ever even studying I was fast becoming an expert. Or maybe I'd been an expert all along.

I slipped back to flesh me. Organizing many shades at the same time was an extension of the skill I already possessed, where I battered shades out of the way using ghost me. Ghost me is an Inmortalis spirit. An Inmortalis spirit is connected to all of ghostkind. So I could either batter each of them individually or ...

Push down.

Every spirit in the living room dropped through the floor. The sound we heard then was the sound of a room full of psychics exhaling in wonder. They'd had doubts I'd pull it off—all except Caroline—but I wasn't offended. It actually made them more sympathetic and relatable. None of us thought I knew what I was doing, like a bond we shared.

Good, nodded Aeternus, who'd had no doubts. *Let us go outside. You'll need your flesh for this.*

He blinked out.

"Let's go," I said. I dove into ghost me, loaded my flesh on him, and now the room was free of shades so we shot the balcony doors in an instant and emerged in beachy afternoon. Afternoon? Not more than an hour had passed since we'd restarted the morning. It'd been no time at all, yet the sun was heading for the horizon. I could practically see it moving, though I know you're not supposed to stare at the sun.

Aeternus hovered at beach level, and I swooped to join him, and we both saw the *Gray* racing up to us. His hair was wet. He still had cop pants. Behind him, he dragged a wet piece of … the pier? Why had he been pulling apart the pier? He was my most active body. Like, *hyper* active. I looked back at the gaggle of psychics staring off the balcony, everybody gathering for a show.

What now? I ghosted. *Let's get this thing moving.*

My technique, he announced softly, forcing me to listen, which is another thing I don't like the feeling of, *is, endow <u>through</u> <u>the</u> <u>ground</u>. The shades below us are in touch with one common surface. If you reach, you will feel them beneath us in the soil. You will feel the objects they hold. You will know their stories.*

"Oh, *I* get it," flesh me said, nodding and looking at his hand.

He knelt and put one palm on the ground. His now familiar pose. He looked up, his eyes, predictably, narrowed in thoughtfulness.

"Just jump into me," he told me. "It's all in my brain. Everything I know."

Were all my bodies one step ahead of me now? It made me feel pretty superfluous, which is a feeling I honestly don't mind. When I jumped, there inside flesh me I found the skill he'd promised. The steps were simple, the order was clear—the worst combination for a procrastinator like people say I am. The earth touched the shades, I touched the earth, I had only to squeeze and their stories would pour forth. Like cracking an entire bowl of nuts at one time.

Aeternus watched. Intense. Probably too intense.

"Why so eager?" I asked. "Is there something about this you're not saying?"

I offer a way to save these shades from the figura. Only that.

"I swear to god if you've got some plan ... "

Asher. Our self-interest aligns. How can I convince you?

"If you were alive you'd convince me by sticking your tongue in my mouth. Is that what you miss? Control?"

I have learned to control only what is in my power. You will learn this yourself. Now. You must raise these shades to save them, as Inmortalis. You must play your inevitable part. We all must.

"Only history's inevitable," I muttered. But my heart wasn't in it. My hand was already pressing the sand, deploying my brand new skill.

The supernatural part of me reached through my palm, into the ground, and felt a company of shades stretching under the beach in total darkness. Their *dominion* was sluggish, it barely moved. They stood in ranks like buried terracotta warriors. Each outstretched hand with its object. Each object with a story. From above, from the sand, as if from the clouds, I reached for the stories.

Then three hundred brain movies began playing all together, projected not *on* me, as much as *through* me, while my focus, despite its known deficits, somehow spread to follow them all. But these stories ... something was different now. Each object held more than a single story. Every shade was now linked, somehow, to an ancient chain of life stories within them, end to end, a story for every body that ghost had sparked to life—thousands, tens of thousands, *more*. Skysill was the story on top and from there they went backward in time.

My life generates endless irony, of which this was simply another example—I'm someone who's made *not* knowing people his life-style. My brand has always been some form of *get the fuck away from me*. For that kind of person, this was nauseating. All these people, their problems, their ideas, rushing through me, all convinced theirs was the most important—it was stomach-turning. Part of the problem was, yes, I recognized my own tendency to self-aggrandize here. But mainly it was, I'm just more comfortable in groups of no one but myself.

Thankfully it was over fast. I was a needle of muscle-bone the stories threaded, pulled farther and farther back in time, all the way back to the very genesis of this world at the moment of the curse and over the border to the Undying Land. There each thread ended. Or rather, began. Each thread began with the story of a life from the Undying Land. An original ghost story from a ghost with an Undying name.

In the real world—if there was such a thing anymore or ever had been—no time passed at all.

I endowed them all. My flesh eyes rolled. I gagged but couldn't retch. Because I'd been through it before I expected swirling *dominion* wings around these figures but that didn't happen. There wasn't enough *dominion* for that. The objects just vanished, and the shades went a little runny, then became ghosts. Easy peasy.

In my flesh I fell, to eat a mouthful of beach. Spent. Under the sand, like I was lying on a plate glass floor, I saw them all. They were hazy, foggy-brained, confused. This was the moment of confusion the figura took advantage of. But even as I watched they began to come awake. I used my mass moving trick to raise them to beach level because I know what it's like being lost in that dark.

Then I rolled on my back and stared at the sky. Ghost me and the *Gray* stood together, sort of companionable. Behind them, the cohort of new ghosts began looking at themselves,

For your first attempt, Aeternus said, examining them, *you did well.*

"These ghosts drive me *crazy,*" I coughed drool from my mouth. "Are they always this whiny and self-involved?"

Yes. It has always been thus.

"These guys are waking up fast." Some of them were even making word noises.

Most are Viaticus. Dead psychics. For a Viaticus this transition is easy.

You need to swim into me, ghost me said. *You have more things you need to do.*

"If it's more skills," I told him, "I'll have to pass. I'm at my limit."

It's not over, my ghost body said.

With a groan, I swam to him, because it was easier than listening to more explanations. I heard flesh me gasp at the shininess I'd left as he came awake behind me. I thought he'd complain but he didn't. I was surprised. I know *I* would have complained.

Caroline blinked down from the balcony to scan the ranks of fresh ghosts coming awake. For the first time, I noticed how tired she looked. Like some yearning was thinning her out. I had a pretty good idea what she yearned for.

Which one are you? she asked, looking from the *Gray* to flesh me to ghost me. The other two pointed to ghost me, and Caroline examined me.

Are you okay? she asked.

There was nothing to it, I told her.

Then she turned to Aeternus, who watched us. He smiled.

As you see, he said. *Asher is fine. More himself than ever.*

Finally, she swung around to study the mass of stirring ghosts. *And how about them?* she asked me. *Will they be alright?*

They'll be excellent? I guessed. *I'm pretty sure.*

You got them herded up nice, she complimented after a moment. *They'll be easy to work with.*

I'm your ghost cowboy.

I get a clear picture of you out on the range. I like you in a saddle.

I'm riding off into the sunset thinking of a girl. Such a beautiful girl. And really missing her.

Stop. You're going to break my heart and I have to go fight figura.

The air rippled and flesh me almost fell. The drums boomed, this time from a specific direction; south, down the coast. Toward Three Paths. *Loud.*

I'm thinking ... I said. I paused for banter but she only listened, like she somehow knew I was serious. I swear if I had her intuition I'd be ... I don't know. Maybe more psychic.

I'm thinking you should get out, I told her. The words came rushed but firm. *Before everything ends. Get through the mural. Let me send you to the Forgiving Sea. Are you ready?*

Ash. Once again we were hit with air ripples. *There's figura coming through the Closure. You heard them this morning ... or, wait ... was that today?*

Yes and no, I said, checking the falling sun. *Doesn't matter. I don't care about figura. I'm thinking of you. Let me send you through. I'm not sure any of this's going to work. I want you to go get ... unburdened. There's not much time left. I'll come through as soon as I can and ... we'll see what you think of me.*

I'm not going anywhere. We have to fight for whatever time we can. Phyllis and Jorge already left for the tower. They took all the living psychics. She pointed at the ghost psychics. *I'm here to get the dead ones. Are these guys ready?*

Caroline! There's no long-term solution up there. There's thousands, there's, who knows—millions—I saw them—please go through the mural. Take these ghosts with you, help <u>them</u> get washed off.

And leave everyone in Skysill for the shifters? Come on, Ash. She turned to yell at the crowd. *Okay, listen up!*

You could clearly see two groups in that ghost crowd. The ghosts who'd been Five Families were still stupefied. Figura food. But the psychic ghosts had popped to life, bright little candles. You could see high alert flare in their faces as they turned to Caroline. High alert and a shit ton of confusion.

Psychics of Three Paths! she ghosted commanded. She was used to being listened to. It was super sexy.

The figura are here! she said. *Here and now. In this world. And we have to hold them. For as long as we can. We have to go now—are you ready?*

There was a murmur. A murmur of ghosts—that's what a collection of ghosts should be called I thought, because my brain picks random tracks. From the murmur issued a rising sound with a lot of wailing in it. Very supernatural. These ghosts didn't sound happy. Though in their defense no ghost I'd ever met had sounded happy. But here I heard a stoney note of sorrow. Then a ghost voice rose from the middle of the murmur.

There's somewhere ... said this ghost ... *there's water ...* It was a woman in a soccer outfit with big glasses shaped like hearts. *I feel ... I think I'm supposed to go ...*

That's the Forgiving Sea, she called, *and yes, it's almost all I can think about. But we have a job. We have to buy what time we can.*

When can we go? cried other ghosts. *When? We want to be clean!*

Caroline seemed to swell and her voice got steely. The ghost psychics fell silent. This was Caroline summoning the full Monarch spectacle, and it brought quiet to the beach.

This is our time. This is our task. I am Queen of the Path Behind and I say, this now falls to us!

They almost seemed convinced.

What are you buying time for, exactly? I asked, softly.

You. To find Ti'eirl.

I was afraid it was that. Because ... at this point how?

Talk to ghosts? Paint a picture? Have a vision—you'll get an idea. I've been in your brain. It's nothing but ideas.

But without the aunties ... I might have to do something I'll probably regret.

Be more specific and talk faster.

The hive queen gave this ... she waited. I did not talk faster. I realized the brand was one part of me I wanted to tell her nothing about. I had too many parts already.

What's a hive queen? she asked.

Figura. I'm thinking of you at Three Paths. There might be a hive queen, or—I mean, these figura <u>eat</u> ghosts like you.

Not like me, she told me. *They're in for a surprise if they try. Now we have to go.* She glanced at Aeternus, floating in supernatural splendor. *He's not on our side, Ash. I don't care what he says.*

Then she blinked out. A second later so did all the other psychic ghosts. Blinking is one of those skill things. You just know how. Like taking a breath or picking a scab.

For a moment there was silence on the beach. Even Aeternus had blinked. Only the sleepy ghosts remained, and beach sand reflecting sunlight in fruit tones; watermelon pink, tangerine, lemon streaks served on a sky of deep blood berry-blue. Almost a regular sunset except it was proceeding at a million miles an hour and it would be a global catastrophe when it happened.

"Thoughts?" I asked ghost me. He shook his body, *no*. I looked at the *Gray,* lying in the sand, who alpha-checked me a look saying this was not his problem.

"I'm serious," I told them. "I'm out of ideas. We have to find Ti'eirl to lift this curse. The more I hear about her the more I think I understand her. She'd want to help. I think. I just don't know how we're going to find her. So, what? Speak up with ideas or hidden skills. Hidden skills you two?"

What kind of skills are you thinking of? ghost me asked.

"I have no idea," I admitted. "Maybe I'll know if I see it. I'm coming to look."

I swam over into ghost me. I rooted around in that mind. It felt rude but I had no time to ask nicely. And ghost me had nothing anyway. I turned in ghost me toward the *Gray.*

What about you? I asked him. *Skills? Ideas?*

"Why don't you come find out?" he asked, sort of daring me.

Tensing up—mentally—I swam into the *Gray.* Under normal circumstances, he's the last body I'd take, because he used to be so hard to get *out* of. But what I found once I took his limbs and legs and brain was, everything felt completely regular. Frightening strong, disturbingly fast, but without any interest in destroying anything, no urge to join or cause a fight—and unfortunately, no ideas for finding Ti'eirl.

I ended up back in ghost me and there I stayed. He just felt most natural by this point. The body I wore no longer affected my mind. I wondered how it would affect my ability to intoxicate myself. These bodies were suits of clothes I put on or took off, but were no longer *me*. Hadn't one of them once been me? Had there ever really been just one of them?

Flesh me and the *Gray* watched as I settled into ghost me, one of them filled with absolute trust, one with complete disinterest, as the sun fell lower and angled through ranks of sloth ghosts listing on the beach. I surveyed that crowd bleakly.

So am I really going to have to do it? I asked the other two-thirds of me. Not expecting or getting an answer. We all knew I was just talking out loud to myself. *Is it actually coming to that? Aeternus's plan?*

Could that be right? I didn't even know how his plan worked. In principle, it was simple: eat a bunch of ghosts, get powerful, use art skills to save everyone by expanding the mural over the planet. Or the planet plus the sun. Or ... what about the rest of the universe? Was I responsible for that? I groaned. Like every plan, the more you thought about it the more impossible it seemed. I have no idea how anybody ever gets anything done.

"Maybe it wouldn't be that bad," flesh me suggested, reading my thoughts.

Eating a bunch of living minds sounds okay?

"No, not that part."

"But think what it'd *feel* like," the *Gray* said. "How would it feel if the whole world was your painting? If *everything* was a painting by you? That'd feel awesome probably!"

"It does sound good," flesh me admitted.

"Let's go check out that mural," the *Gray* said, sitting up. "How's this supposed to work?"

They checked for instructions like the issue was settled. Eat a bunch of ghosts to become the most powerful artist that ever lived— that was their advice. It was so disappointing. The one time I look inside, the one time I ask myself *what should I do*, because I have nowhere else to turn, and the advice I get is completely fucked up. I've never been a person to take his own advice—I'm crazy but not *that* crazy—but I was beginning to think I might have no choice. I was backing myself into a corner.

Someone had once given me a test to determine the severity of my mental handicaps, which had gone off the top of some of their charts and confused them. One question on that test I'd always remembered. It starts with a runaway train. You're in charge of a track switching lever. If you do nothing the runaway train goes straight down the track and hits a terminal and kills hundreds. Or you pull the lever and send the train on a different track, where it only kills one family—a mom, a dad, a daughter, and a son, maybe. A family of painters perhaps. And the question was, which do you pick?

I wracked my brain. Had I passed that test?

But my brain only returned another question. Why, with everything everyone knew about me, would anyone ever put me in charge of a lever like that?

Overhead a gull cried, then a crescendoing round of drums washed through our beach party, and this time it carried a high, shuddering chorus of screams. Monster screams. The figura breaching the tower?

I heard another note as well, a discordant tinkling within the clamor. I couldn't quite ... it seemed to be coming from nearby. A sharp, familiar ... a ringing ... phone? Flesh me reached into our pocket. He looked thrilled at the opportunity to grab something— anything at all, he didn't care. With fingers of amazement, he lifted our ringing phone, scanned the ID, and answered. All I could do was watch as my life proceeded without my participation or permission.

"Hello?" he said.

For a moment he listened, then nodded, then held the phone to ghost me. "Your sister wants to talk to you."

CHAPTER

TWELVE

*hy would you ... I complained, I don't want to talk to my
sister, I have a thousand ... I'm busy!*

"I already answered," he shrugged. "Here."

What, but ... ghost me can't use a phone ... oh my god ...

I slipped back into flesh me and pulled the phone to my mouth.

"What!" I yelled. "What is it Amy I swear to god you call at the
worst—"

"I found Roman," I heard her say. Her voice was a dark, soft hole,
somewhere dreams went to die. My sister can be very dramatic. "He
says there's nothing anyone could have done for Veronica. The
fabrica who initiates a False Death is the only one who can rescind it.
She couldn't rescind it from where she was."

"I mean, are we still talking ... I mean, Veronica, like I already said
... I mean I have a lot going on right now but I'm sorry about Veronica. Did you need something?"

"I don't know what to do. There's nothing left, Ash."

"I know. I do. It's totally fucked. Come over. Come to the Bradley.
I'm on the beach."

173

"I made Roman teach me. I didn't believe him. But it's true. The False Death … "

"Wherever you are, just come over. Hurry. Get here before sunset. Can you?"

"I messed everything up, Ash."

"You didn't mess anything up. Come over."

Then I hung up on her. Because how many tests do these people think I can fail, concurrently? The podcasts all say *pick one test at a time*, fail *that*, and *then* try failing something else if you want. I was already juggling the ghost-eating umbra eye, sunset dooming us, the mural possibly saving us, finding or not finding Ti'eirl, sending or not sending but in the end probably sending Caroline to the Undying Land without me—adding Amy and her relationship problems was too much. I was failing at the very limit of my abilities.

"I guess let's go look at the mural," I agreed to ghost me. He swooshed over and I was climbing up when, through his neck, I saw a new ghost vapor-simmer itself into place with me, there on Ghost Beach.

Ghost Nikita.

She was the oldest ghost I'd ever seen. Most of the other dead people reverted to some younger form but Nikita might actually have become older. She wore the kind of bathrobe you tied with a scarf, and heavy leather boots, and some kind of hat of fur. She looked like a pioneer thrift shopper.

"What the hell're you doing here?" I shouted. "Shouldn't you be up with the Monarchs?"

Yes, hello to see you too.

"Nikita! What's going on?"

Caroline sent me, she said. She rolled her eyes, *You are thorns in her side.*

"She said that?"

Pff, no. But she fights at the Closure. She is distracted by you.

"Is she okay?"

Fine. She said to me go, check on Asher to keep him safe.

"How will you keep me safe?"

She has figura to battle, who knows? I am expendable. We all know this. The figura will easily kill me in battle, I am old and a crosspath. Monarchs are very organized using their human resources. Nikita gave a critical look to the field of non-psychic ghosts waiting, foggy-eyed, on the sand. *But these, they will be easier to eat even than me. Like snack foods, like baby seals in a buffet. They just stand in one place. Why is this?*

"You Viaticus wake up faster," I said, stepping back up onto ghost me. "I have to check my mural. Stay here and keep an eye on them, if you want to be useful."

I do not. I am here for Caroline.

"Well," I said, rising, "I'd rather you stayed with *her* to keep *her* safe, at least—"

I stopped talking as a dark shadow spread across the beach. So acclimated to my recurring crisis had I become that my first thought was *sunset.* But sunset shadows happen everywhere and this shadow was growing, right on top of the ghosts and Nikita, falling only on us, then I heard wings like copter blades roaring and an earwig nightmare plunged from the sky.

It thundered to the beach blowing sand in all directions screaming hate and hunger. From between the pinchers framing its mouth came a shriek, "Viaticus!"

It faced Nikita. She stared right back. I wiped blown sand from my eyes and yelled, "Move Nikita! Blink!" But she didn't. The figura crept closer, almost in disbelief, like a child creeping up on a bird, waiting for it to fly off. Only Nikita didn't.

"What's she *doing*?" I asked out loud of myselves.

She can't leave, look, said ghost me.

I saw. Behind Nikita were three hundred helpless ghosts. If she blinked away, they were the only remaining target. She couldn't move or she'd doom them. It was like the runaway train question, with a supernatural monster and a beach full of ghosts.

The figura suddenly lunged. Nikita didn't budge. I dropped back toward the sand. What could I do? Nothing. Nothing, as Nikita was snatched from the beach into the air.

The earwig raised her, shrieking in anticipation, the bristles on its stomach pulsing, frenzied, but before I could reach her and not help ... the *Gray* sauntered into its view. The figura paused. I thought the *Gray* was a little too casual. I thought he had no idea what he was up against.

I thought wrong.

"Let's play the game where I kill you," he shouted happily.

The figura was surprised, but seemed amused, and dropped a huge claw on him. He reached above his head and just caught it. Laughing.

When he twisted that claw the figura turned—it had to, or it was going to lose the arm, since the *Gray* was bio-magnetized to the ground and made of titanium muscles. And it did try to turn, but then the arm was lying at the *Gray's* feet anyway, dripping oily yellow. He'd stopped laughing but he was definitely having fun. The thing screamed and struck with a different limb, which he caught and tore away. Then it reared, stumbled on missing legs, unfurling its wings.

The *Gray* dodged blows like he was playing tag with a toddler while airplane wings spread and the figura lifted its head toward the sky. Then he jumped from the beach. He rose like a missile. A streaking air blur. He hit the earwig beneath its jaw, arcing it up off the sand and blowing itsd head to pieces. He passed all the way through it. Ams up like Superman.

The figura body spasmed. Shivered, then fell motionless to the sand in a pile of paper-thin wings and sinew, like a broken elephant parachute.

Nikita pried her ghost self from a claw.

Pff, you see? she told me when I landed beside her and jumped to the ground. *You need me.*

"Are you okay?" I asked.

Considering I am dead, eh, I am fine.

"Are there more of these coming?"

Maybe. This one escaped before the Monarchs were ready.

"Then what the hell are we going to do with these ghosts … "

I gestured around helplessly at all the many ghosts swaying on the beach, bleary-minded from the endowment. If a figura trying to eat them hadn't woken them up, I didn't know how to help them. They appeared to be shocked, like a group of tourists mass married in those cult ceremonies where the preacher's a charismatic, godly sex criminal. Like they'd just discovered themselves in the wrong place at the wrong time, but now the chapel doors were locked.

"Hey you all," I yelled. "You can't just *stay* here, you have to … "

The Gray walked up, wiping bug mulch from his arms, having the time of his life, and I got an idea.

"I'm going to take care of these ghosts," I told him. "I want you to go to the Closure and protect Caroline. Kill anything that tries to hurt her."

"Ohhhh," he crooned and nodded, filled with anticipation. "That's more like it!"

And he was gone in a shower of sand.

Smooth move, hyena boy, Nikita told me, *now we have no chance here.*

"I have an idea."

Yes I am sure, what is this idea?

"I going to move these ghosts up and shove them through the mural into the Undying Land. Where no figura can get them."

Huh. This is excellent idea. I will watch.

"That's sure to speed everything up."

I used the trick Aeternus had taught me, a trick that no doubt had ancient ghost blood all over it, though beggars can't be choosers. Scanning the sky for incoming ghost eaters I visualized my murmur of beach ghosts and cast my imaginary net, woven to catch and hold ghosts. I gave them a yank and they bunched together like captured fish. Then I slung them at the penthouse. It was easy. They weighed literally nothing. I lofted them four floors then pushed them through the balcony wall. They vanished.

There, Nikita said, pointing behind me. *Is one you missed.*

Turning, I saw her; one supernatural figure remained behind, timid green surf visible through her chest. Samantha. She was still a shade. She'd slipped through my net—it'd been designed to hold ghosts—and been left behind. I knew she was perfectly capable of locomoting herself wherever she wanted to go. I waved.

She looked lonely. What else could I do? She wasn't a ghost and she'd never be one. Despite months of trying, there was no way I could help her. She'd appeared very sparingly since she'd killed Aeternus at the quorum. Keeping to herself, I assumed, because it was only a matter of time, and she knew she was doomed. For me at least, that's an interlude to spend alone, thinking about your life and getting drunk. For me, I'm saying.

I left her on the beach. I mounted ghost me and rode him to the penthouse, through the ghosts I'd netted, and landed myselves before the mural. It was not in good shape. If this painting was part of my plan to keep the world going, I'd have to move fast—the entire wall was dimming. The edges of the painting were fading to shadow as the *light* of it contracted, the four corners now entirely dark. It had a familiar feel, like end-stage liver failure—deterioration that would pick up speed as the end approached. And then I turned and surveyed the room, remembering not to narrow my eyes.

Nikita stood in front of the assembled murmur, looking not at all curious about what I had to say. Behind her some of the other ghosts were finally beginning to wake, shaking heads like newborn fawns, tottery and uncertain. Some whimpering. Pretty soon the questions would start, a stage I wanted to avoid because it's annoying. And all of them, the comatose and the conscious, fixated on the mural behind me. On what they sensed waiting for them on the other side.

"Listen up ghosts," I yelled. I glanced at Nikita. "Can they understand what I'm saying?"

Almost no one understands what you are saying. This shrouds you in mystery. Go.

"Listen to me ghosts," I told them. "Here's the thing, you're waking up—no, save all the questions for when I'm not here—you're waking up and now you're ghosts, and the first thing you'll want to do is wash off the pains of your old life. Now, inside this mural, there's an ocean. You feel it. No—comments and questions later, time's very extremely short."

Many ghosts now held their arms out towards the throne, like it had heat, or gravity, or beauty. Nikita saw this and rolled her eyes since she's less affected by any of those things.

"I'm not *exactly* sure how that works, but get ready, I'm going to give you permission and ... send you through. Ready—no don't answer. Ready?"

Oh, they are ready. Look at them. Like kindergarteners before recess.

"This includes you," I told Nikita. "You go to."

Wash off these pains? Please. Where would I start?

"Your call I guess." To my murmur, I called, "I herby grant you permission. Go ahead, get started. Is there a problem? You in front. Go."

They must touch you. Nikita said. *I feel it too. This will release them.*

"It's always something," I sighed. "Let's move, then. Come on people. Ghost people. Form a line."

A ghost with long hair and leather moved forward, arms toward the mural. When he passed, I held my hand out, so he could high-five me. His fingers passed right through mine. He bumped the mural and bounced.

"Fuck! Ghost me, here, *now!*" I yelled, and in he popped. I positioned him, arm out sideways, and the leather jacket ghost made another stumble run, and this time touched my ghost hand, and suddenly, like paper down a toilet, he was vacuumed into the mural and sent spinning away, off of Mount Obitus and into the Undying Land far below. In seconds he was out of sight.

After that it was easy. Ghost me did all the work. I sat on the couch and watched. Delegating was turning out to be a strength of mine—who knew? Ghost me was my turnstile, the *Gray* was off protecting my girlfriend. Like I was running a temp agency. Flesh me was weak from lack of food, water, sleep, and stress overload. It was a relief to sit him.

I spent the time watching the mural fade, darkness creeping in from its corners.

The line funneling ghosts into the Undying land went fast but even in that short span the sun dropped nearly to the horizon. The light through my beach windows darkened from fruit loops to an oily, orange smolder. The final ghost plunged through. Nikita and I watched her fall. For a moment we said nothing. I wished them well.

Eh, she told me. *Good to be rid of them. Maybe they will survive.*

"They'll wash off, they'll be golden."

Or something terrible will happen. So. You failed with the aunties. What is next plan? Caroline says you always have plans. I am listening.

"For one thing, the aunties were dead when I got there, I didn't fail."

People are often dead when you get to them, do you notice this pattern?

"Of course I do. What's your point?"

No point. How will we find Ti'eirl?

"I'm not doing that anymore. I have a worse plan."

Back when I was alive, she continued, ignoring me, *if a client came in the store, a hypothetical old lady say, who lost her dog—what do I do? I am crosspath. Unreliable psychic powers. As soon as hypothetical ladies come in, I am already looking for information; how does she walk? Breath? Talk? What are her problems. You see? Often, looking is better than being psychic. So tell me. What are things we know about Ti'eirl?*

"Nikita, I have no idea. You're not helping."

Wrong. When I study hypothetical lady, to help her to give me her money, I look everywhere. Tone of voice. Pocketbook or purse. Hurrying, sad, suspicious—you see? What do we know about Ti'eirl?

"Oh my god."

Family? Friends? Enemies?

And there. At the edge of perception. I heard them again. Investigator bells. Something ... something Nikita was saying ...

"Actually," I said, "we do know something about her, now that I ... we know about her love life. That was her big problem."

Nikita nodded. *This is typical. Either lost dogs or love life. Sometimes both. Even hypothetical old lady—her dog is gone, but ten minutes later she is telling me stories of the boy she loved in high school. A boy soon to return, maybe, if she knows what to look for. So romantic. Who can say?*

"We know Ti'eirl and Aeternus were bound together. She tried to save him by trading places, taking his pain. That's why the curse went bonkers. You can't do that. Apparently."

Yes. Universal law of fate, own the consequences of your actions. Everyone knows this. They were in love?

The bells were louder. I felt ideas slipping around my brain. Maybe one of them was the idea Caroline had hoped I'd have. It occurred to me I'd done a fair job investigating the other mysteries I'd been presented since I'd accepted Waylon's bullying and gone to see his dead daughter. And this investigator feeling, only now did I recognize it. Investigation is a lot like art. You need intuitions, impulses, combining impossible factors and connecting polarized elements. Connecting the impossible.

Art is just an exercise in problem-solving. A balanced piece of art is balanced because you leave out everything that doesn't matter. Practice that over and over, eventually you can build a pyramid of precedence with only the essential pieces showing. That's art. Look at this, not at that. The irony is, artists are supposed to be so disorganized, but at some level, they're more organized than anyone on Earth.

Investigators do the same thing. Order information. Sift for only the most essential pieces. Create a work of ... realization.

"The goblet," I said.

Yes, what now? I thought she might have nodded off while I ordered my pieces. Was that possible for a ghost?

"The goblet—Aeternus created each goblet from a Keystone. The Keystones go back to the Undying Land. To him and Ti'eirl. Maybe the goblet can take us back."

The goblet is gone.

Nikita was pointing at Samantha, holding out her hand full of nothing. Had Samantha appeared just as I began outlining my plan? My needle in a haystack plan. If she was here, maybe I was onto something.

"*Samantha's* goblet is gone," I said, pointing to the living room steps where flesh me had put Amelia's goblet, "but one goblet's as good as another to get the story we want. If we can get a good look at Ti'eirl we can get a clue, like you and the hypothetical lady."

Hmm. This is very thin gruel. Do you not think?

"I think this way, maybe I eat fewer ghosts. What's thin gruel?"

Like … to kill a vulture with a dewdrop. Very unlikely.

It was unexpected comfort to walk across the living room. There were no encumbering ghosts, no shades, no spirits of the dead, though there were a lot of corpses. However, dead bodies by that point I categorized with hotel art or potted plants—meaningless scenery. I lifted the goblet and showed it to Nikita, and the sinking sun glanced red along its delicate edges.

"We need one clue," I told her. "Anything. … the psychic vision in this goblet … there's still hope."

Pff. The psychics have no visions. Time is gone. Objects have no stories. So. We are doomed after all. Hope has vanished.

"I'll fill the goblet with *dominion* when I relight the sun."

I see. Hope is barely alive. How will you do this?

"It's complicated."

Good, I am not interested.

Even as I watched, the sun dropped to lip the sea. A golden apocalypse glow flooded the balcony to light the penthouse in marmalade. The world was about to go black. If I could just get us one more day. I hoped that would be enough. It would have to be.

"We'll need a Monarch to read the goblet when it's ready," I said. "Wait here."

I dove into ghost me, left flesh me to carry on his own confounding conversation with Nikita, and good luck to both of them. Then I blinked to Three Paths.

I appeared above the psychic estate, my familiar blinking pad, and was instantly assaulted by noise coming down the ravine. Something like drums, but arrhythmic, like a hundred trash trucks all loading cans and roaring. The garbage fleet at the end of the world. I headed toward the Closure.

The air shivered and rippled like I'd fallen to the bottom of a swimming pool. The sunlight bent hell-colored reflections up canyon walls while thunderous blows shook rocks and debris to the canyon floor and filled the air with dust. Like the mountain was coming down. I passed an unmoving figura on the ground, head partially torn off, leaking yellow. I didn't know if that was a good sign or a bad. But *go toward the dead figura* was the rule I decided to make up for myself and follow, just to build my confidence. To make me feel like I knew what I was doing.

I twisted the canyon curves past more dead earwigs, strung out like soldiers fallen in a running battle—a figura retreat. The cacophony grew as I flew until I rounded a final turn and beheld the Viaticus. Beholding was the only word that did them justice.

Their tower lay in ruins, burst from the inside. A black and spiraling hole gaped into space where it once had stood. From that hole flowed a weak rivulet of *dominion*—just a trickle, all that remained of the Paths of time. The psychic ghosts had used that *light* to build a tunnel, of sorts. A floating lattice of ghosts and *light,* one end enclosing the ruined tower, the other open fifty feet down the canyon. At the open end stood the *Gray.*

His clothes were shredded. Insect gore clotted him, slicked his hair, dripped from his fingers, while around him figura corpses lay in piles. There were dozens. He seemed to be waiting for more, bouncing on his toes and laughing.

Above it all Caroline flew, organizing and syncing the ghosts, shifting *dominion* around the tunnel, calling orders. I ghosted to a stop where Jorge and Phylis stood, on an outcrop, watching in their flesh bodies, looking out of place.

From their backs arose their grotesque, screaming spirits, straining up, hands and feet buried, weightless horror statues. Phylis had found a long, thick length of pipe, and Jorge had one of his sabers. She swung it, glowering, but neither of them was exactly outfitted for the battle at hand.

Phylis saw ghost me. "That thing of yours's fucking *insane*," she said, never taking her eyes from the *Gray,* who was yelling at the tower, goading the figura and laughing. "He's incredible."

What's going on? I demanded.

"The shifters broke through the closure before we got here," Jorge said. "There were too many, they spread out. Then he came. Fighting his way up the canyon. We got them bottled in the mouth of the Closure. But they're coming in off the Path. It's bad."

What's this tunnel? I asked about the tunnel. *You're doing that?*

"Twilight House isn't the only Closure with scholars. The figura can come one way now. He has them spooked—maybe they think we have more like him. Pretty soon they're going to rush us, though. That's what I'd do. I don't know how long our path walkers can keep it up."

How's Caroline?

"She's just as fucked as the rest of us—what are you *doing* here?" Phylis shouted. The *Gray* heard her, turned, saw me, and laughed. Just innocent, pathological happiness. It was nice to see someone enjoying themselves.

"Did you find Ti'eirl?" Phylis demanded.

Not yet, I told her. *I have an idea. I need one of you at the Bradley.*

"Fuck that, not leaving my people," Phylis snarled. "If you're not—

At that moment an atmospheric ripple slammed the canyon, and directly in front of the tower, a massive earwig emerged. It came through mad, immediately tried to fly, but the supernatural tunnel gave no room for that so it tucked its wings, bent its legs, and launched toward the *Gray*. More followed immediately. Many, many more.

Jorge was yelling at me, "We'll come when we can but—"

And I was screaming, *I need a psychic back at the Bradley—*

And the light went out.

Sunset.

The scene before me froze in the dark. The ghosts in the air became immaterial afterimage blurs. Phylis, Jorge, the few other living psychics, all were frozen. The charging figura were frozen. Caroline was barely visible.

I had only seconds. I blinked back to flesh me.

He'd already moved to the lightless beach, posed on a hand and a knee. He'd even brought the goblet and set it in the sand. On the horizon our blackout sun hung, just a hole in the universal backdrop of failing stars. Time to merge.

I superimposed. I focused. The merge.

The merge was ... nothing happened.

Nothing flowed through me. Nothing was left to flow. There *had* to be something. Somewhere? The Closure was still leaking a trickle. Could I prime the pump somehow? What if I pushed in my reserves? I had reserves. I remembered them. But they could only be pushed into something that already existed. I could expand a stream but not start one from scratch, and though flesh me was eye-crossed so hard it ripped our suborbitals, my merge produced no stream.

Cold grew. Starlight faded. Constellations faltered. The sea stilled and began to vanish. I wrenched *all* my selves open, demanding, pulling, calling down whatever perverse power the universe could force through me, *please*, I thought *Dominion*. Where are you?

In my chest something stirred, twisting, reaching. Burning. And the umbra eye awoke. The brand, on the *inside,* stirring to life in answer to my need for *power*. Power was the thing it was built to provide. All I had to do was bring it to the surface. And eat.

But my problem is I habituate so fast. Addiction's a process by which we habituate ourselves, compulsively, and it only ever takes one for me—one hit, one shot, one taste and I'm habituated. That's my personality, I'm all in. And since I've recently become what they call a functional addict, and I know my habituation weaknesses, I stick to my core competencies, which are vodka and self-deprecation. If I ever tasted a ghost ... it'd only take one.

And then who would I be?

Fortunately, it was not a question I had to answer. Because, finally, it came.

Like a sun rising it started. A trickle of *light*. A streamlet. It got me started. Around me I accumulated a ball of *dominion*, babying it up like a magic balloon. The force of the stream built, filled us, and with it rose hope, since I never learned my lesson about hope. I tell people that's my natural optimism, but it's really just me not paying attention. And I thought, if the force kept building, maybe I wouldn't have to tap my reserves at all.

I reached for the goblet. If we were lucky—and I *knew* someday that was going to happen—the goblet would point us to Ti'eirl. If we got lucky enough we might find that this goblet was the very Keystone Aeternus had been holding when the curse was imposed. And yes, you never want your plan to depend as much on luck as mine always seem to. But what am I going to do?

The nimbus around me shot my arm and hit the goblet and electron by electron began to fill it. I don't know if they were really electrons. I'm not an electrician. But the goblet sucked *light* like an empty sponge. When it was filled, it flamed up.

Then the *glow* around me thickened and expanded and some final upstream supply broke free. After that, I could only cling and scream. I lost track of the goblet. Wild *light* took me. I rode a torrent through the dark to the cold core of the planet. A raging discordance shook me. And pain. You'd think familiarity would increase your tolerance, but that's not how it works. But I preferred pain to the end of the world though. Didn't I? Wasn't it better than the void of nothing, waiting as the only other option?

From the inside out I lit it up. I re-fleshed the supernatural skeleton of the Earth. From the inside to the outside the *light* of me spread, from a disco ball to a ravaging inferno, and rising with it I emerged through the planet's crust.

Everything was ruin and darkness. Across all the lands, shades spread. Nothing but shades. Billions dead. Everywhere on Earth but Skysill, life had stopped. Even in Skysill, only the strongest remained—the psychics and a few of the Family. Even the figura had fled the world outside Skysill. Or died in it. A film of proto ghosts and human corpses covered our world. And somewhere among them, Ti'eirl floated. I hoped.

I rose off the surface toward our inkwell sun and felt the *dominion* flood falter. I focused. Light the sun. Fill the cup. Find the ghost who cursed the world. Live. If the universal *dominion* was failing, then the time had come to use my own.

The extent of my reservoir when I finally, at twenty-six years of age, was forced to confront it, astounded me. All seven Highers spread inside me, fanning their ultraviolet rainbow of *choke, compulsion, reason, crush, farewell, wander* and *bleed.* Added to that was another, eighth—undiscovered—color.

Dominion.

Undiscovered no longer. *Dominion* belonged on that rainbow. It was the inverse of *bleed.* They were the two ends of the Higher spectrum. The poles.

Bleed, the color of destruction. And *dominion,* the color of creation.

This rainbow was my night charge. My own night charge though I was not *fabrica.* Though I'd never been tapped, still I had this resource, entirely personal. A sense of self-sufficiency overcame me, though of course, that's one of my most misleading senses, behind only my senses of self-worth and direction.

So like an old-time locomotive engineer, I began shoveling my *light* into the engine of the sun. Load it, light it, start it the fuck up. All while screaming. Those were my thoughts.

And I tried. I cleared my decks. I reached so deep. I did all the cliches. But it was obvious the sun was too big, which, hello? Of course. And there wouldn't be enough *light.* I couldn't call any more *dominion* from the Paths, which were dry as desert riverbeds. It was just my night charge against ... the sun. Unsurprisingly what I had was not sufficient.

My charge dropped toward zero. My failing strength slowed me. I strained, I was mere inches from success—though *inches* measure nothing remotely like the distance I had to cross. The world below had almost stabilized, the sun had almost filled—almost. It needed but a thimble of *light* and one struck match. But my charge was gone.

I felt myself choke, black space pressed, and I thrashed, like Veronica had, and strained, and—

Pulse, went the brand in my chest. *Pulse. Eat.*

Everywhere were shades. I had only to endow one, eat, and my problems were solved. How easy it would be.

On the pitch-dark beach sand, flesh me had withered. He was thinned, wrinkled—old and emptied of *light,* just as Julian had been when he'd died on Waylon's ridge. A sickening memory. Julian dead because I'd taken his deepest *light.* The creator *light,* the animating light—*dominion,* Higher color of creation—Samantha and I drained him of everything that made him an artist, and once that was gone, he died. Which ...

I was an artist. Could I drain my own animating *dominion?* Would it be enough?

Earth's window nearly closed. But a second remained. On the sand, deep in our merging bodies, in the emptied core of me, I felt for the place the artist lived. I felt the creator, I felt all my inspiration, a paint box of Asher Gale color.

I took the paintbox and ripped it open, raised it, and thrust *light* in living streamers into Earth's cold sun.

And then I fell.

CHAPTER

THIRTEEN

Clawing back up from unconsciousness may be my worst habit. But even when it's against my best interests, which is almost always, I can't help myself. I do it the old-fashioned way, the way people do crosswords with coffee; just a box to check, a part of the ritual starting your day. I did it the way I always have, matching a pinky and a little toe, an ankle and a wrist, etcetera, until I'd filled all the blanks and puzzled my way awake, to survey whatever new wonders the world had waiting for me this time.

What waited was the new wonder of laying on my side at the bottom of a hole with sand in my face. I knew I was embodied in flesh me because of the pain. I rolled him onto my back slowly. The sky over the hole was the blue of asphyxiated skin, though that was better than the endless black of the void. Morning sun fell past the rim. The sun had reset. It was already morning. The day had restarted while I slept, or lacked consciousness, or whatever I'd been doing. Things that needed to get done were not getting done. I knew there were things. There always are.

But first, sit up. The act was almost beyond my strength, but I groaned and levered my elbows into the sand, then paused, panting and light-headed. Had I just done something I was going to regret for the rest of my life? Something I didn't even want to think about? If history was a guide, like they say it's supposed to be, then yes—I'd done something so horrific to myself that, I wondered ... was this the end? And I wondered ... would I ever again get out of this hole? And I asked, why did I feel so ... empty?

Deep inside—where I usually keep my alcohol—something was different. I felt an imbalance. Was I less real? Because I felt less real. Like a sacrificial limb, like an arm the rest of me had chewed off to escape a trap. I was what was left behind. I was diminished. The better parts had fled.

Again I groaned, which made me gasp, and I drew a breath and tried to fill the space in my chest that I knew all the world's oxygen could never fill again. In some ways, despite all the evidence, I'd always believed myself invulnerable. But now I'd ripped out the part of me that created art, the only part with any real value, and what did that make me? Just an ordinary drunk?

Surprisingly, that thought was not a relief.

I had no time to waste, yet here I was, wasting it in a hole. I puffed at the sand on my face and blew it into my eye. Blinking and spitting I struggled up and leaned my head over my knees, wasting even more time managing dizziness. And then finally I thought—*the goblet.*

Complaining to myself as I will I heaved up, and turning, saw ghost me and ghost Nikita floating at the edge of my sand trap. The *Gray* must still be with Caroline, I thought. Hoped. The ghosts were not watching flesh me—because why would they care, I guess?—but rather, the beach at their feet, where a little Higher-sun-chalice beat out *dominion* in waves that spread over the beach. The goblet was alive. So all that ... had worked? I was amazed.

The problem now was that the two ghosts were the only people on the beach.

"Where are the fucking psychics?" I demanded, the way people love. "Where's Jorge or Phyllis?"

Who knows? Nikita shrugged.

"They're supposed to be ... Jorge said they'd come, god damn it ... "

Never rely on Monarchs, Nikita scoffed. *In the old country, we have saying: Monarchs are like a rockslide.*

"In what way?"

No one knows.

"Well thanks for the ancient ignorance, but if someone doesn't get here and read this goblet ... "

My thoughts were: *as usual, this was about to become my job.* And I also thought: *it's going to be a relief to swim into ghost me and get my numbness back and blink and scream at the Monarchs.* But I found I just didn't have the strength. I was gutted. All I could do was stand in my hole.

"Someone needs to get a flesh psychic here *now,*" I told her, pointing at the sky, where the sun was already rising toward noon. "This is about to be our last day. Sunset's permanent this time and it's coming on fast. Go tell the psychics the goblet's full and get down here it's our last hope!"

Yes. Why, again? I do not like bringing them nonsense.

"So they can read the goblet and trace it to Ti'eirl!"

That thin gruel again? All our hopes riding on—

"God damn it it's our *only* gruel Nikita," I screamed, "go!"

Yes, fine, first I will clarify how thin I think—

"Don't bring up gruel to them Nikita just *go!*"

With absolutely no sound or buildup she blinked off of the beach. I wanted to collapse. I crouched. Yelling that way, everything wobbled. I felt like a car, fleeing an accident in slow motion, rolling forward on three tires and a hubcap.

The thing to do next, I thought, was get this goblet inside. The *dominion* coming off the mural might help the psychics with the reading. Assuming the mural was giving off *dominion* still. Every time the sun set the mural got dimmer—plus there was another piece to the sunset pattern, which was that every time the sun set ... I spent a numb moment thinking. I knew something horrible happened, but I couldn't think what.

It was now or never for climbing from my hole, but scooping and clawing got me nowhere until I remembered to call ghost me. He ferried me up. I stepped from his arms to lean on my knees on the beach. Panting. I was getting my strength back but slowly. Years ago I'd promised Amy I'd stay off meth. But there's a reason they invented that stuff. Because sometimes the world is ending, and you're afraid you'll never be whole again, and you need a little goose.

It was my own turn now, to stare at the goblet blazing with my *light.* I'd emptied my cells in there. I wondered if that was the way to think about it. Had it ever really been my *light*? *Dominion* wasn't like blood, it was nothing that personal. No single creator owned that *light.* I'd just been a vessel. Now empty. Don't think about that, I said, encouraging, like a docent at a museum. Let's just move to another gallery.

I bent to lift the goblet. My hand slowed as a distinct electric trickle built in my fingertips. Coming from the goblet? The *light* felt supercharged.

And from behind I heard, *I wouldn't touch that. If I were you.*

Aeternus. I almost did that thing where you have a conversation with another person without ever turning around, just to show your disdain, but that seemed like it would take more energy than just turning so I turned. I scowled to show my disdain instead. He didn't look impressed. Though he's a hard one to read.

"What's?" I asked. "Don't touch the goblet? That's what you're saying?"

He scowled back at me then and showed how it was really done. With flowing hair and his cheekbone salutes and his casual loincloth he was like a sexy, self-aware, super-criminal Gandhi. He really did know how to scowl.

The goblet will kill you if you touch it, he said. He wasn't totally happy.

I looked back down. Looking and turning so much, for a person unsteady like I was, is not advisable but ... what was he saying?

"Why not touch it?" I asked, trying to sound suspicious, which also took energy. "Is something different about it?"

The goblet has not changed. His scowl deepened. *You are different.*

He watched me digest that. The gulls watched too.

"In a good way?" I asked. Without hope, because it's never that. "Or what?"

Do you feel it tingle? The goblet will tear you apart in a proximal, multi-variant purgation.

"Says you—what? I'm confused." You could tell how confused I was by how sincere I accidentally sounded. Aeternus floated forward and circled to examine all my sides. I suspected it was for effect, which I will admit worked pretty well.

I do not understand, he admitted. *But your body is changed. There will be a purgation.*

"Purgations happen to untapped Aspectu," I said. "Don't they?"

Untapped. Just so, he agreed, peering, stripping me with his eyes. Maybe putting a loincloth on me. It was creepy. *What is this change in you?*

"Small problem restarting the sun," I guessed for him. *And now the cells of my body are empty and my art is stripped away and I'm worthless,* I did not say, because it sounded whiny, but that's how I felt. So now I was an untapped Aspectu. I'd been turned off. Did I need a *relino*? Were there any left alive?

"Okay," I said, thinking out loud, "maybe this is true about the purgation ... "

It is.

"But it doesn't matter. What about the psychics, though? Will they blow up?"

The psychics ... he said, looking uncertain, *no, the change is in you. But you don't have time for the psychics! There is one way to save this world. One. You must expand your painting. You need the umbra eye! I can give it to you!*

"There's a lot of moving pieces to that, as far as making art, which was always a bad plan and now it's impossible. And the umbra eye. And all the rest of it. I'm just going to sum up here with *no*. Stop bringing any of that up. If you really want to help, then go get the psychics!"

This plan of yours ... reading the goblet ... even if you find Ti'eirl, she will not help to lift this curse.

"And you say that why?"

Because I know. Ti'eirl and I have a history. She is ... troubled.

"Well, that makes you an ex-lover with an axe to grind. Let's let her speak for herself."

He gave me a sharp look. Like he'd revealed something he hadn't intended. He's not the kind who's comfortable being revealed. Something drove him to keep talking, though.

That is a waste of time. She will never help lift the curse.

"She's got to regret how everything turned out."

How little you know.

"What are we even *arguing* about? You're as bad as Amelia."

You imagine she'll want the curse lifted but <u>listen</u>! Ti'eirl ... this curse is a product of her hatred. Her hatred of me. It is hate that goes beyond reason. Beyond logic. She will not help, not as long as I am alive to suffer at her hand.

"Okay ... there's hatred, and there's *crazy*. Are you saying Ti'eirl's crazy? She's going to doom the world just to hurt you?"

Ti'eirl would rather the universe fail than my suffering end. Look around you. The evidence is plain.

Arguing with him was so tiring. And confusing. The hive queen already told me this story, I thought. Was it the same story? I had only enough energy for questions, knowing that answers would only confuse me more.

"Why's Ti'eirl hate you?" I asked.

He took a moment looking at his past, while I watched waves

throb through his chest. Finally he held his arms wide, as though at a loss for words.

A broken heart, a broken soul ... drive her to madness. She held forces that can never be contained. These are the forces which burst us. She ... you must trust me. She is beyond reason. And then he made a slightly quizzical squint, then took one finger to stroke his forehead. Having a thought. *Unless ... yes, unless ...*

I guess I should have seen it coming. Waylon used to pull this kind of shit too. Like an idea had *just occurred to him*, I was supposed to believe. An idea that could solve all my problems. He'd been leading to this the whole time. *Unless*, he says, and I'm supposed to jump in and ask, *what? unless <u>what</u>?*

Which, mostly from laziness, I did.

"Unless *what?*"

Unless I am already dead when you find her.

"Unless you're—how can ... oh."

It is the only way. Consume me. Eliminate me from the many worlds. Ti'eirl will help you then. This is my destiny. I see it now. My only chance for redemption. So I am not remembered as the Inmortalis who broke the all worlds. Eat me. End me. I will show you how.

After a moment I gave him my narrow eyes, but this time the weight of incredulous disbelief finally gave it some gravitas. Later I'd ask ghost me exactly how it looked. Assuming he was paying attention.

"I'm supposed to believe," I started, "that you're willing to sacrifice your life to save the lives of all these ghosts? *Now?* Out of guilt for everything you did, or whatever? When you just spent the last three billion years *not-dying-under-any-circumstances?* Plotting, slaughtering, torturing—*now* you feel really bad and willing to die for the rest of us? Eat you? That's your story?"

Is it so hard to believe? The guilt a ghost suffers ... you cannot imagine.

"It's laughably weak gruel. You're a world-shattering psychopath!"

Ask Caroline how devastating this murder guilt can be. She's as much a murderer as I. In my case, at least, it was the result of my sickness. Caroline made a choice to do what she did. Is she any better than I? Am I worse than she?

"Leave Caroline out of it."

I must teach you to eat! It is all I have left. Then I am yours. Do Ti'eirl's job for her.

This complicated set of competing concepts was exactly the kind I'm least qualified to handle sober. Aeternus, offering to teach me to do a thing I already knew how to do—or *could* know, by activating the brand in my chest. And offering to sacrifice himself when I could eat the shit out of him right now if I even wanted to, which I did not. I almost threw it all back in his face but the hive queen said don't trust him. Though what was the reason I should trust the hive queen, who was part of the monster horde eating humanity? Her resume was as dark as his.

Could Ti'eirl be this crazy? I mean yes, Aeternus was a guy you either loved or hated but mostly hated, but enough for her to end the world to see him suffer? Was that possible, I started to wonder, then I thought oh yes, that was possible. Polarized does crazy things to a brain. Was she still polarized, a billion years later? Did it last that long?

And there, in the midst of my philosophizing self-reflection— which is where I'm most confused and vulnerable—I heard Amelia. Who ... oh, I remembered, I'd told her meet me on the beach. For what reason?

"It's him," I heard behind me. Like a gasp. I turned. And wished I hadn't.

She stood on the sand pointing my way with a spirit emerging from her back that had ... mutated. Grown twice her size—*bloated*. It gave off an air of ... being absolutely *wrong*. Its feet were completely free of her and dangled just above the sand. Its face was frozen elaborately gruesome, horror eyes wide, mouth stretched in silent scream, tendons bulging.

The only parts still touching her were its hands. Its hands were wrapped around her throat.

She staggered toward me in an upright zombie tilt, eyes arctic saucers. Gasping for breath. One hand pointing, the other wiping her throat.

"Amy ... " I started, but that's as far as I got. There weren't words. Usually, that won't stop me.

"It's him," she grated again. She wasn't pointing me out. She pointed at Aeternus.

"Maybe you should sit down," I told her. I'm like a doctor.

"*I ... want ... him ... dead!*" she screamed, not loud but very, very violent, scraping her throat raw around some pressure. She seemed to run out of energy to scream then.

Ironically, Aeternus told her, *Asher and I were discussing that. If you can persuade him—*

But Amy hadn't stopped screaming, she'd just taken a breath to force out more rage words, "*You ... you killed her ... and my ...*" then she screamed at me, "*he killed Veronica!*"

"Okay, hey, let's take—"

Her polar cap eyes—I kept forgetting they actually worked to see things—fell to the hole I'd climbed from. No. Not the hole. To the goblet blasting *dominion.*

"*I'm killing him!*" she strangled, stumbling toward it.

"He's a ghost," I said, gesturing *stop,* "you can't kill—"

She reached me, went to her knees for the cup, but I couldn't touch it or I'd blow us apart in frozen strings like Celine's car, so I grappled her hand, but she had another hand—then she was lifting the cup. Screaming more. Oh my god my sister can scream.

She filled with *light.* She became the brightest thing in our world. The weakened sun could not compare. I fell and covered my eyes. *Light* still came through. I had to turn, so I was facing Aeternus when his face went from disdain to surprise to something like uncertainty —some dramatic, charismatic form of uncertainty.

He blinked off the beach. Escaping somewhere.

Amy, still screaming, raised a veil of *wander* around her and I know what they use *wander* for so I screamed.

"Amy I need that goblet!"

But she vanished too. Looking for Aeternus. She took the goblet.

I stood alone on the beach except for ghost me. So technically, alone on the beach.

It was a lot of inconvenient things happening in a very short time and none of them what I'd have preferred, like it always is. I gave myself a minute to turn back and face the ocean, stand without expression, and have no idea what could possibly happen next. That's shock. In many ways, it's the story of my life.

Even with the goblet, our chances were thin gruel. And I had no way to find my sister. I screamed her name out at the surf. Then I remembered we had phones and I screamed into that without any hope. I could barely feel mad at her—she was out of her mind from grief and the brain melt of Higher *light*. She'd never give that goblet up I knew, even if I found her. I know my sister. She's like a crazy fucking magpie with a marble. If I did somehow find her and tried to take it, I'd blow us up. And there was no time for a manhunt. This sun was a one-way pendulum, speeding toward ruin.

The beach was super quiet. The drums of the figura were gone. They'd been silent since I woke in my hole this morning. It was well past noon now. *Noon?* And peaceful on the sand. A gull or two cried —some of the only gulls left in the universe, I'd been given to under-stand—and waves rolled in, not so much breaking onto the shore as laying down in surrender on it. Maybe that was me projecting, a habit I'm told I have.

Nikita said, *They're here,* from behind me.

Ghosts are so quiet. I wondered, how long had she been waiting back there? Probably not long. She has less patience than I do. Today was just the day everyone snuck up and announced themselves from behind.

So I turned, again, thinking of the swivel chair they'd put in my office before it became a public park, a chair a person could spin, tracking arrivals in all directions and issuing observations and working a bottle. I hadn't really taken advantage of that chair. Now it was too late.

Nikita floated between me and the Bradley and behind her came all three Monarchs, two living, one dead, and the *Gray*, spattered yellow with insect. The *Gray* continued across the beach toward me, while Phyllis and Jorge stopped. They were horrifying to look at. Huge, mutant spirits rose behind them, choking or pulling their heads off or whatever—they were Monarchs though, and it hardly fazed them.

But behind *them* came a flood of regular psychics—also living and dead—and the living ones had massive issues with the grotesqueries riding them. Many were losing their shit completely, all of them grabbing their throats and gasping. Every time the sun set, these spirit bodies looked crazier.

I notice a lot of new shades in that crowd. The figura battle toll, I assumed.

But through all of them—the dead, the disappointed, the dispirited—I had eyes for Caroline alone. It was riveting, the way she moved. Like a ghost of course, only she didn't just float. She flexed, she pushed, her hips and arms and belly shifted as she came, lithe as a stream. She dug her feet into the world. As beautiful as a ghost as ever she'd been in life, outlined in beach-light on the last day of the world.

Then the beach light framing her faltered. I looked to the asphyxiated sky to see the sun well down, nearing the horizon. The whole day gone? It'd lasted an *hour*—it was over, how can you get any plans done with days this length? But as Caroline came toward me in rapture glow all I wanted was to feel her lips on mine. The thing I couldn't. To feel her touch. Sadness washed me.

We weren't going to make it, I saw. We weren't getting out of this together. This world was ending. Whatever we could have offered each other, or been together, wasn't going to happen. Polarized, at best we'd be adjacent. Never together.

Why I had those realizations at that moment, on that chaos beach, I do not know. I never know. It had to do with the part of me I'd given up, I think. This was the clarity that comes from emptiness. Nothing to cloud your judgment. As if my self-delusions and unrealistic expectations had been lost with those artist parts of me.

She and I were on different paths, I admitted. Now I could try to save her.

Hey cowboy, she shouted, herding a confused shade into the group.

"We're here," Phylis shouted at me, the words forced past ghost fingers crushing her windpipe. "Where's the goblet?"

"Excellent question," I said. "My sister stole it so I don't know."

"What the *hell?*" Phylis raged. "You let her *steal* it? Why'd you let her *steal it?*"

"Just to annoy you," I said. Arguing with her was less sad than thinking about Caroline, so I leaned into it a little. Phylis carried a long piece of pipe stained with gore. She swung it in circles pretending in her mind to smash me.

"Does anything you try ever work?" she raged.

"I'm trying to piss you off, how's that—"

"You little prick—" she raised her pipe and came for me.

"Quiet!" Jorge lurched between us, desperate for peace, whatever that would get us at this stage. He took a deep breath. It didn't look easy. He glanced over his shoulder at the monstrous, transparent Jorge throttling him. Then he ground out, "No time for that. The plan was ... use the goblet, find Ti'eirl. The goblet's gone. We need a new plan."

We all nodded, we pretty obviously needed a new plan. Usually that's where I shine, when the old plan's fucked and the time comes to make everything up as you go along. The instinct of trusting that there's always a next step for me to take, that's how I used to do my whole life. Every painting I ever started. You don't know how it'll end, but you land the brush and you start.

Now I couldn't. I couldn't land the brush. I couldn't paint, I couldn't plan—none of it made sense. The part of me that made new things was gone. I'd given it up. What did that leave me? I did not know. It left basically nothing.

Ash? Caroline worried. *You okay?*

"Just thinking," I said, worrying her more.

And then Samantha, who'd been hiding wherever hopeless shades spend the final hours of the universe, shimmered in. Right in front of me. And it was nice, how everyone else could see her too. How everyone stared. It made me feel less lonely. Though not less sad.

For a moment she floated facing me then turned, empty hand frozen in front of her, and floated toward the crowd of psychics and shades. From that herd she separated a shade, a bearded man in a mini skirt holding an empty box, and bumped him toward me. He drifted a few feet, and Samantha came behind and guided him right up to me. Then backed away. They both faced me. Like they always do. In fact, everyone faced me now, the living and the others. Everyone watched.

"What?" I said to Samantha. I looked at the *Gray* and ghost me. "What's up with you two? Do you have any idea what this is?"

The *Gray* flicked gore off his shoulder and shrugged. He didn't care and was thinking about his battle. Ghost me shrugged in his mind. They were as much help as I myself would have been, in their shoes. No help.

"*What* Samantha?" I demanded. "You're saying there's something about this shade?"

I looked him over. I didn't recognize him. He looked good in his skirt.

"Are you saying endow him?" I asked. "Is that … ?"

I didn't need more clues, though. Shade charades. I'm an expert.

"I don't even know if I even can anymore," I complained. "Shit's broken in me."

But that wasn't true. I mean yes, I'd given up the one thing, art or whatever, but the other thing was still there. The Inmortalis thing. I could feel that still. I'd given up inspiration, but my death skills were strong as ever.

And then the drums came back.

"Fucking hell just *do it!*" Phylis shouted.

So I did. I palmed the shade's empty box.

It all happened in an instant. And just as when I'd endowed my beach full of psychic shades a few days ago— or earlier today, or later last afternoon—his story came in a millisecond. It was a story about an empty box. It poured out without me noticing a single detail, thankfully, and after that the stories from the life before this Skysill one, and then all the way back until we crossed into the Undying Land to an original ghost, who'd been named Me'sorl. I'd never heard of him.

The mini skirt shade became a ghost. A psychic ghost who started recovering right away, drifting back to his people.

"Now what? Who's Me'sorl?" I demanded of Samantha.

The drums throbbed down the coast from the Psychic District, louder, faster. The sun dropped closer to the sea.

"Seriously, what's the *point* of this?" I yelled at her.

Samantha blinked back and bounced another shade to stop in front of me. She was like a sheepdog for ghosts. Before Phylis could yell I sighed and touched the object. Like a good Inmortalis. I had no idea what the object even was, I didn't even look, just a bunch of fears welded together. The story came, followed by all the stories of all the lives down the millennia, then across the border of the Undying Land to a ghost named Da'Neysien.

As this shade became a ghost and drifted away, waking up, Samantha was already rushing the next lamb into position for reverse slaughter. They took no energy. Doing hundreds at a time on the beach had been a little tiring, but this pace I could keep up all day. Especially considering how much time remained in this day. Not more than an hour. What the hell were we doing here?

But still I endowed them, one after another as Samantha brought them, the drums hammering, the sun falling. I did it because all my inspiration was gone. All I could do was whatever was in front of me, over and over, counting down the seconds.

Again and again I stamped the ghost passports to Happy Land. Until finally I saw. As I traced another one over the border. To a final, Undying ghost. With a name. The pattern. The audacious ... was *that* what she wanted?

The one similarity each and every ghost shared was ... they were all named something, but not named Ti'eirl.

If I endowed a shade I could tell exactly who its Undying ghost was.

Samantha could see I understood because I objected.

"Wait ... you want me," I sputtered, "to ... *endow every shade in the world? To find one ghost?*"

The beach people and ghosts had all been watching my show and now we'd finally come to the plot twist which made the whole thing a blockbuster. A murmur started among them. Particularly among the ghosts.

"Can you do it?" Jorge asked, urgent and incisive. He'd been paying attention, a skill I wish I shared. He saw the whole idea at once. "*Can* you endow them all? Is that possible?"

"I don't think so," I said, furious at Samantha for this idea about me she'd put in people's heads, where ideas about me do the most damage. The beach was quiet except for the ghost murmur and the waves and the gulls and the drums and a hundred and fifty living psychics getting choked to death. Samantha's plan was ridiculous. It was the kind of plan people make when they're not the ones responsible for living through it.

The scope was ... what? *What?* What would it take to endow every shade on the entire planet? I'd been there. I'd seen them.

I sank, hands to knees. Then knees to ground. Out of reasonable options. I couldn't expand the mural by painting. I couldn't even touch the goblet. Now I was supposed to do *what?*

Me, the drums, the ghosts, it was too much for Phylis to sit still for so she flamed impatience and called a three-person Monarch conference. It was quick. They broke like a football huddle while I watched from my knees, my mind overloaded. I wanted to get up, or say something useful or even something snarky, but my brain was short-looping.

When the huddle broke, Phylis and Jorge went shouting to their psychics, waking them and organizing them, prepping them for one last battle. When Phylis says she's going out fighting, she's not kidding. Nothing else mattered to her. Just don't give up.

And the other Monarch, the beautiful one, came my way.

What do you think? she asked, floating in and squatting beside me on the sand.

"I'm out," I admitted, "of thoughts."

She looked at Phylis.

As soon as these new ghosts wake up enough, Phylis and Jorge are going to Three Paths. We'll buy as much time as we can at the Closure. Can you do this? It seems like a pretty big project. Endowing every ghost. What do you need from me? How can I help?

"I need ... " I was surprised to find myself shivering. The day was not cold. It was not warm. It was a nothing temperature. My body had simply had enough. There, folded on the sand, it began softly weeping. It didn't even feel sad. It didn't feel anything. It was just out of options. That's what weeping is. Your body's last option.

Oh Ash, Caroline said, reaching to my cheek. She put her hand through my face and shook her head.

"I messed up," I said. "I gave it away, it's gone ... I can't do any more ... "

Yes you can. You only have one job. I've seen you do it, Ash. No one else can.

"What job have you seen?" I wept. "Me having a fit and passing out on your sidewalk?"

That's not your job, honey, that's just your hobby. Jorge had a vision. You're the one.

"There's no way I can do this..."

Jorge thinks you can. This was the last vision he ever had. Before the Paths collapsed. A vision of something Peter said.

"Peter?" I snot whispered, just a mess. It was hard thinking back that far. So much since then had gone wrong. So many people had gone ... just gone. Something Peter said?

Caroline tried touching me again, because trying's a hard habit to break. But she'd learn. She knew it as well as I did. We'd never touch again. I appreciated her effort, though.

"Jorge saw Peter in a cloud of sound, dying. He was talking to you as he did. He said, *There's only starting again. It's our hope. It's our only hope. Start again, Asher.*"

His last words. I remembered them. *Start again.* What art used to be for me. A way to say I don't give up. I take another look. I'm not dead. The process and not the product. *Look again.*

Caroline bent near me, so serious and confident, so haggard, resisting the penthouse mural, holding on and remaining behind. Working this beach in thinning ghost *light* with just ... guts. Remaining, despite the song calling her to the only place she'd ever find peace.

Jorge and Phylis were badgering psychics but throwing us looks. Caroline'd obviously been given the *deal with Asher* assignment. The prize everybody wanted. And oh how I wished for our old telepathy. She went forward so clear-headed. The only person on that beach who seemed hopeful. I wanted inside her brain to know—was she as fucking crazy as it seemed she had to be, to feel hope here?

"Endowing them all, I wouldn't even know ... how to start," my body said, fighting trouble with its voice. I wanted to be what Caroline was. That confident. But I never would be. So I used the skills I did have, skills honed convincing police officers I wasn't drunk. I controlled my voice.

"Endow every shade—what's it even look like? How many can I do at once, I mean, I don't know— but the entire world?" I shook my head, watched her watching me. Using her secret calm. "What would *you* do?" I asked after a moment.

I'd do a trial run, she said immediately, organized and certain. *You did a beach full of them. Try a town. What's the worst that could happen? You die?* She smiled.

"You make it sound pretty easy," I said. "Have you done this before?"

Nope, it's my first apocalypse. Pretty exciting though. So what if you started with shades from Skysill? There's a lot. Everyone in town's dead. Do what you did on the beach. Just do a few more. A few thousand more. Look for Ti'eirl. Just work up to the entire world. You can do it. I know you can.

"You'd make a great fitness coach."

Em hm. She smiled. *Plus remember, I've been in your brain. I know what you're capable of.*

"So this confidence in me. All your belief in ... what is this about? I mean, I've been in my brain. I'm in there right now. It's a mess. You're super sexy, but honestly are you crazy? What do you really see in me?"

I told you the first time we kissed. Boys who cry are my terrible weakness. I'd do anything for one.

So I tried Samantha's plan. Because who am I to argue with a Monarch?

FOURTEEN

It's comforting having a person with her kind of authority give you permission to try the impossible things you keep getting assigned. If you fuck it up, as you're likely to do, there's someone to take responsibility.

What Aeternus had said about his *technique* ... push them underground. A technique to get masses of shades ready for him to eat all at the same time. Awesome. Feeling dramatic as fuck I closed my eyes, and felt around with my arms in front of me. The shades were out there. They were spread through the town. How do you connect to ghosts you can't see? I'd only done ghost manipulation by sight or touch. When I tried picturing them in my mind the picture failed. My days picturing things were over, donated to the sun.

All I knew was, the shades were there. Staring at me.

Staring. They saw *me* though I couldn't see them. In fact, I might be the only thing they *could* see. The center of their universe. Was that enough? I had their attention. Were they just waiting to see what I'd tell them to do? Much the way I felt about myself?

Sink down, I told them, and made pretend grabby hands, wrapping shades in imaginary nothing nets and pulling down. I couldn't picture them, but I could still picture Skysill. I'd lived here so long, I didn't need imagination. I pictured the city like I had a map burned into my brain, and every shade on that map, I took.

Around us the few psychic shades I hadn't already endowed dropped under the beach. Just like that. So easy. Just pretend to grab with pretend hands. If pretending had always worked this well I'd already be the owner of my own all-in-one bar and 12-step recovery facility.

Nice, Caroline cried. *That's cowboy shit Ash. What next?*

"Well ... last time ... " what had he said? *Touch the ground and touch them all.* Though out of sight, though underground, they were just a touch away. I reached.

The shades hung *everywhere* under Skysill. Ten, twenty, a hundred thousand—too many to count, even if I'd been one of those people who liked counting things, which I was not. But the technique worked as well for a beach of shades as for a city full. All at the same time I felt them, with their objects, and *touched* them. All at once. And *squeezed.* That's how it worked. A bowl of nuts, all cracking together. Their objects opened and stories poured out.

It happened fast. Ghosts poured toward me from everywhere. As each got in range it unloaded its story. I braced myself—which, why I still even try is a mystery, it's *never* helped—as history rivered through me, each ghost with its lifeline trailing all the way to the Undying Land. From everywhere in Skysill they came. And every one of them showed me their original, Undying ghost. It wasn't even hard.

I entertained the fantasy that I was about to find Ti'eirl right there in Skysill Beach, on my very first go. I mean everyone else was in Skysill. The psychics, the painters, Aeternus and the Families— why wouldn't Ti'eirl be there? But none of the Skysill ghosts was named Ti'eirl. And then it was over. The experience left me chilled but untroubled. I could just tell—I was pretty fucking good at this.

I'd found my thing. My shadowy, horrible, necromancer thing. Death guy.

When they'd all been endowed, they gathered under the beach beneath the Bradley. It was dense with ghosts down there. None were psychics, so they weren't doing anything on their own. I used my death skills to levitate them out of the ground, and all the psychics on the beach and even the Monarchs and Caroline gasped. For one awesome moment I was one of those magicians who did tricks that only work on TV. Ghost legions rose from the ground.

But it was only awesome for a second and than it was unsettling. Soon there were layers of ghosts backed up under the exposed layer on the beach, a silo of ghosts going down, all massing like people waiting to get into a concert. I knew what they *really* wanted: a bath. The ghosts at the very bottom of the pile, the farthest away, were sort of ... screaming?

So much screaming on this beach. It occurred to me that eight billion ghosts under this beach would be a problem, if I got that far. I had to drag them in range to endow them, but if they kept piling up eventually I wouldn't be able to get them close enough.

"I need room," I told Caroline. "These ghosts are piling up. I'm going to push them through the mural and make space for more, and hope I get the timing right."

That's so organized, Ash. I think I might be in love with you.

"Really? What if I bought a calendar?"

Do you really know how one of those works?

"They have a course you can take."

"Hurry the fuck up!" shouted Phylis.

"Ghost me," I screamed. He was floating ten feet off the beach because he couldn't wedge down into the dense ghost crowd at ground level. He got low enough for me to grab his foot, but I was too weak to hold it. When the *Gray* saw what I was doing he just grabbed me and threw me up to my ghost back. We were like like a troupe of identical, supernatural gymnasts.

"To the mural," I instructed ghost me.

Wait, Nikita called. Just when I was getting some momentum. She floated over to me at the old country pace she preferred.

"What?" I said. "Hurry."

You will push these flipper brains through your graffiti wall? Like the others?

"Yes, Nikita, I'm going to ..." I had to ask. "You have something to say about it?"

No. Every one of them will die. But do whatever you like.

"And why do you say they'll die? What is the reason you say that?"

That's what happened to your first batch.

Jorge called from the beach, the words barely forcing their way past the spirit fingers squeezing his larynx, "What are you saying Nikita?"

Inside that mural is crawling with figura. Just waiting with mouths open like famine rats. Very horrible deaths for ghosts. Certain death. All those ghosts you sent earlier are gone.

"What?" I demanded. "You never said anything!"

She shrugged. *Eh. I was tired of talking. You are exhausting.*

"So ... " I said, like I knew what I was going to say next, which is a trick I used to use to inspire more words or an idea to come out of my mouth when I'd run out of them. A trick that would never work for me again. I had to move these ghosts off the beach or there'd be no room for more ghosts. There was no place other than the mural. But killing every ghost on Earth by sending them through the mural in order to find Ti'eirl so I could try to save every ghost on Earth was bad math. Even I saw that. I swear to god, if a math class ever had word problems about the end of the world and eating ghosts, I'd be much better prepared for the life I've ended up living.

We're going to have to go through first, Caroline called to the Monarchs.

Phylis and Jorge were already nodding, like they'd had the same thought. A Monarch thought.

"If we get in there and our weapons are embodied, like when we walk the Paths … " Phylis said, her eyes gleaming. She still had her piece of pipe but she was dreaming of her magic ball and chain.

Caroline had returned to confer with the other Monarchs. They seemed to know what they were talking about and I'm attracted to that, all their furious planning. Then an argument broke out. It grew louder and then it was bordering on a full blown, regicidal cage fight.

"What now?" I asked. Caroline turned to me, furious.

They want us all through, she said. *And leave you out here. Alone. Unprotected.*

"That's okay," I said. Oh my god, she was the best—I think she really *liked* me. "Go. Go protect them as I send them. I'll get the curse thing figured out. I'll join you. Or you come here. Anything could happen."

But there's figura coming through the closure right now, she said. *If we're gone and they get here … what if you …*

"We can't split our forces," Phylis yelled. "We go where we do the most good."

I'm not leaving him alone, Caroline said. *If the figura get this far, he's a sitting duck!*

It was a standoff that only lasted a second.

"I'll go to the Closure," said my own voice behind me. The *Gray*. He'd cleaned a lot of gore from what clothes he wore with a dive in the sea. He looked fresh and happy. He had on only underwear, like a comic book man—the Amazing Sociopatho who all our hopes hinged on.

"Stay away from the Closure," said Phylis. "What are you talking about?"

"I'll go stop the figura," said the *Gray*, shrugging.

"There are tens of thousands," Jorge said. "You're no match for that."

The *Gray* gave him a look, pretty amused, and his eyes got bright.

"We'll see who's a match!" he laughed, and his laugh faded as he sped down the beach, where we watched him cut inland in a spray of sand and vanish. Racing to meet his match. To see what could finally kill him. I know that's what he ultimately wanted. A match. I guess that's what we all want. Maybe he had a chance, though I doubted it.

"Caroline," said Phylis, all reasonable impatience, "it'll be fine, that buys the time we need. You've seen that thing fight."

He's supposed to fight thousands? Caroline protested. *By himself?*

"He probably can, for a while at least," I told her. "For long enough. Get your people up to the mural. Hurry."

Phylis was screaming at psychics, pulling and pushing, the living among them stumbling into motion, gasping under their choking spirit homunculuses. Two groups of ghosts populated the beach. The slack-jawed, newly endowed Skysill ghosts, and the Viaticus. The Viaticus moved as a phalanx, organized by the Monarchs.

And all around us the beach darkened, the sun gagging out dimming light near the very bottom of the sky. How much time we had left I did not know, but less than we needed. I knew that. It would never enough.

I rose up to the balcony and ran inside, and as I went through the door it occurred to me too late—what was going to happen when *new me* looked at the mural? Would I get blasted like Amy and Veronica? Or killed like Victors?

The best way to find out was go stand in front of the mural, which I did because momentum dictates nearly everything I do, where it turned out I was perfectly safe. Who knew what the rules were any more? I presumed there were still rules. Maybe I'm immune to murals? Or maybe nothing happened to me this time because the mural itself barely existed anymore.

Black shadows crowded across the wall, moving as I watched, pressing to cover the painting. It was irising closed. The part of the image that remained visible featured the view across the Undying Land past the back of the throne. *Dominion* no longer blew though like a tempest. It barely blew a tea kettle. It faded as every second passed.

Ghost psychics looked at that wall, appalled. Deep down every single one of them heard the call. Their only hope of peace seemed to be slipping closed. None of them could cross. They looked confused and desperate. A few pleaded with me to let them go. They knew it was my call. And suddenly I had yet another problem.

The living psychics all dragged their monsters in among the couches and bodies and stalled, prying their necks and looking confused, and I realized that all those flesh bodies were going to have to die before they could get through—the ghost psychics could go, but the Monarchs and the other living psychics would have to die. And I did not want anything to do with that. I had that line, at least. That line I will not cross. Didn't I? You have to have a line. Mass slaughter in your living room has got to be a line. I'm sure people say that.

The screams and drums surged in volume. A thunderous boom rattled the windows. It sounded like war. Like enemies. Like finality.

"Well?" Phylis was screaming. "Let's go! Send us. The mural's fading!"

"Someone needs to kill you," I said, "and I'm not doing it! That's where I draw the—"

"Ready people?" Jorge yelled, disinterested in all my drawing lines. The living psychics nodded. They looked ready to die. They were exhausted, struggling to breathe. Terrified. But they had a plan in place, apparently—Jorge had them organized. He counted down.

"Three ... two ... one ... " he gasped, "... good luck to you all ... "

One after the other the psychics let their hands drop from their throats. Either in surrender, or sacrifice, or exhaustion. And those terrifying, neck-wrapped spirits pinched them all out. Snuffed them like candles. Psychics started dropping dead. More and more fell. It was basically a breath holding contest where the penalty for winning was, you suffered a few extra seconds of agony and fear before you died. In thirty seconds every person in the room other than the two Monarchs and flesh me had fallen dead to the floor. Shades rose.

Philip and Jorge, faces purple, surveyed their tribe of fallen soothsayers calmly, in case anyone needed help choking to death, maybe. Then they nodded to each other. Then went down.

Outside on the beach I was hearing moans as a whole city's worth of ghosts began coming awake, and feeling the sorrow and pain and yearning. They wanted to be free of it. They wanted to come through.

We better get moving, Caroline called to me. She heard the throng on the beach too, and knew exactly how they felt. Her own eyes went to the mural, watching it dwindle.

Because of my love of efficiency and my laziness, I wondered, were there steps I could skip? Endowing these psychic shades, flying flesh me back and forth out to the beach to touch the ground, seemed like wasted effort and also boring. So I used my death skills to push the shades under the ground, then knelt in the living room and palmed the hard wood. Did I have to touch the actual ground? Was that a real rule?

No it was not. Deep under the Bradley I found all the psychic shades and squeezed. All their life defining stories poured through me. I ignored what I could. I was just there checking names. None of them were Ti'eirl. The chill of these stories bit harder than the first set, like I'd accidentally swallowed a chunk of ice I'd been cleaning of vodka. I didn't like the feeling. But if that was the worst problem I had to face, I'd feel lucky.

I yanked them up, and a murmur of ghosts rose from the ground into the penthouse. I'd planted shades and now I harvested ghosts. Most were already coming awake, unhappy and confused. Phylis and Jorge transitioned instantly.

What's next, Phylis asked, then was drawn, as if against her will, to the mural. *What's this feeling ...*

Ignore it Phylis, Caroline told her. *That's for later. Hey! Everyone! Listen up!*

She reviewed the plan. The wings would leave in order—Before, with Phylis, Beneath, with Jorge, and Behind, with Caroline. Once through, they'd drop to the Undying Land and form a perimeter. This made them all nervous—every psychic is familiar with the Paths. But the Undying Land was something else. This was asking them to do what they'd feared all their lives—leave the Path. Only the Monarchs did that. Now they were all about to enter the Undying Land.

I hoped these Monarchs knew what they were doing because *eight billion* more ghosts would come pouring through as soon as they landed. And that stream wouldn't stop until I found Ti'eirl.

I understand you're afraid, Caroline was urging them, *but Phylis and Jorge and I will be with you. When the Monarchs get through this wall we'll have our weapons. All of you will be full fledged Viaticus. The figura are afraid of Viaticus. We'll have a chance. A good chance.*

Jorge, carefully examining the mural, longing in his eyes but iron in his voice, said, *And if I understand this correctly, as Viaticus we'll all have the power to curse. As Monarchs, our curses will carry even greater weight. It's going to be enough. It's a terrifying power.*

All I need's my god damn ball, Phylis growled. *Let's get going!*

They arranged themselves in three groups, a Monarch with each. The first was Phylis, with Before. I made the announcement they were free to enter the Undying Land and kick figura ass. I meant to give it an inspiring, storm-the-beaches tone but it came out sounding more like a question. Because who am I, General Patton?

Phylis didn't need inspiration anyway. She sliced forward, her cohort watching. When she came to the wall she had ghost hands up. Ghost me waited to touch her. She screamed a war cry—or some kind of cry—and was through.

On the other side she appeared in plate armor, looking solid as a mountainside. Both her hands raised in exhortation. Murals are silent but her head was back and her cry was obvious, you knew how she sounded. In one fist she had a chain, and a ball glowing *dominion* whirled at the end. The *light* was weak, but maybe it'd be enough. As she fell from view her path walkers charged after her, arcing out past the throne and down, like paratroopers from a plane.

It was pretty tightly organized for something they'd thought up a minute earlier. Organization like that in the face of such ridiculous odds had an unexpected majesty. I'm almost never impressed by organization *or* by majesty but there it was. The end of the world. It affects everyone differently.

Jorge went next. His phalanx poured through in a waterfall of Viaticus taking a glide path down. I remembered what it was like on the other side. A billboard sized portal floating in a night sky behind you and far below, the top of a mountain and the Path stretching out. Soon all of Jorge's psychics were gone too.

All I could see was Caroline. All she could see was me.

Lie Wie, she shouted, not looking at him. One of the ghosts in her crew spun and rose. *Take this group through, I'll bring up the rear—go!*

Lie Wie turned and flung himself forward. Now that he'd been endowed he looked majestic in his own way. More majesty to move me. You could see it just looking at him—he was a former Monarch.

His entire corp moved together as the ghost psychics of the Path Behind passed through the mural, appeared beyond the throne, and fell. And then at last only Caroline remained. The smell of smoke was strong in the air. Smoke that darkened the sunset. The figura, lighting final fires. Was the *Gray* alive still? Should I be able to tell without asking? And what was Caroline thinking? I should have been able to tell that too, but couldn't.

I remember the first time I saw you, I said. *You fed me water in a bowl.*

After Romeo died I got a thing for strays. Sure glad I did.

I stepped up to her. She hovered down six inches. We met eye to eye and despite myself I reached both hands for her, though she wasn't there of course. All I wanted was to give something to her. Anything. Before it was too late.

I wish I'd met him, I said. *I wish I could give something to you. To remember me.*

You let me in your brain, that was the most amazing gift I ever got. I saw freedom. Possibility. You showed me a talking water heater.

I wanted to give you something less weird like chocolate. Like ...

She smiled, because she appreciated the effort I was making, but we had serious subjects to cover and not a lot of time, and she was the only one paying attention. It's a lot of work, probably, being my girlfriend.

Listen Ash, how's this work out here? For you? What's your plan after we're inside?

The plan's loose, but I'm confident.

I'm not leaving til I hear it.

Okay. Part one is I endow all the ghosts on Earth looking for Ti'eirl. That's part one.

She waited a moment. Then as a formality, she asked, *And is there a part two?*

All the rest of it is part two. There's only two parts. It's a simple plan.

That's what I was afraid of. What happens if you don't find Ti'eirl?

I'll find her.

We don't know she's here. We don't <u>know</u>. What if she's not?

She saw she'd got me confused. Though honestly how hard is that really? Sixty percent of the time I'm confused. She was just playing the odds.

Her hands went up around both my cheeks. I held very still. For a moment it was like she had my face in her hands, looking deep in my eyes. Like we were normal.

Listen. Please listen. I'm serious.

I'm listening. I said. The weirdest thing was happening. All the other sounds, all the other smells, the smoke, the drums, the lights in the room—it all went soft focus. It didn't fade, but it lost any relevance. The brain cells I used, processing reality, had no need for anything other than her eyes holding mine.

If it goes wrong, she was saying, *you come through the mural. You hear me? I'll wait for you. If this doesn't ... if the world's ending you come through to me. I'm not going to the Sea without you. I'm going to wait.*

Don't wait.

Promise me. Promise you'll come. Do you promise?

I promise to try. But listen don't wait!

No more sacrifices! The two of us already did that. We deserve some-

thing. This is not the last time I'm ever seeing you, Ash. It is not, do you hear me?

And then my focus racked back to the room, the beach, our shadow-darkened star. The smoke so thick that sunlight weighed like heavy oil. A growing chill sealed me to the present. It was cold everywhere, getting colder.

Don't, she said, and stopped me saying what she saw I was going to. She swallowed.

When ghost cry, I saw, their tears go up. Now, pearls of *light* floated from the corners of her eyes. Frustration consumed me. We couldn't hug. We couldn't *anything* but watch each other across the curve of time, through the door of space. Watch each other say goodbye without saying it.

I thought I wanted us normal, she said as she began floating backward. *But now I see what we have is better. Come back to me.*

And before I could speak she turned and fell through the mural. I'd wanted to say goodbye. But what else had this relationship ever been, from the very first moment, but two people saying goodbye? Moving farther apart. From a kiss on a sidewalk further and further until we'd come to this; we were people in separate worlds. What was the point of saying goodbye when we'd been living it since we met?

She appeared beyond the throne in her green archery outfit, holding aloft her bow, plunging toward the Path and the Undying Land below. And was gone.

The time had come—a saying that means nothing to a person in my position—to go dig up Ti'eirl. Whoever she was hiding inside of. I thought of all the parts of this plan I still hadn't figured out. Because for once in her life, Caroline hadn't been asking the right question. *What do I do if I don't find Ti'eirl?* she wanted to know, when I was certain I *was* going to find Ti'eirl. Call it necromantic intuition.

She hadn't asked the important question because it was an Inmortalis question. It hadn't occurred to her. I turned toward the mural and for a moment stood immobile, watching black shadows inch ever closer to the throne. The all worlds closing. I sighed, for luck. Then I raised my right hand over my chest, where I felt the dark shape deep inside. Deep within me, I felt it go … *pulse*. The umbra eye *pulsed*. My brand pulsed.

And I called it to the surface of my skin.

Because Ti'eirl was a complete unknown, and the question Caroline hadn't asked, the only relevant question, was; what was I going to do when I *did* find her?

CHAPTER

FIFTEEN

The brand throbbed beneath my shirt. I felt it. I didn't need to look to know it was raised like a scar. Black as a coal mine shadow. I'd never had a tattoo. I wondered if they all felt this way. Cold. Hard. Puckered and pulling the skin around it.

In case I'd forgotten that the end times were here, at that moment the sun began to shake. The dull orange light in the living room went quivery, like a flashlight through a bowl of jello. I looked to the sky to see the sun shivering as though resisting some inexorable force, its final strength almost gone. Our star, not ready to set. But resistance would not hold it aloft. There was no going back.

The trembling, light-carved shadows flickered through the living room across piled psychic bodies. Hundreds of them. Hard as I tried to clean it up, every time I turn around this penthouse filled with corpses. I watched in disappointment as psychic bodies strobed. Like a dance floor where everyone was napping. I felt the chill growing.

"It's like The Triumph of Death in here," I said to ghost me, who hung near the balcony doors.

I don't know what that is, he said.

220

"Bruegel the Elder, 1562." I had the sense he was shrugging. "You're no art historian I guess."

Why are we talking about this? Shouldn't you hurry?

He was right. I'd need to pick up the pace from here. From here until the end I needed speed more than I needed history. I held my palms out, gathering my powers of concentration, which is not something that can be rushed because they are limited and shy. And then I heard him. Behind me.

Can it be true? he said.

Because of course. It's always something. I turned. Aeternus looked perfectly comfortable among the corpses, stargazing at the front of my shirt. He blinked up close to me, and from a foot away reached for my buttons. His hand went through my chest. He grimaced.

I'm very easy to distract. I know that about myself. It's literally a disorder I have. Though anyone would have been distracted by the most ancient ghost in the universe sticking their arm through your lungs. I forgot what I was doing for a second.

"Back off," I said.

You have it. Don't you? You've done it.

Now he was watching my face. I recognized the look. I'd seen it on the faces of all my official, law enforcement interrogators. Aeternus was sure I was guilty. But for inconvenient, constitutional reasons, he needed me to say it out loud.

"I don't know what you mean," I told him. I'm not even sure why I decided to lie. Not knowing things is just my habit when I'm being questioned. It worked as well with Aeternus as it did with the Skysill PD.

The hive queen branded you. But she warned you against me.

"Hive queen?"

And now you can eat. Am I right? Can you eat?

"You're like a broken fucking record," I complained. But he hardly heard me. He was back to scanning my chest.

Show me. Please. I must know, before the end.

His eyes shot to my face, just a flicker, and away. He was looking desperate. Freaking out. Very off-brand, which is like catnip for the brain of a person like me who, as I keep saying, is so easily distracted.

"You're afraid you'll never get to the Forgiving Sea. Is that what this is?"

Please. If you have the gift, show me. Let me see. Before we perish.

"Is that what you think is happening? Perishing?"

Show me. Then do what you must to me. I accept your judgment.

"Judgment? I have a lot of other things to … I'm not like you. Just go through."

With what seemed like the greatest effort he dragged his gaze to my face. He searched there a moment. As though trying to remember what I'd just said.

Go through?

"I'm letting you through." I pointed at the mural. "Nolear Fa, I give you permission to leave. Go to the Undying Land and wash off your pain."

At some level, I suspected this decision was a mistake, because of how the others have all been mistakes. Because, could you commit the crimes he'd committed, transgressing every boundary you saw, then just skip free? Without consequence? Was that justice? One part of me saw the justice in letting him suffer right to the end, if there was going to be an end, because suffering might be the only justice he ever saw.

But who am I, Thurgood Marshall? Justice isn't my job. I say, everyone starts over if they can. It took him a moment. Then he was laughing.

Oh, Asher, he said. *You really do not understand, do you?*

"That takes too much energy. Are you leaving?"

His laughter died. Just like the rest of the world. He took a pose. It was instinct with him. He knew the angles and couldn't stop himself from using them.

I will not leave. My only chance was to bring Agape back. What was done to me when I was killed—I am a ghost now, so the curse will not recognize me if it is lifted. To the curse, I was a body, while Ti'eirl was a ghost. If the curse is lifted now, I will not be recognized. I will cease to exist. And if the curse is not lifted, if it ends the all worlds ... the same result. The Forgiving Sea? What good is momentary peace? I will remain where I can affect the manner of my end. I can still help you. Just let me see it. Please. Let me see the gift. To know for sure.

Something about his plight had nobility—the nobility of failure. The only kind I know. His explanation was too complicated, and I wasn't paying attention, but basically he seemed to be saying he was doomed. Which is another position with which I'm familiar.

I reached for my shirt.

Are you sure you want to show him? wondered ghost me as I did. *Maybe—*

But my shirt was open, and the brand was out. I stared, just like everyone else. The black sigil spread over my heart as it once had Aeternus's. I'd never gotten a tattoo because there wasn't an artist in the world I respected enough for that. But now I had one, and I understood the appeal. It grounded you. It made you something.

At last, Aeternus whispered.

Then he blinked. He was gone.

Umm... ghost me said, pointing behind me. I turned.

Aeternus hovered, facing down, slowly dropping toward the floor.

Or ... not the floor. Toward a corpse. Phylis's corpse. He made contact. He disappeared within it. And the corpse stirred. Limbs spasmed, jerked, and it groaned. Phylis groaned? Then, slowly at first but with increasing confidence, it got to its knees and stood.

"Phylis ... ?" I asked.

That's not ... said ghost me.

Phylis held her figura pipe, stained with gore, looking at me. I felt a cold shiver go down my back. Even now, here, there are things that creep me out. Corpses getting to their feet was one of those.

She was ten feet off when she launched herself at me. It only took a second. The way she moved. She leapt. She spun in the air for momentum, raising her pipe behind her. Like ballet. Like a zero-gravity rhino. Like a Monarch fighting shape shifters.

She reached me. I started to duck. Too late. Her pipe flashed down on my skull. The room blurred and I was falling.

I knew it was happening but kept thinking it wasn't real because that's a problem I have—hardly anything's real. But the pipe blew my head back. And as I fell I was losing consciousness—one skill I've retained, through all my trials, is my heightened sensitivity to loss of consciousness—and so, confused, I dove out toward ghost me.

Flesh me hit the floor as I left him, definitely breaking his nose if not his entire face, eyes rolled up. He was out when he hit, head spilling blood from the pipe gash, and out the front of his pretty smile onto the floor. Lots of blood. What was happening?

Phylis stood over him with the pipe, considering her next blow. Flesh me did not move.

What's ... hey! I ghosted. *Phylis? Or ...*

Phylis? Phylis said. *She's dead ... oh I see. I'd given you too much credit, Asher. Apologies. I have taken Phylis's corpse.*

Aeternus? She smiled. Or he did. Aeternus. I hadn't recognized him without his loincloth, but now I saw it. A hint of self-loathing. Or just regular loathing. And cruelty.

I thought it likely, the Phylis corpse said, *after seeing Li Wei's corpse animate, you'd figure out ... I overplayed my hand there. I had to know. Had you been branded? I've been worried ... but you simply don't have the framework. Even now ... do you understand what is happening?*

So an Inmortalis ghost can animate a corpse. That's your big secret?

I was mostly talking to myself, of course, as I've been doing all my life, though from shock in this case and not alcoholism. But along with shock ... something wasn't tracking. And that also makes me verbose. I had a crucial piece of information missing.

An Inmortalis ghost can animate a corpse. Aeternus had been keeping it from me. Because Li Wei's corpse—I *had* seen it moving, but like so many other things I'd neglected to pay attention—that had been Aeternus, trying to see if my flesh body had been branded by the hive queen? Which—wasn't that basically what he'd been trying to do himself? Why attack me now?

Blood spreading from my motionless skull pooled on the hardwood. The light in the room grew darker. Time running off. What was I missing? I saw again the look on the Phylis corpse as it spun with precision battle frenzy through the air—that had been hunger.

Precision battle frenzy. *That.* Phylis's Monarch skills lived in her corpse. And now Aeternus had them because he had the corpse. Like I'd had Officer Smith's skills.

I understood at last. Because yes, I'm quite simple, but it wasn't that complicated. It was just hard to fucking fathom.

This is why you wanted to teach me, I said. *Teach my body. You wanted my body to know how to eat.*

Ah. You <u>are</u> putting it together. You are a wonder.

You needed my body to know how to eat before you killed it. That's what you're going to do. Kill it.

I am. I knew I'd have a chance, as long as I had surprise.

And then you'll animate it yourself.

I will possess it. And finally …

I said it out loud. One of us needed to.

You're going to eat the ghosts.

I feel sorry for you Asher. You were so close. I wish we could have shared this.

It was hard putting my outrage into words, which never happens to me, so you know the world had to be ending.

But there's still a chance we can lift the curse. If we don't, the world is done.

My curse cannot be lifted.

Fine, yeah—but the rest of them … what the <u>fuck</u>? Can you not see how <u>wrong</u> this is?

He shrugged her massive shoulders. *Of course I see.*

Then stop!

Aeternus turned Phylis away from my flesh, momentarily facing me, and I knew what he was about to say. *But I cannot stop. I do not want to stop. Nothing this sweet has ever existed. The end of the world? That is nothing. The world ended for me the first time I tasted it. You of all people understand. I am powerless. I am an addict, as you are.*

No. Because I'd try!

Would you, though? Don't we owe ourselves the peace we seek, he asked, pointing Phylis's gore pipe at the sun. *And this? This is inevitable. This is the inevitable history of light, Asher—it goes out. In the end it always goes out.*

And he raised her pipe. And began beating me.

And I blinked to Three Paths screaming *HELP!*

And I saw the *Gray* battling figura with ultra-violence.

And I saw my sister battling beside him in a raging ball of *light.*

And my sister heard me and a ball of *wander* clouded her from sight.

And the Gray heard me and like lightning sped toward the Bradley but was too far away, the pipe was falling.

And I blinked back and my sister was in the penthouse.

She filled the room with *dominion,* from both her eyes and her cup. As I watched she *wander* beamed Phylis's corpse, who was in the process of raining killing blows on my flesh head, and Phylis's corpse disappeared.

Her pipe hung in the air. Then it fell onto my flesh leg. And for a second there was silence.

It was Aeternus, I ghosted then, pivoting around the rest of the room, filled in my gut with a not-good feeling, watching a room full of motionless corpses, *he's trying to kill me so—*

We all know you can't *wander* a supernatural body—Veronica already tried that on me. So we still had Aeternus with us somewhere. In the room was my guess. A guess confirmed when one of the other corpses suddenly jerked.

Amelia snarled, frowning. A crazy goddess of rage.

The course charged flesh me. Amy vanished it.

He was so good, you didn't even see his ghost flicker. He just blinked away and raised another corpse. And another. She sent them off, but there were a lot of corpses, and every time, the glow of her dimmed. *Wander* drains her fast. Though there was a different strategy here, I thought. Something else she should do. What?

But the bodies kept coming, and Amy was wearing down. Screaming of course, since it's all she knows to do anymore—her clothes in tatters, figura blooded and filthy, a massive, mutant spirit-body choking the fuck out of her from behind—spending her *light* on a platoon of corpses. She needed a better plan. This math wasn't going to work. Too many bodies—another reached my flesh, pressing dead fingers around my throat.

Then she was pushing all the *light* in her body into the goblet. She'd seen the math. She was … draining herself into the goblet? Pouring out her life's *light*. It was familiar in the most sickening way. This was not my other plan. Whatever she was doing. What was she thinking?

She emptied herself and her features softened, body bending like Julian's had, still holding her goblet, stumbling toward the blood-red mess on the floor that was me getting throttled by an Aeternus-powered corpse.

The ghost with his fingers on my throat laughed, dismissing her. "This is what happens. There is nothing you can do. My life is endless, and beyond your reach."

"Then you'll have your endless life," she gasped as he reached him, and, collapsing, brought the cup to his shoulder, *"and I'll have your False Death."*

It was super dramatic and for a minute it didn't make sense. Aeternus understood what she was doing before I did. The corpse jerked desperately. But too late. Too slow.

The first thing that happened then was my sister died and her spirit rose up. The other first thing that happened was, from the goblet came a multi variant cloudburst of *light*. Like there'd be some explosion. But there was none. There was an implosion.

Light vacuum sealed around Aeternus's borrowed corpse. *Tight.* A shadowy ghost face pushed into that surface from inside. Pounding. But trapped. The shrink wrap kept tightening, vanished inside the corpse, and the corpse stopped moving. It stayed upright a second, straddling flesh me, then fell sideways.

A thin thread of *dominion* disappeared off the top of its head.

Then the *Gray* arrived.

SIXTEEN

Then things started moving *really* fast. Really faster I guess I mean. Is there a miles-per-hour rating for the speed of shit happening, where it's one thing after another blurring together? Because this was that.

When the *Gray* rushed in he stopped, looked at Amy where she'd fallen on bloody flesh me, and at flesh me who was not technically dead yet. But his skull was a gaping ruin. Amy's shade hung to one side of him. Below the shade her goblet, drained to a star flicker of *light,* rolled on the floor

"He's a goner," said the *Gray* at flesh me. He sounded fascinated.

We don't know that, I said, even though we did.

Then the part of me that gets distracted started thinking. How disappointing was it going to be, dying this way? While at the same time the *other* part of me, that part that looks around at stuff, was looking at the goblet rolling out of Amy's corpse hand and rolling up to my flesh fingers, still with a spark of *dominion.*

They were going to touch.

The rules had changed, distractible me thought, hadn't they? Like, was I *not* supposed to touch *dominion* objects? Yes, I *was not* supposed to, because of explosions. But flesh was coma bleeding and it was going to happen. I blinked into his chest but of course, a ghost can't stop a rolling goblet, and with rising panic, the goblet inches—

STOP THAT! I ghosted at the *Gray*. He's so fast. Like those vampires on that show. When he moves it's a blur. But for the first time—and the last—the *Gray* wasn't fast enough.

So when flesh me exploded, the *Gray* was mid-dive, chest to chest above him, with ghost me floating in the same place so all three of me connected in space. And when that tiniest flicker of *dominion* in the goblet blew us up, it didn't kill us. Not instantly.

As we vaporized, *dominion* rushed to fill us all. As we splattered in all the directions Asher Gale can splatter—many directions—we were filled with *dominion* and became *dominion*. Together. A kind of fourth body. And as tendrils of Asher Gale arced through the air I caught them.

By *caught,* I mean something completely different that I don't have words for, of course. But I kept doing it. Our bodies spread through the air like Celine's car had, like Tilly's body had when she touched my tube of paint. We sprayed up and out in threads—an Asher filigree—while I continued catching strands, gathering them in using some other body, some alchemical, separate body.

Until it was time to merge forever.

One last time my bodies did.

There was no pain. I'd become so good by then. And I found myself staring at the ceiling, facing up from the floor, with blood in my eyes and my sister's corpse, and other corpses, lying on me. Like the end of a horror movie birthday party.

I pushed myself up far enough to see the brand on my chest. My palms slipped in the blood behind me and I fell back and hit my head. My head. I felt my head. It had no holes. I was not dead. Had this happened, really, I wondered, because of the things which were impossible to understand. I looked for the *Gray.* He was gone. Where? *Exactly who am I right now,* I asked?

Then I saw Amy.

My sister was a shade. She had her hair in a bun. She wore an apron stained with paint. In her motionless hand, she held a torn paper ticket, and I recognized the logo. It was a ticket to Shay's Wonder Faire.

"Ames," I choked out, already crying, standing. Crying? That was weird. She was just a shade. She'd become a ghost. Like all the others. They went on. Everybody just ... went on. Why was I crying?

"That's not the plan I was *thinking*!" I shouted at her. "The False Death? *My* plan was, don't *wander* the Aeternus corpses, *wander my body*. To a hospital, that would have been good, or ... "

Oh my god. She drives me crazy.

Then, still crying, I reached for her ticket, and her story came out.

It was evening in Skysill Park, high on the ridge. Above us trees framed a dark sky with bright stars beyond our borealis. Before us lights and music spun a frothy blur, down a path opening onto Shay's Wonder Faire. All four of us were there. Me as a toddler. Amy, maybe six. Katerina Gale, and beside her Marlon. All of us in the happiest vigor of life well lived.

We entered the Faire gaily chatting, heading for the goat pen. That was for me. I loved the goats. And there at the fence, we stopped. My sister watched my dad lift me on his shoulder. I laughed, looking down on the goat heads. My mom stepped close to Amy and held her with one arm, so dancer graceful, then pulled the two of them to hug my dad and me.

And for an impossible moment we stood there, in popcorn fairground moonlight. My mom looked at the stars. She said, "Isn't this wonderful?"

And the story ended. After that all the other stories this ghost knew funneled through me, all the way back to the Undying Land and a ghost named Si'mallama. For a few seconds, Amy's shade was covered in light bubbles as something percolated. And then there she floated. Ghost Amy.

"Hey Ames," I said. She could only blink. Her pupils were still missing. That was disconcerting. And she was going to take a while to wake up, since she was no psychic. So I started her toward the mural.

"Okay Ames. Time to go. I give you permission. You can go. I'll help."

The shadows in the room were deep. It was really cold. Maybe freezing. Everywhere except the mural the illumination was match sticks—the sun trembled, just a reflection at the bottom of a distant well, and I wondered if it would simply fail before it even had a chance to set.

But it held on. For what I did not know. Probably just habit.

And I realized, I'd endowed Amy without moving to ghost me. Usually, I have to watch an endowment happen from ghost me. But ghost me was gone. The *Gray* was gone. Was it just me?

I gave Amelia a push and she drifted across the room of corpses toward the mural. In the past I interacted with ghosts by bouncing ghost me off them. Now I touched them with my hands. All the rules had changed again. I mean, yes, of course. And now I could push my own sister's ghost through the air. She had all the weight of a cup of water. She drifted to stop a few feet from the mural.

"I know you can hear me," I said. "It'll take a few minutes to wake up. I'm going to push you through and psychics will protect you. And when you get in there, will you give Caroline a message for me?"

She blinked again. She sort of turned her head. She was coming around fast. The fastest I'd seen from any non-psychic. It's almost impossible to keep my sister unconscious. She hardly sleeps. I needed to get her through while I had a chance. She'd try to stay with me if she had a choice.

"Tell Caroline," I said, "do not wait. You understand? Tell her I said *don't wait for me*. I don't know ... it's pretty complicated out here. There's no margin for error. And I always need a margin. Tell her *get to the ocean while she can*. Can you hear me, Amelia?"

"Don't ... " Amy mouthed, pieces coming together, "wait for you ... what?"

"Just tell her. Goodbye Ames. I feel like I was a shitty brother. But I was trying. If that matters."

Then I pushed. She drifted away, face puzzled, and her back hit the only patch of the mural with any colored *light* left. She fell through. And I turned to survey my apocalypse penthouse. Strewn with bodies and growing ever darker.

A single corpse trailed a *dominion* thread from its head like a marionette, all strings sliced but one. Aeternus. Nolear Fa. Now that Amelia was dead he'd be there forever. She was the only one who could free him. Would he be there until the inevitable end of history? Was the light really going out?

I dropped to a knee. My palm to the floor.

Fuck inevitable, I said. And went looking for ghosts.

Instantly I found myself with a three-dimensional picture of the planet; a globe with one, continuous glowing surface. I wasn't seeing it. Also not *seeing* it. This sense I used was my Inmortalis connection to the dead. I perceived all the dead at once, crowded over the crust of the Earth, a pulsing film of shades. I beheld them all. They beheld me—I was the only living body on Earth. I was the last. My species was gone. The planet was dead.

So that's where I started: eight billion blank shades to endow.

At first, it was too many stories. Too many at once. But get organized, I thought. What would Caroline do? Endow in batches. Start in rings—start with a ring around Skysill, a hundred miles deep. I took all the shades in that band, four hundred thousand. I touched them, I heard them, and as their stories went by I sifted them for the nugget at the end—the name of a ghost in the Undying Land.

None of these four hundred thousand were Ti'eirl.

I pushed them through the mural and they were happy to go. That's the way it seemed. The planet's temperature dropped again. I expanded my search, endowed a wider ring, sifted their stories for Ti'eirl, then shoved them through. And the cold grew. A freeze spread. My face stung. Ice built around the planet. I went faster. Took larger rings. Great swaths of shades. I listened to all of them. I moved them on.

I cleared the near continents. Then I went wide, ringing the globe. I hadn't found her yet but she was there. I knew she was. I went around the poles, endowing ghosts in longitudinal stripes, and as milliseconds passed and darkness spread I did not find her. I did a ring of five hundred million shades. I rounded the planet flinging them behind me.

No Ti'eirl.

I worked the system, wishing Caroline could see how methodical I can be when I put my mind to it. Such a lonely thought. Focus. I rounded the far side of the planet, went over the poles and back the opposite way, and my rings got smaller again. four billion shades down. I was getting faster. I was meant for this. The last Inmortalis, really hitting his stride. Really letting them fly. Not getting worried.

Five billion down. Because it's like the lottery, I told myself, where you might lose over and over but eventually you'll be a millionaire. Five point five billion shades. Above the planet, all the stars were gone. On the planet all the heat was gone. And I wasn't worried but I was irritated because of course she's going to be on the farthest side of the world. She's going to be the furthest ghost. She's the perfect example of everything that's least convenient in my life.

Six billion gone.

The planet encrusted in ice. In my penthouse, my body sheeted in frost. I shook frost from my face. The sun was dissolving. Almost gone. Where was she?

Seven billion. Not there.

Seven and a half billion.

Five hundred thousand left. And yes, now I was worried. I realized too late I should have been searching only for psychics. Ti'eirl was Viaticus and that meant she was a psychic and I could have saved precious seconds. But for what? Time ... what if ... was it possible she wasn't *here*? Where else, though? All these shades, *but the one shade I want is missing?*

Three hundred thousand.

I pushed them through the picture hole.

One hundred thousand. And really? *Really?*

Nine thousand ... *what? ...*

One hundred shades left one Earth ... no ...

One endowable shade remained. I touched her hairbrush and heard her sob story. Sifted her back to an Undying Land ghost named Bu'namana. Pushed her through the mural like someone cutting an anchor. And was adrift.

That was it.

Ti'eirl had never been here? Was that what just happened? No.

Like a starving dog licking an empty bowl I swept the world for something more to endow. Anything. One shade. Just one endowable shade. But there was none. Nothing. Only shadows. Just emptiness. The end of it. The history of light was over.

From frozen open flesh eyes I saw the final inch of mural peeling closed. It was now or never. I had to leave. Join Caroline for the end. Because this was it.

Which is when I noticed I *wasn't* alone in the penthouse. I'd been looking for an endowable shade. But here beside me ... on the shrinking patch of hardwood floor ... shadows melting to nothing ... was Samantha.

All the world shrank.

She held out her banished goblet hand. The goblet she'd found only because she had been able to see *dominion.* Samantha saw *time.* Samantha was psychic.

Samantha. In the middle of everything. Killing Aeternus.

"Ti'eirl?" I whispered.

The two of us hung in darkness, on a vanishing, ice-slick, three-foot platform of dark floor, the rest of the world gone. One postage stamp aglimmer where the mural irised closed, hanging on nothing. She *had* been in Skysill all along. Collected here with every other player in Nolear Fa's tragedy. Put here by the curse, by magnetism, by fate. By the curse.

And she was the one shade I couldn't endow. She'd tell no curse secrets. That plan had always been a thin gruel. Now here we were, in a final pocket of space, tucked together at the blackness at the end of reality, the two of us and nothing.

She flashed toward me, sank through the floor so her outstretched hand pointed at my chest. The umbra eye went *pulse*. *Pulse.* Toward her fingers.

The terrible charades of it all.

Eat a shade and you're gone. You end. You both end.

And here it was. The only kind of choice I'm ever given—take it, or leave it.

As the thumbnail patch on the not-wall vanished, I chose leave it. Because, either way, the light was going out for me.

CHAPTER

SEVENTEEN

I ate her to death through the umbra eye. Like lemonade through a straw. And the world vanished.

Despite what Aeternus claimed, Ti'eirl tasted like nothing. Although he'd been eating ghosts, and Ti'eirl was a shade. So she not only had no taste but eating her killed me at the same time it killed her. I felt such disappointment. No rush, no joy wave, no endless desire fulfilled. More like I was at the bar and accidentally poured a glass of water in my mouth. It was nothing.

And then I swallowed her. And even that was over. And all I had was an empty glass.

And when the glass was gone ... all I had was emptiness.

I was in a familiar void, antithetical to the existence of all the kinds of things. It was the space between, where I fell when I was lost between my bodies. It was the deep black void tearing Veronica apart. It was a lightless endlessness. The reason I was not being torn apart now was, I fit here. I was no longer a thing. I was of the void.

But I wasn't the only one here of the void.

"At last, it is over," I heard her say.

Ti'eirl was with me. I wasn't seeing, like eyes see things, because things were obliterated here. But still, I knew what she looked like. She could have been Samantha's cousin, born a billion years apart. Ti'eirl had mad waves of hair, wide eyes, a serious mouth. She wore something you'd call a gown if you were writing a poem.

In the background between us was nothing.

"I ate you and we died," I said. Because even in a void, it helps to start with the obvious. Helps *me* I mean.

"We have come to the end," she agreed.

"Is this ... what you wanted?" I said. "Why ... is this happening ... ?"

"I attempted the forbidden. Out of love. Which made it worse. The fault for this, all of it, is mine."

For a suspended moment we said nothing, did nothing, felt nothing and went nowhere. We were the void. But I felt a threshold coming. This was the darkness at the end of the movie, just before they turned the projector off. It wouldn't last.

"But if you're Ti'eirl," I complained, because why change now, "then I mean ... why all the charades? All that time ... "

"Inside a shade are multitudes. Lost amidst them, I could only send intentions out and hope. Call up out of the dark. Hope was all I had."

"Like Peter."

"And now, at last, the cycle is done. Something new can happen."

"What cycle?"

"The endless. The revolving. Two beings, the poles, the end of the world. Though you and I are no longer of that world, behind us those who remain will now find their way."

"Those who remain? Who does remain?"

"You lifted the Curse. You restored the all worlds. Everyone remains."

"Caroline? Amelia?"

"They will have lives, long, fair, to do with as they wish. They live on."

"And us? What happens here?"

"Well. That is the great mystery. The one each of us must confront alone."

Somewhere—ahead or above or behind, there was no context for this—a light appeared. A fucking light.

"Is that … where we're going now?" I wondered. It was all out of my control. I'm not sure why I even wanted answers. One of my bad habits.

"That is our destination. Though we go alone from here," she said.

"We go where?"

"They are called the many worlds for a reason," she said, smiling.

"So wait a minute. You're a zillion-year-old ghost, right? Let me ask you … "

"Yes? Our time grows short. Ask your question."

We could both tell I was going to make this all about me. But I swear to god it feels like it is all about me.

"What now?" I asked. "For me I mean? What am I? If I'm not … whatever I was."

"What are you? What could you ever be, but an artist? In the all worlds, the artists are those driven to investigation, to combination, to the pursuit of wholeness. Successfully, self-destructively, but their goal never changes: to make existence increasingly whole. To put the pieces together."

"I left my pieces … I left them."

I thought of my pieces, scattered over the sands of the city I'd grown up and died in. I thought of them all, though only one mattered. A brown-eyed psychic girl with Yosemite Sam socks. Archer, Monarch, telepathic lover, literally the other half of me. Who I'd never see now, who was off living a life fair and long. A happy one, after she washed herself free. I hoped. So I had that at least— those pieces remained. It would be enough.

"Perhaps you will find new pieces, Asher. You are formidable. And now … ?"

"Is this it? It's over?"

"Either that, or it has only begun. Goodbye, Asher Gale, you … "

And then, with no warning, an invisible meat hook pierced my guts and ripped me, yanked me, spun me. It spun Ti'eirl too.

"What …?" I heard her say. "No. No, no, what is this?"

I had no idea what it was but I liked it not at all, and it was getting worse *fast*. It was car sickness in a universal sedan, yanking, losing equilibrium—

"What *is* this?" I cried out.

"No! It cannot … " she muttered, then yelled, "no no, not this! Not again!"

"Explain—what the fuck is going on?" I screamed as reality bucked.

"A curse," she wailed. "She is laying another curse!"

"Explain *more!*"

"The Viaticus, she will not let you … it is the curse I used. A curse exchanging two people … she will break the all worlds again—she will ruin us!"

"*Who are you talking about?*"

"The Monarch of the Path Behind. The one who's bound to you. She is trading places—"

"*Caroline?* Caroline knows we can't—I don't want to trade—"

And I felt that I was falling, and saw Ti'eirl vanishing above me, growing dim and small … falling upward … no. The perspective flipped. I wasn't falling. It wasn't me going anywhere. I remained behind. It was Ti'eirl going away.

She dwindled, fading, and was gone. Far, far away gone. The void was truly empty now. With only myself and a distant light. What'd Caroline done? What kind of disaster had we—

"Hey, baby," I heard from behind me. Always behind. Where it's most dramatic.

I turned and saw her. Not the old way. Not with photons. Some kind of mental picture. But all of her. Brown eyes. Psychic. The works.

"So," I wondered after a moment, "do you think we should stop meeting like this?"

"I do. We lack imagination."

I stared into my mind. Where she was. Where I'd always wanted her.

I asked, "Did you just end the world? With another curse? What just happened?"

"It was a curse. But everything's great in the world," she said. "A little weirder than it used to be. It'll be fun for them. People are going to be fine."

"I thought the thing was ... you can't take anybody's *place.* Their fate or whatever. I thought you couldn't do that or we get the curse at the end of the world again."

"You can't trade places to save someone else. But you can do it to save yourself. That was Ti'eirl's mistake. Not mine."

It took a moment. Because it always does with me plus the world just ended and I was woozy.

"So this is you saving yourself?" I clarified.

"I was going to die without you, Ash. I had to come."

"You traded places with Ti'eirl and ... you know where we are, right? This is like ... super death. The end. We're not going back."

"I know but I missed you."

"I love how you might be crazier than me."

"It's not a competition. But if it was we'd be tied. I thought I'd come here because we needed someplace people would finally leave us alone. That was never going to happen anywhere else."

"Oh my god that's true. So I guess Amy gave you my message?"

"Message?"

"Don't wait for me? Go leave your worries behind in the Forgiving Sea ... "

"I never made it to the Sea. I had to come find you."

For a moment I tried to understand the peace she'd given up to follow me into death. And all I could think was, in a lot of ways we'd given up similar things. Except—was she a murderer now for the rest of eternity?

"So you'll carry that ... burden or whatever ... forever?" I asked.

"I guess. What's forever even mean? Might not be that long. Who knows? There's no going back, I do know that. Anyway don't feel sorry for me, what about *you*? Your burdens, oh my god Ash ... "

"Mine? What? Mine are nothing."

"Yours are so heavy, so ... yours are ... oh, la, I guess we're lucky you lack introspection."

"Yes. My charm is I have no idea what's going on inside. People love it."

"I know. You're super cute." Then she pointed at the light that'd first appeared for Ti'eirl and me, some distance off. It was brighter now. Most insistent. "So that's where we go next?"

"That's what I heard, but ... " I hesitated.

"Ah, you're nervous. Like our first train ride. Don't worry. We'll go together."

"That's the thing," I said, "I asked Ti'eirl, she was no help, but it's not clear we *can* go together. She said alone."

Caroline thought for a moment. I imagined her moving through the rooms in her mind house, the yellow one with the garden and the shady porch, solving this problem.

"No," she said. "After everything we've been through, my bet's on us together."

"A girl with a gambler's heart. That's my favorite."

"I say let's just go. Let's just go and see what happens."

To go and see what happens, she held out her hand. A question filled her eyes. The one I'd always known how to answer. I held out my own hand and somehow, there in that void of no-things, where literally nothing was allowed, we laced our fingers. Hers were warm, and strong, and happy. They were perfect.

When her lips met mine, they were soft. Exactly as soft as I remembered. It was a normal kiss. It went on a long time.

Then together we went to see what happens.

THE END

AFTERWORD

The Curse at the End of the World: The Book of Touch ends here, and so does the series, *The History of Light.*

The time may come when I return to Skysill Beach in other books, but the story of Asher and Caroline ends here and they will never return. That, afterall, is the inevitable history of stories. However, after I finished the final lines, I did wonder what the two of them found, going together toward the light to see what happens. So I gave them a few pages more.

If you'd like to read a final few pages of Asher and Caroline crossing boundaries never to return, go to kevinhincker.com/goodbye.html and join the list.

THE HISTORY OF LIGHT
BOOKS 1 THROUGH 5

~

ALSO BY KEVIN HINCKER

The Little Queen

The Einstein Object

A Debt to the Stars

About the Author

Kevin Hincker writes speculative fiction for curious readers. If you'd like to join his mailing list, or find extra information about his books, you can signup, or just explore, at https://kevinhincker.com/

If you want Amazon to deliver you information about his future releases, such as Book Five of this series, go to his Amazon page, https://www.amazon.com/author/kevinhincker and click the "Follow" button in the upper left next to his picture.